DAZZLING PRAISE FOR
THE AWARD-WINNING
ROMANCES OF
MARION CHESNEY

"All the elements for a good Regency come together....Witty, charming, touching."
—*Library Journal*

"Warm-hearted, hilarious reading."
—Baton Rouge *Sunday Magazine*

"Entertaining."
—*Booklist*

"Amusing."
—*Kirkus Reviews*

"Well-written and easy to read."
—*News-Sentinel*, Knoxville, TN

Also by Marion Chesney

Henrietta

Marion Chesney

ST. MARTIN'S PRESS/NEW YORK

Henrietta was previously published by Jove with the author pseudonym of Ann Fairfax.

HENRIETTA

Copyright © 1979 by Marion Chesney.

ISBN: 0-312-91364-8   Can. ISBN: 0-312-91373-7

Printed in the United States of America

Jove edition/October 1979
First St. Martin's Press mass market edition/January 1989

10 9 8 7 6 5 4 3 2 1

To my friend Madeline Trezza,
her husband Tony,
and her children Dana and Anthony.

Chapter One

SO THIS WAS LONDON!

Miss Henrietta Sandford cowered in the corner of the carriage and fervently wished that she had never left the quiet county town of Nethercote to answer the mysterious summons she had received only that morning. The noise of the city streets was deafening as crowds jostled along the pavements under the old overhanging buildings. The smell from the kennels in the middle of the street was nigh overwhelming.

The hack negotiated the filth of Ludgate Hill and then picked its leisurely way up Fleet Street past the red latticed windows of the taverns. The shop signs rattled and creaked mournfully as they swung back and forth in the bitter November wind.

The hack came to a halt in the press of traffic. Suddenly a drunk pressed his face against the carriage window, staring mindlessly at Henrietta with wild red eyes peering out from a forest of long, greasy unkempt hair.

She gave a squeak of alarm and turned her head away. The carriage jerked forward and she went over the events of the morning in an effort to settle her mind.

She had been going about her parish duties of visiting the poor—or rather her brother, the vicar's duties—when suddenly an unfamiliar soberly dressed servant appeared by her side.

He had a message for her from her Great-Aunt, Mrs. Hester Tankerton. Henrietta was not aware until that moment that she had a Great-Aunt or indeed any other living relative apart from her brother, Henry. Mrs. Tankerton feared she was dying, explained the servant and was desirous of seeing Miss Sandford without delay. He cautioned, she *must not tell* anyone, especially her brother, of her visit.

Henrietta had been first frightened and then intrigued. Bullied by her brother and treated as little better than a servant, Henrietta had experienced very little excitement in her life. London was only a few hours ride from Nethercote, and all at once, Henrietta had decided to go. The servant seemed respectable. And before she had had time to draw breath, she was swaying and bumping along the London road. Now as she stared out at the strange sights and sounds of the metropolis, she felt she had been indeed mad to go on such a wild venture.

With a sigh of relief, she noticed that the streets seemed to be getting broader and quieter and at last the coach came to a stop in front of an imposing mansion.

Feeling suddenly quite shabby in her outmoded pelisse and refurbished poke bonnet, Henrietta knocked firmly on the door. It was opened by a middle-aged butler who bowed her into a shadowy hallway with various servants sitting around on wooden benches. Obviously Mrs. Tankerton's staff was taking advantage of her illness, thought Henrietta. Even in provincial Nethercote, the servants were expected to remain in their own quarters unless they were actively engaged in work. Evidence of Mrs. Tankerton's old-fashioned ways was amply illustrated when Henrietta was ushered into a cedar parlor on the first floor to await her Great-Aunt's summons. A ring of hard upright chairs stood in a circle on an uncarpeted floor where the ladies were supposed to sit and coze. Obviously Mrs. Tankerton did not believe in the more relaxed atmosphere of the modern drawingroom with its oriental rugs and scattered chairs.

There was no fire in the grate and the wind howled dismally in the chimney. After what seemed like an age, the butler reappeared to inform Miss Sandford in hushed accents that Mrs. Tankerton awaited her.

She passed up another narrow flight of stairs to a massive oak door and into a dark bedroom dominated by a huge four-poster on which a small figure lay hunched against the pillows. Henrietta hesitated on the threshold, her heart beating fast. The curtains were tightly drawn and the only light came from a single candle beside the bed. The bare floor was waxed to a high shine. The only other furniture was a table beside the bed, laden with phials and medicine bottles and a few occasional chairs crowded against the far wall.

"Is that Miss Sandford, Hobbard?" came a querulous voice from the bed. The butler placed a chair beside the bed and withdrew. Henrietta moved slowly forward.

"Come here child and let me have a look at you." Mrs. Hester Tankerton raised herself slightly on the pillows. She was an elderly woman with thin wisps of grey hair escaping from under an enormous lace cap. The face was waxen, almost translucent, held to this world by a pair of small bright eyes like a bird's. Henrietta stood before her, her hazel eyes looking wonderingly at the small figure on the bed. Mrs. Tankerton sank back on the pillows as if the small effort had completely exhausted her. "You don't look like your brother," said Mrs. Tankerton, "but that's about all I can say for you."

"You know Henry?" asked Henrietta in surprise.

" 'Course I know Henry," snapped the invalid. "I know Henry and about every other toady in London. I'm very rich and I'm about to make my will. What d'ye think of that?"

9

Henrietta moved her hands in a sort of bewildered embarrassment and remained silent.

"Faugh!" said Mrs. Tankerton in disgust. "Milk and water miss! I am looking for an heir worthy of my fortune. Not some countrified, dowdy miss, frightened to open her mouth. Be off with you!"

She struggled to reach a small handbell beside the bed.

"Allow me, madame," said a voice like ice. Mrs. Tankerton looked up and encountered such a blazing look of dislike in Henrietta's large eyes that she remained frozen, her withered hand stopped motionless in mid air.

"You," said Miss Sandford, clearly and distinctly, "are a horrible old woman. No amount of money in the world gives you the right to be uncivil, madame. Good day to you!"

She marched past the astounded butler who had just arrived at the door of the room, and ran lightly down the stairs. She gave vent to her lacerated feelings by slamming the street door behind her with a resounding and most unladylike bang, and jumped into the coach.

Hobbard went forward anxiously to where his old mistress lay shaking on the bed. To his surprise he found that Mrs. Tankerton was convulsed with laughter.

"By George, Hobbard," she gasped. "Send for my lawyers. This'll put the cat among the pigeons. I'd give a monkey to see the look on Henry Sandford's face when the will is read.

"She'll do. Yes, I really think she'll do. . . ."

Chapter Two

"DEAR HENRIETTA, I FEEL you should pay a call on Miss Scattersworth," said the vicar of St. Anne's, Mr. Henry Sandford. "I myself will call on Lord and Lady Belding."

Miss Henrietta Sandford twitched the curtains and stared out at the rain which was blanketing the county town of Nethercote. "You will be taking the carriage then," she remarked in her placid voice.

"Of course," remarked the vicar, preening himself in the looking glass and straightening his cravat. "One must keep up appearances. But you will find the walk to Miss Scattersworth's invigorating. We should not put off our calls simply because one of our parishoners lives in the poorer section of the town."

Henrietta reflected that her brother, the vicar, did not at any time feel obliged to put his glossy hessians inside the door of any low class house. He left that duty to his sister. But she was fond of Miss Mattie Scattersworth who was an elderly spinster of the parish and one of her few close friends. She made a move to leave the room.

But her brother was not finished with her. He felt irritated that Henrietta had accepted the duty of a walk in the rain without fuss. He racked his brain for some way to annoy her.

"It is very gracious of the Beldings to include you in their invitation to the ball. It promises to be a very grand affair. Ah! If only you were as beautiful as Miss Alice Belding, we should have you married to some fine London Lord."

Miss Henrietta Sandford's one claim to beauty lay in a pair of magnificent hazel eyes. And with them, she surveyed her plump and pompous brother with an unfathomable expression. "Well, Henry, since I am six and twenty and practically an ape leader, you should realize that there is no hope for me," she finally remarked with an edge to her voice.

"And who's fault is that?" said her brother, turning an unflattering shade of red. "You could have been married to the squire had you not been so stubborn." The squire, Sir Arthur Cromer, was a widower of fifty-eight with daughters as old as Henrietta herself. It was an old argument and Henrietta decided to make her escape. She was entirely dependent on her brother for the roof over her head and the clothes on her back and he unfortunately topped every argument by reminding her of that unpleasant fact.

Henrietta escaped up the stairs to her room and began to prepare for the wet walk ahead. She pulled the heavy wooden pattens over her shoes and put that dowdy piece of headgear called a calash over her bonnet to protect her from the elements, reflecting that it would have cost her brother very little to allow her to hire a chair. But Henry delighted in penny-pinching—as far as his sister was concerned. His own clothes leaned almost to dandyism and would not have disgraced a Bond Street beau.

The town of Nethercote was considered by the few visitors from London to be a charming seventeenth-century village and by its residents as a bustling metropolis. Most of the town was centered round the central market square with its Assembly Rooms and posting house, The George and Dragon. Why go to London when the shops of Nethercote had everything there was to buy from the best of plain English fare to a real French dressmaker, Madame Aimée? The fact that Madame Aimée was once a Clapham seamstress called Bertha Battersby had been long forgotten and the townspeople did as much to foster her French image as Madame Aimée did herself.

Aristocracy was in residence just outside the town in the shape of the Beldings; and Sir Arthur Cromer, Henrietta's rejected squire, lived in a brand new cottage *ornée* to remind the sophisticates of Nethercote of the simple joys of country life despite the fact that his vast thatched-roofed residence could have housed a whole army of tenant farmers and their laborers.

Henrietta picked her way across the slippery cobbles of the market square, with the heavy ring on the soles of her pattens making an ugly clanking sound and the rain beginning to trickle down her neck.

The visit to Mrs. Tankerton seemed to be a long, long way away. She had told no one of her visit, not even Miss Scattersworth. Miss Mattie Scattersworth would have thought her mad for not trying to ingratiate herself into the rich lady's graces.

Miss Scattersworth lived above the bakery at the corner of the square. She was one of Nethercote's many indigent gentlewomen, keeping the body and soul together by sharing each other's modest tea trays, and perpetually living in the grim and awful shadow of the poorhouse.

As she climbed the stairs to Miss Scattersworth's lodgings, Henrietta composed her features into their usual outward calm.

"My dear Henrietta!" gasped Miss Scattersworth, "So delighted! But in this terrible weather. You must be chilled to the bone."

"I am," said Henrietta matter-of-factly. "Do let me in, Mattie."

Miss Scattersworth stood aside with profuse apologies and followed her young friend into the tiny parlor where a meager fire fought a losing battle with the all-pervading chill of the bleak November day.

Henrietta placed a basket of victuals tactfully on a small table but Miss Mattie's quick eyes had caught the action and filled with grateful tears. "So good of your dear brother," she said in a choked voice.

"Fustian!" said Henrietta sharply. "You know he would not even give you a piece of bread. I stole these from the kitchens."

Only in front of her elderly friend did Henrietta put off her carefully cultivated social mask. Miss Mattie gave a delighted gasp and covered her mouth with her long, bony freckled fingers.

A lifetime of genteel poverty had not dimmed Miss Mattie's spirit for adventure. A thin angular female of sixty-two with thick grey hair in neat bunches of ringlets under a modest cap, she had never given up hoping that something exciting would happen to change her drab life. She was an avid reader of novels and Henrietta thought that her friend lived more between the pages of her favorite romances than in the real world.

When they were both seated in front of the fire, Mattie leaned forward and grasped Henrietta's hand. "Now tell me all about your going to the Beldings' ball. What are you going to wear? Do you think you are going to fall in love? I can see it all. He will cover your face with impassioned kisses and ..."

"And throw me across his saddle-bow," grinned Henrietta. "And of course Miss Alice Belding will be so madly jealous that she will ..."

"Take poison and in a fit of remorse for all the bad things she has said to you, will leave you all her money in her will and ..." cried Mattie.

"And," interrupted Henrietta, "we will both go to London for the Season where we will dazzle all the gentlemen with our unique beauty and ..."

"I shall marry an Earl and you a Duke," finished Mattie triumphantly.

Both burst out laughing. Then Henrietta shook her head. "You know what it will be like, Mattie. I shall sit in the corner with the chaperones and occasionally be singled out by Alice who will deign to drop a few crumbs of gossip to me from her lofty height."

"What will you be wearing?" asked Mattie.

"Oh, I shall be very fine," said Henrietta. "Henry has spared no expense on this occasion. Alice made a derisory remark about my dowdy gowns in his hearing. It was only meant to hurt me, of course, but it made Henry determined to dress me as richly as possible . . . if only for the ball. I turn back to a pumpkin when the dance is over. What am I wearing? Rose silk, my dear, cut dangerously low on the bosom but vastly pretty for all that. I shall at least *feel* pretty."

Miss Mattie hesitated and then said timidly, "I have noticed that when you are animated and your eyes sparkle . . . why I think you look very well indeed."

Henrietta blinked in surprise. She was not accustomed to compliments even from her old friend. "Why, thank you, Mattie. I shall endeavour to sparkle to the best of my ability. Oh, I had almost forgot. A splendid piece of news. No less a personage than Beau Reckford is to attend. The Beldings are all a-flutter and hope for a match between Miss Alice and the Beau."

"Who on earth is Beau Reckford? Is he a dandy?" asked Miss Mattie.

Henrietta laughed. "No. He is a Corinthian and a very Top of the Trees. He is an expert swordsman and pugilist and drives to an inch. He has broken more hearts than we have had hot dinners and is said to be prodigious handsome."

Miss Mattie's eyes misted over with emotion. "He sounds like the very man for *you*, my dear Henrietta."

"Stuff!" retorted Henrietta. "He will not even notice me with Alice Belding around."

"She *is* terribly pretty," sighed Miss Mattie. "And

15

the gentlemen never seem to notice what she is like underneath . . . spoiled and cruel. Surely she is too young, though. She is only eighteen and does not make her come-out till next Season."

"*That* will not stop my lord and lady or their daughter," said Henrietta. "The paragon is very rich as well."

"How did you find out so much about him?" asked Mattie, carefully giving the fire its ration of one lump of coal.

"Oh, from Henry. He lives in the Beldings' pockets, you know. What else do I know of the famous Beau? Let me see . . . he is nine-and-twenty, real name, Lord Guy Reckford, reputation . . . rake and sportsman."

"Oh, if only he would fall in love with you," twittered Miss Mattie, jumping to her feet and pacing up and down the room.

"And *then*," smiled Henrietta, "he would immediately reform . . ."

"And give up his evil ways. . . ." said Mattie.

"And all his opera dancers and gambling hells. . . ."

"And you will have lots and lots of children and live happily ever after," said Miss Mattie triumphantly, her ringlets bobbing and her face flushed.

"Really, Mattie," protested Henrietta. "I think you half believe our fantasies."

"And why not?" said the spinster defiantly. "I'm sure it only takes a bit of energy and courage to bring it about."

"Well, all my energy and courage will go into simply enduring the evening," said Henrietta and with that she took her leave.

The days before the ball were mercifully free of Henry's pompous and overbearing presence. He had posted up to town to order a new suit of evening clothes from Stultz. He had confided to Henrietta that he had chosen blue silk as the most suitable material.

His sister had tried to point out that in view of her brother's increasing age—he was nearing forty—and waistline, the current mode set by Mr. Brummell for severe black and white evening dress might be more suitable. Henry had merely pooh-poohed. "I do not follow the dictates of that popinjay Brummell. Why, I don't believe the fellow even knows his own parents. Fellow asked him the other day about his parents and Brummell replied that it had been a long time since he had seen them but that he imagined that the worthy couple must have cut their throats by this time because when he last saw them they were eating peas with their knives! What d'ye think of that?"

Henrietta had merely smiled and commented that since George Brummell's father had been able to place him in a most fashionable regiment, then he must be all that was respectable.

But on the evening of the ball, there was Henry, tight blue silk encasing his rotund form, and panting and gasping under the restriction of a pair of Cumberland corsets. A handsome powdered wig covered his sparse hair and his waistcoat rattled with fobs and seals of all kinds. The points of his cravat were so high that he could hardly turn his head.

His protruding eyes bulged even more as he surveyed his sister. The simple Empire lines of her rose silk gown were very flattering to her plump figure and showed her white arms and bosom to advantage. Her heavy blonde hair which was usually worn under a cap was dressed in one of the latest styles, rioting in a mass of loose curls confined with a rose silk ribbon.

"Well, well, I suppose you'll do," said the vicar in a dampening voice. "Remember to cultivate the friendship of Miss Belding. She is all gracious condecension."

"Exactly," remarked Henrietta. "I sometimes think that Alice seeks me out as a friend only to use me as a foil for her beauty."

"Nonsense! How dare you speak like that! Miss Alice is an angel!" raged the vicar. "How dare you

17

presume to be impertinent to me . . . me who has to share my daily bread with you because you have nothing of your own. Without me, you would be starving in the gutter."

All animation drained from Henrietta's face leaving the usual placid mask. "Yes, Henry," she said in a deceptively mild voice.

"That's better," said her brother surveying her bowed head. "Miss Alice Belding, as I pointed out, is an angel. You agree?"

"Yes, Henry," said Henrietta meekly with her outer voice while her inner voice raged. "You wouldn't know the first thing about angels, you old hypocrite, and you're not likely to find out in the after life because you will be burning in hell."

Gathering up her reticule, fan and Norfolk shawl, Henrietta wondered for the hundredth time how there could be so little love between a brother and sister.

Their father, Sir James Sandford, had died after an accident on the hunting field; and their mother, Isabella, had died giving birth to Henrietta, a fact that her elder brother never let her forget. Since he did not mean to get married, Henry Sandford had long ago found out that Henrietta adequately accomplished the duties which were usually assigned to the vicar's wife. With the exception of the aforementioned squire, he had discouraged all possible suitors and denied Henrietta a Season in London.

Henrietta assumed that they must have been left a comfortable income. The vicar's clothes were so expensive and so dandified that several people in the town were apt to remark that his dress was unsuited to his calling. He had an excellent hardworking curate in an elderly man called John Symes who fulfilled most of the vicar's ecclesiastical duties, leaving Henry free to toady to the Beldings.

There had been Beldings in Nethercote since the Norman Conquest. Theirs was an ancient, if undistinguished, line, the ancestral Beldings having had a deft habit of changing their politics and religion to suit the current ruler. The present family followed in the pattern of their forebears, having a great deal of money, incredible arrogance and very little else worthy of comment.

When they arrived at Belding Court, Henrietta pasted a fixed social smile on her face and prepared to sit out the evening as she had done many times before. Alice Belding was wearing a slim white high-waisted dress which set off her blonde beauty to perfection. She was as fair as Henrietta but there the similarity ended. Where Henrietta was plump, Alice was slender, where Henrietta's face was round and placid, Alice's sparkled with animation, all wide blue eyes and dimples.

"You are looking very fine, Henrietta," remarked Alice. "Although perhaps your hairstyle is a little bit too young for you. Turbans are quite suitable for a girl of your age, you know. I shall call on you tomorrow and we shall have a comfortable coze and I will tell you all about my admirers. I am sure it will be just like having them yourself. We are such dear friends." She smiled brilliantly at the vicar who complimented her fulsomely on her appearance and then drew his infuriating sister aside.

"Why didn't you reply when she said you were 'such dear friends,' " he hissed, holding her above the elbow in a painful grip. "Such condescension!"

"Sorry, Henry," said Henrietta quietly, smiling warmly at Alice Belding while her inner voice said caustically, "I wish, just once, that some man would see her for what she is . . . an empty-headed, cruel, vicious little. . . ."

"Look!" exclaimed the vicar. "Beau Reckford has arrived."

Henrietta looked across the room with interest. Her first emotion was one of surprise. Surely no one could consider the Beau handsome. His harsh aquiline features and light tawny eyes gave him a look of a bird of prey. He was very tall, well over six feet and impeccably dressed in black evening coat and knee breeches. His snowy cravat was tied in the Waterfall and he wore his black hair unpowdered. Then he smiled down at his hostess and his whole face was transformed. No woman could resist that smile, thought Henrietta, feeling a painful lurch inside her. Lady Belding was positively fluttering, the end of her high patrician nose turning absolutely pink with delight. Alice was radiant. She fluttered her long eyelashes demurely behind her fan. Feeling suddenly old and chubby, Henrietta trailed off miserably to take her usual place with the chaperones.

Lord Reckford led Alice out for the first dance and Henrietta stared down at her slippers and tried not to look. This is ridiculous, she chided herself. One just does not fall in love at first sight. "Oh, yes one does," snarled her inner voice, "and you've just done it."

She tried to concentrate on the conversation of the two elderly chaperones next to her. "I hear they are going to waltz this evening," said one to the other. "I can't help feeling that the waltz is . . . well . . . *fast*. Now, in our day, the minuet was all the rage. That really was dancing. One needed to have so much poise and grace. And we wore a special little lappet in our headdress to show that we could perform the minuet or was it to show that we meant to perform the minuet. Oh, dear! I do forget things these days." "It's our age," replied her companion. "But I do remember how much I loved watching the minuet performed. Now a gentleman had to have a very good leg for that! Legs are terribly important in a gentleman. They must be muscular but not *too* thick. And the ankle must be well-turned."

Henrietta's sense of the ridiculous was fairly tickled and her face lit up in a smile. Then to her confusion, she noticed Lord Reckford studying her from the other side of the floor and she began looking at her slippers again.

"Who is that pretty girl over there?" said Beau

Reckford to Lady Belding. She and her daughter, Alice, looked across the floor in a bewildered way. "Over there," repeated his lordship, waving his quizzing glass in the direction of Henrietta.

Lady Belding looked at him in pure amazement. "You can't possibly mean Henrietta Sandford—the girl in the pink gown."

"Yes," said Lord Reckford, "I mean the girl in the pink gown." Three pairs of eyes surveyed Henrietta who was now scowling horribly and staring at the floor. Beau Reckford would have left matters as they were because when he had first noticed Henrietta as she smiled at the conversation of the chaperones with her large hazel eyes twinkling, he had thought her an attractive girl. Now she simply seemed plain and plump. But Alice Belding was outraged.

"You are funning, of course! Henrietta pretty! She is a pleasant girl, I allow, but she is all of six-and-twenty and has no beaux."

"Indeed! She is younger than I," commented Lord Reckford. He considered Alice pretty but spiteful. He would dance with the girl in the pink gown after all. He turned to Lady Belding, "Please present me, madame."

Henrietta looked up and blushed as she saw her hostess standing in front of her with Lord Reckford. With an icy glare, Lady Belding made the introductions and after the couple had murmured to each other that they were enjoying the dance, took hold of the gentleman's arm to lead him back to her daughter. With horror, she heard his lordship asking Henrietta to stand up with him for the waltz. There was nothing she could do but return to her furious daughter. Alice had told the whole of Nethercote that she would dance the waltz with Beau Reckford and there went that dumpy little Henrietta, floating round in his lordship's arms. He was laughing! What was Henrietta saying? Alice accepted a partner for the waltz with bad grace and nearly injured her neck by craning over her partner's shoulder to catch a glimpse of the maddening couple.

Henrietta had never been happier in her life. After her initial shyness, she had found herself chatting quite easily with her formidable partner. For his part, the Beau gave the dazzled Henrietta the full benefit of his considerable charm.

"Where did you learn to waltz?" he asked.

She gave an infectious giggle. "I studied the steps by sitting watching the dancers at my last ball and then practised them with my old friend, Miss Scattersworth. She will be so pleased that I found a gentleman to waltz with!"

"I am sure many gentlemen would wish to waltz with such a charming partner," he said gallantly.

"Very nicely put," said Henrietta admiringly. "The next time I sit with the chaperones and wallflowers, I shall treasure your words."

He looked down into the hazel eyes with a startled expression in his own. "If we go on like this," he said lightly, "we shall make honesty positively fashionable. What an unusual girl you are!"

"Oh, I do so hope honesty never becomes the *crack*," said his partner following a neatly executed turn with an expertise she would previously have thought impossible. "Cannot you imagine, my lord, what a flutter *that* would cause? 'I am compelled to dance with you Miss X because my mama is interested in your fortune. But I would infinitely prefer to be dancing with the beautiful Miss Y.'"

His eyes held a mocking look. "Ah, but you see, Miss Sandford, honesty holds no pitfalls for me. I dance with exactly whom I please."

"Gentlemen are indeed fortunate," replied Henrietta. "Now ladies really have to accept *anyone* and with very good grace too. Of course, we have our little excuses. We can plead the headache or the vapors. But I am sure that has never happened to you."

"No," he said cynically. "Since we are both being so

honest, I would hasten to point out that the ladies' compliance is because of my fortune rather than my face or figure. Sometimes I feel like a great bag of sovereigns balanced on two legs."

"Now that I would not mind in the least," said Henrietta. "I adore dancing and should not care in the least for my partner's motives provided I could dance all night!"

The waltz came to an end and Lord Reckford suddenly made up his mind. He would take Henrietta into supper. Little chits like Alice Belding were ten a penny, despite her looks, but this girl was really something different.

But Henry Sandford was waiting to accost them, his face crimson with fury and embarrassment. He had just had his marching orders from Lady Belding in no uncertain terms.

"My dear vicar," she had fluted, never taking her eyes from Henrietta or her partner for a minute, "I note that your sister is not in looks. In fact, she is decidedly peaked. You must take her home."

"But Henrietta is never ill," protested Henry.

Lady Belding gave him the full benefit of an icy glare. "I said take her home," she said between her teeth. "You are not usually so obtuse regarding my wishes."

Accordingly, Henry grasped his sister's arm as Lord Reckford was in the middle of his invitation to supper.

"We must go home immediately," said Henry. "I am not well."

"You certaintly look extremely red," said Lord Reckford dryly. "Do you really need your sister's help?"

"Yes," snapped Henry. "I am afraid I might faint."

"In that case," said his lordship, "I shall escort you myself. You obviously need a man's strong arm. You will want your sister to stay and enjoy the ball."

"Yes . . . no . . . that is . . . ," Henry broke off and gave his sister a venomous look. Henrietta found she was receiving the same look from both Lady Belding and her daughter. Her face resumed its customary mask.

"Thank you, my lord, but your services will not be necessary. I understand exactly how to minister to my brother's complaint."

Had there been a trace of irony in her voice? But the hazel eyes were politely devoid of expression. "As you wish," said his lordship, giving the pair a formal bow. He strode off to the other side of the room and took the whole of Henrietta's heart with him.

Henrietta was to remember that terrible ride home with brother Henry to the end of her days. She had been presumptuous, said Henry. She knew how much his friendship with the Beldings meant to him and had deliberately gone out of her way to destroy it. If this was all the thanks he was to receive for years of room and board and loving kindness, then she could go out and earn her own bread. She was not qualified for much except the post of paid companion. Yes, yes, that was it. He would consult Lady Belding on the morrow. And having successfully disposed of Henrietta's future, he entered the house and took himself off to bed in a more tranquil frame of mind.

His sister cried herself to sleep. The future looked grim indeed. Paid companions led a life of genteel drudgery and although it would be much the same existence as she now had, there would be no more chance of dancing the waltz with handsome rakes like Lord Reckford.

Chapter Three

THE MORNING DAWNED AS gray and leaden as her spirits. There was a fine sprinkling of snow on the ground and the clouds above the square Norman tower of St. Anne's beside the vicarage, were swollen and black with the threat of more to come. The vicarage emulated the style of a country house on a small scale. The public rooms were on the ground floor with the drawingroom to one side of the hallway and the diningroom on the other. The parlor, which had been on the first floor, had been redesigned by Henry into a master bedroom for himself.

Henrietta often wondered where her brother had found the money to carry out the expensive improvements, from the rich rugs on the polished floors to the removal of the ivy which had formally clung to the mellow brickwork of the Queen Ann house.

"We live on the grand scale but in miniature," Henry would say to visitors, with a deprecatory wave of his plump hands.

Henrietta sat down at the pianoforte in the drawingroom to play some sonatas to calm her jangled nerves. She was so intent on the music that she did not hear a visitor being announced and it was only when a discreet cough from the housekeeper penetrated her thoughts that she gave a start and turned round.

There stood Beau Reckford, impeccable in morningdress from his blue swallowtail coat of Bath Superfine to his glossy hessians, giving her a courtly bow. Henrietta was wearing her oldest dress of grey Kerseymere wool and she blushed painfully as she got to her feet. "I am sure my brother will be down d-directly," she stammered.

The Beau nodded and stood for a minute, wondering if she were ever going to ask him to sit down. Custom dictated that he should make calls on all the ladies he had danced with the night before and he had hoped that the visit to Henrietta would at least prove to be an amusing interlude. But the girl seemed to be painfully awkward and shy.

"Aren't you going to ask me to sit down?" he asked in his pleasant, husky voice.

"Please . . . please do . . . sit, I mean," said poor Henrietta, looking at him as if he had risen from the pit.

"I think we are going to have a heavy fall of snow. Do not you?" said Lord Reckford, stretching his long legs out in front of him.

"What! Oh, yes . . . snow. Yes . . . lots . . . I suppose," replied Henrietta faintly, knowing that she sounded hen-witted but unable to gain any sort of composure.

"Well, that disposes of the weather," said his lordship. "Now we shall discuss your brother's health. He did not have an apoplexy, I trust?"

Henrietta suddenly smiled and sat down. "No, of course not. He was much improved when he reached the fresh air. Fresh air is very beneficial to his complaint."

The tawny eyes surveyed her with a mocking look. "It's the first time I've heard of fresh air curing anyone suffering from Lady Belding's wrath."

A delighted smile lit up Henrietta's face. "How on earth did you . . ." she began.

"I noticed the little by-play," he drawled. "Alice goes to her mother and whispers fiercely, Lady Belding goes to your brother and whispers fiercely, and your brother is suddenly smitten with some strange disease. If you will forgive me for speaking so freely, I assure you I did not enjoy the ball after you left."

Henrietta's large eyes shone with a gleam of mischief. "Thank you for the pretty compliment, my lord. The sudden loss of your company quite devastated me, myself, I must admit."

The Beau, who had expected her to simper, looked at her in some surprise. He was not used to having his gallantries neatly returned, especially by country misses.

He leaned forward and said with mock intensity, "I am glad my feelings are reciprocated, Miss Sandford. May I kiss your hand?" He dropped a light kiss on her wrist and glanced up at her from under his lashes. Now how would Miss Sandford of the vicarage cope with that!

Henrietta's heart had given a painful lurch but not by one flicker would she betray to this heartbreaker the strength of her feeling for him. She held her wrist to her cheek and looked at him soulfully. "I may never wash this poor hand again," she said on a fluttering sigh.

Something remarkably like a giggle escaped from her elegant companion. "Why, you are the veriest minx," he remarked rising to his feet and crossing to the pianoforte. "You were playing very beautifully when I came in," he said flicking through the music. "What have we here . . . do you know this one . . . 'Early One Morning?'" Without waiting for her reply, he started to sing in a loud baritone and was soon joined by Henrietta's clear soprano.

"How could you use a poor maiden so," they were carolling happily, when they were interrupted by an enraged voice from the doorway. "What is going on here?" It was Henry puffing and goggling like a turkeycock. Both singers stopped and stared at him, Henrietta in consternation and the Beau in surprise.

"I repeat, what is going on here?" demanded Henry, strutting into the room. Lord Reckford raised his quizzing glass and glared awfully at the irate vicar. "I think you should explain your manner," he drawled. "I am not accustomed to provincial drawingrooms."

Henry flushed in confusion. He did not want to offend Lady Belding but, on the other hand, he did not wish to annoy such a notable man of fashion as Lord Reckford. "I was taken by surprise, my lord," he explained hurriedly. "My little sister has led a very sheltered life and perhaps I am over-protective. You were coming to the end of your call no doubt."

To his horror, Lord Reckford ignored this patent hint and sat down on the piano stool next to Henrietta and began turning over the music.

The vicar sat on the edge of the sofa and surveyed the pair in dismay. Why they had their heads nearly together as they discussed various composers. With relief, he rose to meet a new pair of arrivals. Lady Belding and her daughter sailed in and halted in frozen dismay at the sight of Henrietta and her companion. Alice and her mother had spent a frustrating morning chasing from house to house after the Beau. They had run through all his dancing partners of the night before and had finally thought of Henrietta. Lord Reckford had made his first duty call on Alice but he had stayed only for a few minutes to say that he would be departing for London that day. So the redoubtable Lady Belding had decided to hunt him down to acquaint him further with the charms of her daughter.

They were further frustrated when the infuriating lord rose immediately to his feet, made a magnificent leg, and departed. Alice and her mother ran to the window and watched him drive away through the now heavily falling snow. To Henrietta, it was as if the last little bit of light had left the room.

She looked at the company and three pairs of baleful eyes stared back at her.

Before Lady Belding could speak, Henry hurriedly outlined his plan of sending his sister out to earn her living as a paid companion "in order to teach her the virtues of Christian humility."

Immediately Lady Belding was all smiles. She knew the very lady, a Mrs. Grammiweather who lived in the next county. Mrs. Grammiweather, it appeared, was ailing and had run through a selection of paid companions in the past two years.

Alice had recovered all her radiance. "It will serve very well, Henrietta," she said taking that girl's hand in a warm clasp. "And you will not be out of touch for I shall write to you from London when I have my Season and tell you all about the balls and routs and parties."

Henrietta made a last bid for independence. "I would rather you didn't," she said. "Since I shall no longer be able to take part in social occasions except as a kind of servant, I would rather forget that such a world exists."

And to united shouts of 'impertinent' and 'ungrateful,' she hurried from the room to indulge in yet another hearty cry. She hardly knew whether she was weeping over her future as a companion to a sick old lady or whether it was because she would never see Lord Reckford again.

Downstairs Lady Belding was rising to take her leave. "You have done very well, Mr. Sandford, very well indeed. I shall not forget. Perhaps I was a trifle abrupt last night but Alice has set her heart on marrying Lord Reckford and since she is the only child I have, I mean to see that she gets what she wants. Pray ring for our carriage."

By mid-afternoon, the snow had ceased, leaving the town of Nethercote sparkling like a Christmas card.

Henrietta watched the housekeeper, Mrs. Ballis, hurrying off with her shopping basket, and crept down to the kitchen on stockinged feet to raid the larder for food to take to her friend, Miss Mattie. Then silently pulling on her pattens and shoes, she slipped quietly out by way of the area steps and took a deep breath of cold clear air. If only she had enough money just to keep on walking and never return.

The heroines in the novels she and Miss Mattie read would not be so poor spirited. They would become governesses and marry their employer's handsome son or dress up as boys and become smugglers, but never, thought Henrietta savagely, would they sit and accept their fate with a meek 'Yes, Henry.' Well, their spirits had not been broken as hers had been and they did not live in the harsh world of reality. "If only I were a man!" muttered Henrietta through clenched teeth. Then she remembered the Beau and was heartily glad she was not.

She suddenly thought of Mrs. Tankerton. Surely she had been a fool to throw away the chance of a fortune! Then she mentally shrugged. The old woman had simply been playing a game of power. She would probably live to a hundred, threatening and blackmailing her friends and relatives and changing her will and her mind every few days. Henry had still not even admitted to her existence.

Miss Mattie was twittering with excitement at the prospect of hearing some delightful gossip about the ball. But her sympathetic eyes filled with their ready tears when Henrietta outlined her fate.

"But why should your brother suddenly decide on such a cruel idea," cried Miss Mattie.

Henrietta told her about Lord Reckford. Miss Mattie's eyes flashed with optimism. "There you are! He *did* fall in love with you. Now your worries are over. He will ride post-haste and *ventre à terre* to this Mrs. Grammiweather and demand that his affianced wife be released from bondage and Mrs. Grammiweather will say . . ."

"Don't make such a cake of yourself, my lord," finished Henrietta dismally. "It's no good, Mattie. I can't play that sort of game any more."

"It's *not* a game," said Mattie intensely. "You must *hope*. Something will happen to you . . . oh . . . tomorrow, which will make your sun shine again!" As if in contradiction to her optimism, a gust of wind sobbed and cried in the chimney and escaped in the room where it set the flames of the tallow candles dancing.

"I must go, Mattie, before I get snowed in. Look . . . it's started falling again." Both women looked out of the tiny window. A link boy trudged along the street and in the light of his lantern they could see the snow falling thick and fast.

By the time Henrietta reached home, the snow was well above her ankles, she was late for dinner, and was forced to listen to a long and spiteful lecture from her brother about punctuality being the first duty of a good servant and, since she was shortly to enter that class, she should bear it in mind.

Despising herself, Henrietta said, "Yes. Henry dear," and wondered to herself how her brother envisaged his Maker. Probably as some superior member of the aristocracy, she thought bitterly, who placed his angels carefully on clouds at a height according to their social station.

"Lady Belding has written to Mrs. Grammiweather this very day," said Henry, dabbing at his rosebud mouth with his napkin. "You must call on her tomorrow and thank her most humbly for her efforts. Why! What a peculiar look you have on your face!"

He did not know that in her mind his sister had removed the chafing dish and was holding his head face down over the flames of the spirit lamp.

"It is merely a touch of indigestion," explained Henrietta.

"You eat too much," remarked her brother. Henrietta opened her mouth to point out that it was an obvious family failing since they were both overweight but tactfully held her tongue. She wondered if her brother ate too much for the same reasons as herself—waiting for the heavy weight of food to tranquilise her mind—but looking at his pompous face she doubted it.

She kept her replies to polite monosyllables until the vicar rang the claret bell and signalled to her with a wave of his plump beringed hand that she had his permission to retire.

The next morning Henrietta descended to the breakfast parlor early in the hope of avoiding her brother but he was already there, leafing through the morning post which had managed to arrive despite the heavy snow.

Suddenly with a quickening heartbeat, Henrietta noticed him picking up a heavy letter addressed to herself. Without even looking at her, he opened it with a paper knife and started to read. Henry read all her letters.

"Bless my soul!" gasped the vicar, rattling the pages of the letter. "Why, bless my soul."

"What is it, Henry dear?" asked Henrietta watching her brother's prominent Adam's apple bobbing up and down over the edge of his tight cravat. "If I painted little red eyes on it," mused Henrietta, "it would look just like a puppet in a Punch and Judy show."

"Bless my soul!" gasped the vicar for the third time.

"What is it Henry?" asked Henrietta and thinking, "if he doesn't tell me soon, I shall pour his tankard of small beer slowly onto his head."

Her brother at last surveyed her in amazement. "Henrietta! Did I ever tell you of our Great Aunt Hester Tankerton?"

"No," lied Henrietta with forced calm. "You have always told me that we have no living relatives."

"Well, this is from her solicitors and I can hardly believe my eyes. The old lady who was prodigious rich has passed away . . . and left you her entire fortune.

You! I can't believe it. Why, I could have sworn she did not know of your existence. In fact, I took pains to. . . ." He broke off in some confusion and unwillingly put the letter into his sister's hands.

It stated simply that Miss Henrietta Sandford was the sole inheritor of Mrs. Emily Tankerton's fortune and the lawyer would be pleased to call on her during the month to explain the terms of the will. Failing that, if Miss Sandford would present herself at his chambers in Cheapside, London, the whole affair could be transacted quickly and to their mutual satisfaction. It was signed 'Yr. obliged and faithful humble servant, James Twiddle.'

Henry Sandford was getting over his first shock. He surveyed his sister with her placid round features under her neat cap and suddenly smiled. "Well, well, it is not so bad after all," he said, rubbing his hands. "The money is in the family after all, heh! I must apprise everyone of our good fortune." He dropped a kiss on top of his sister's cap. She winced in surprise and turned to watch him hurrying from the room.

Henrietta sat for a long time staring at the letter until the hawk-like features of Lord Reckford seemed to swim in front of the paper. A slow smile gradually spread over her face.

Half an hour later, several of the townspeople were shocked to see the respectable Miss Henrietta Sandford entering the portals of the town pawnbroker without even a veil to cover her face. Others later caught a glimpse of her looking out of the window of a smart rented carriage and pair which took the London road at breakneck speed despite the deep snow.

Chapter Four

THE LAMPS HAD BEEN lit for several hours in the vicarage drawingroom and still there was no sign of Miss Henrietta Sandford.

Henry paced up and down, occasionally rushing to the window at the sound of an approaching carriage. Three women sat and watched him—Lady Belding, her daughter, Alice and Miss Mattie Scattersworth. The latter had been sent for in the hope that she might know the whereabouts of her young friend.

"You say Henrietta is now a very wealthy woman?" queried Lady Belding, breaking the funereal silence.

"Very rich indeed," answered Henry. "But of course her money is mine, so to speak."

"But according to the terms of the will—or what you gathered from the letter—the fortune has been left absolutely and completely to Henrietta?"

"Indeed, yes," said Henry. "But Henrietta will leave the managing of it to me. What do women know of money? Dear, dear, what could have become of her?"

"Perhaps," began Miss Mattie with an apologetic cough, "she has been waylaid by highwaymen. Or perhaps," she added more hopefully, "by a *very* handsome highwayman who is really the younger son of a lord who is a kind of Robin Hood and who will fall in love with her and . . ."

"Nonsense," said Lady Belding roundly and Alice looked at Miss Mattie and slowly tapped her forehead. Miss Mattie blushed and relapsed into silence.

The wind howled in the chimney and the snow whispered against the window panes as if trying to get in and impart the whereabouts of Henrietta.

"Oh, do let's go, mother," pouted Alice, getting to her feet. Lady Belding held up her hand and in the ensuing silence, they could hear the muffled clop of horses hooves. They all rushed to the window and there was Henrietta descending from a rented carriage drawn by two tired and steaming horses.

In a few minutes, she burst into the drawingroom, her face flushed with the cold and then stopped short at the sight of her waiting audience. All began to speak at once.

"How dare you." (Henry)

"Positively gothic behavior." (Lady Belding)

"Dear Henrietta, your nose is quite red with cold!" (Alice Belding)

"Did a handsome highwayman accost you . . . ?" (Miss Mattie)

Henrietta sank down on to a chair and grinned unrepently at them all. "I posted up to town to see the lawyer . . ."

"How unladylike!" screamed Lady Belding.

"And he told me the extent of my fortune. I will not bore you with the amount since you, my lady, have always told me it is exceeding vulgar to discuss money. But I am mistress of a very fine house in Brook Street."

Henry went to stand over her, his fat white face a mask of rage. "Did you say *you* owned this property? No! *We* own it. And you will oblige me by ceasing to trouble your head about affairs of property. That is a man's business."

Henrietta surveyed him from top to toe, her face a mask. Then she took a deep breath. "My dear brother, you have pointed out to me for as long as I can remember that I am a sore burden on you. I am about to remove that burden. I leave on the morrow to take up residence in my house in Brook Street to prepare for the Season."

"You have gone raving mad," screamed Lady Belding, before Henry could speak. "It is unheard of . . . a spinster of your years living alone."

"Oh, I shall not be living alone," replied Henrietta sweetly. "I am sure Miss Mattie will be happy to chaperone me."

Miss Mattie Scattersworth gasped and clutched her hands in front of her scrawny bosom. "Too honored . . . delighted. Oh, Henrietta, am I to have a Season too?"

"Of course," said Henrietta, smiling at her.

Lady Belding was beside herself with rage. She had shared Henry's favorite pastime of bullying his sister and now felt as if one of her hounds had suddenly bitten her in the ankle.

She stamped her foot in rage. "A touch of the riding crop is what you need to bring you to your senses. You! A Season! I tell you my girl, I happen to be acquainted with the patronesses of Almack's and by the time I am through, you will not be allowed to cross the portals of any respectable drawingroom in London."

"Really, mother, you are too harsh," whispered Alice. "I fear Henrietta forgets her age and thinks she is once again a debutante. Her head has been turned by the attentions of a certain Beau."

Henrietta heard the whisper and flushed as red as fire. She got to her feet. "Come, Mattie," said Henrietta, turning her back on her tormenters, "and help me to pack my trunks."

"I forbid this," roared Henry. "You are not right in your mind. I forbid you to leave this house."

Goaded beyond reason, Henrietta turned back and faced them. "Do what you will. I tell you for the first and last time. I shall have my Season in London *and* I shall marry Lord Reckford. So there! Come Mattie," and she swept from the room in the middle of a stunned silence.

Upstairs in the privacy of her bedroom, she stared triumphantly at Miss Mattie. "Well, we make our escape tonight. Henry will only think to bar the doors in the morning."

Miss Mattie was pink with pleasure. "Oh, dear, Henrietta, do you think it will take us long to pack your belongings?"

"Not in the slightest. I am only taking one bandbox," said Henrietta. "We are going to buy lots of lovely new clothes and be all the crack. Come let's move quickly. I shall stay with you for the night and we shall quit Nethercote first thing in the morning."

The packing was accomplished quickly and both women sat in silence waiting for the sound of Henry retiring for the night. At last, they heard him mount the stairs. He stopped outside Henrietta's door and rattled the knob furiously but she had placed a chair under the handle. After what seemed like ages, he went away. They waited another half hour and then Henrietta whispered that it was time to leave. Holding their heavy pattens in their hands, the two women crept downstairs, feeling their way in the dark. "We had best leave by the kitchen entrance," whispered Henrietta. Stealthily, they moved through the kitchen and quietly edged the heavy door open onto the area, up the snow-covered stairs to the street—and freedom.

The heavy snow tugged at their long skirts and froze their feet but neither noticed the discomfort on the road to Miss Mattie's modest lodgings.

Once inside, Miss Mattie began to ration her small stock of coals, dropping them carefully one by one on top of the sticks on the fireplace.

"Drop them all on," said Henrietta cheerfully.

Mattie looked at her in horror and Henrietta gave her infectious giggle. "We're rich now, Mattie. Have a great, big beautiful blaze for once in your life."

Miss Mattie clapped her hands in delight and began gaily throwing on all her small stock of wood and coal until the flames roared up the chimney. Then she went to a small cupboard and produced six whole new candles and began to light them one by one, banishing the black shadows and miserable poverty of the small room with a blaze of light.

Then she scurried back to the cupboard and proudly produced a bottle which she held up triumphantly. "French brandy!" exclaimed Henrietta.

"A gentleman gave it to me one Christmas many years ago," said Miss Mattie. "I saved it for a very special occasion and this is it!" She produced glasses and poured two huge measures with the carefree generosity of someone unaccustomed to hard liquor.

Both sat toasting their wet feet at the roaring fire, sipping their brandy and dreaming their dreams.

Henrietta looked across at her elderly friend and guiltily wished there was some—well—some less *eccentric* female she could ask to chaperone her. But there *was* no one else. And how could she possibly run away and enjoy her new found wealth and leave poor Mattie behind? Miss Scattersworth was more starved for adventure than she was for food. Lady Belding had often commented acidly that London society was simply crawling with elderly quizzes and eccentrics.

Her mind moved on to a more pressing worry. "What on earth made me say I was going to marry Lord Reckford," she wailed. "Lady Belding will make sure he hears of it!"

"Never mind," said Miss Mattie soothingly. "Perhaps it will just put the idea of marriage into Lord Reckford's head. And, in any case, everyone will just think she is being spiteful as usual.

"Now let us talk of more cheerful things. We must re-decorate the house in Brook Street. We shall have the drawingroom downstairs in, say, the Egyptian mode. I hear it is all the crack. . . ."

Chapter Five

SEVERAL MONTHS HAD PASSED since Henrietta's flight. London had been thin of company but, with the beginning of the Season close at hand, the fashionable ten thousand had mostly all taken up residence in the metropolis.

The Georgian house in Brook Street had been redecorated from cellar to attic. The grim cedar parlor had been turned into a charming morning room in varying shades of rose and cream with a work table, a writing desk and comfortable chairs. Miss Scattersworth had had her way with the drawingroom which was in the Egyptian style with a great number of sphynxes heads glaring from the carved feet of the chairs and from the ends of a remarkably uncomfortable backless sofa. She had then planned to turn an adjoining saloon into an Etruscan room but Henrietta had put her foot down and had had it decorated in blue and white with Wedgewood ornaments and Chinese rugs.

The cornices and mouldings of the square entrance hall were picked out in gold and white with white Brussels lace curtains at the windows overlooking the street. A charming Louis Quatorze table was strategically placed near the door bearing a large silver tray to receive the cards of the visitors who never came to call.

As far as the fashionable world was concerned, Miss Henrietta Sandford did not exist. This sad state of affairs could have gone on indefinitely but fortunately for Henrietta, Lord Reckford's closest friend was that renowned gossip and man-about-Town, Mr. Jeremy Holmes.

Mr. Holmes burst in upon his lordship unceremoniously one morning as Lord Reckford was preparing to depart for his club.

"Thought you had made all the conquests there was to make," he announced cheerfully. "Now it seems as if the vicar's sister from some godforsaken place is after you with the leg-shackles."

The Beau put an unintentional crease in his cravat, swore, ripped it off and took up another. He waved Jeremy to silence until he was satisfied with the results and then turned to survey his friend.

Mr. Holmes had draped his elegant form over a chair showing a pair of canary yellow Inexpressibles to their best advantage. Although he was the same age as the Beau, his cherubic countenance and mop of golden curls made him appear much younger.

Like the Beau, he had long been the despair of every matchmaking mama and had been castigated as a hardened flirt.

Lord Reckford looked at the breeches and at his friend's silk waistcoat which was embellished with broad orange stripes and shuddered. "If you get any noisier in your dress, Jeremy, they'll be taking you for a Macaroni."

"What's up with it!" exclaimed Mr. Holmes peevishly. "Met Brummell himself on m'way here and asked him for his opinion and he closed his eyes and said 'It berefts me of the power of speech.' So there. Stop changing the subject. Who's this Friday-faced female Lady Belding's telling everyone is going to marry you?"

"I know a great number of Friday-faced females but, for the moment, I cannot understand who it is you mean. Wait a bit! Vicar's sister. Does she come from a place called Nethercote?"

"That's it!" said Mr. Holmes.

"Well, for your information, she is not bad looking at all and since she is not likely to be in town for the Season, I fail to see how she can go about talking to me let alone marrying me."

"Ah, but she came into a fortune," explained Mr. Holmes. "And she's all set up right and tight in Brook Street. But you're right in a way. You ain't going to get a chance to meet her. Lady Belding's put about that she's strange in the head and that no respectable hostess should give her house room."

His lordship's thin brows snapped together. "And since when has my Lady Belding been such a social arbiter?"

Mr. Holmes leaned forward earnestly. "Well, she ain't exactly but the girl has no social connections. No one's heard of her before. So everyone just goes by what Lady Belding says."

Lord Reckford shrugged himself into his coat. "I can't say that I approve of Lady Belding—or her daughter for that matter."

"What!" Mr. Holmes nearly screamed. "Alice Belding is an angel. What's up with you? I've never seen such a beautiful face."

His lordship smiled. "I must be getting old. I think I shall go and call on my sister."

"Thought you was going to your club?"

"No, I have decided that the company of my sister Ann is just what I need at the moment."

Lord Reckford settled his curly-brimmed beaver on his head and telling his friend that he would see him later, he ordered his curricle and drove off at a smart pace, engrossed in thought. Lady Belding, he decided, needed to be taught a lesson. And so did Miss Henrietta. Then, he would kill two birds with one stone. He would flirt with Henrietta to infuriate Lady Belding and it would teach Henrietta a lesson when he dropped her. Anyway, by the time he dropped her, he would make sure she was firmly entrenched in the London scene.

Lord Reckford's sister, Ann, had married a retired Colonel, Sir Geoffrey Courtney, on her thirty-second birthday. As the Colonel was in his late fifties, friends and relatives moaned over the disparity of the ages. But the marriage, now two years old, seemed to work perfectly. Theirs was a harmonious household and Lord Reckford vowed to begin making his visits more frequent.

Ann was small and plump with her brother's hawk-like features and tawny eyes. After the welcomes were over and Ann had rung for the tea tray, her brother leaned his arm negligently along the mantlepiece and began, "I have come to talk to you about a certain young lady."

His sister brightened. "You are to be married at last. Will I like her?"

He shook his head. "Last winter when I was staying near Nethercote, I attended a ball at the Beldings. There was a young lady there, the vicar's sister, who seemed to be unmercifully bullied by her brother and Lady Belding alike. Now it seems she has come into a fortune and plans to make a late debut on the London social scene—she is in her middle twenties—with, according to Lady Belding, the object of marrying me."

"How dreadful!" said Lady Courtney. "What an encroaching female."

"I am not so sure," said her brother thoughtfully. "Lady Belding is a spiteful, malicious woman. If Miss Henrietta indeed plans to marry me, then I shall flirt with her and give her a subsequent set down. But first, to punish Lady Belding, I mean to bring Miss Henrietta Sandford into society."

A worried frown creased Lady Courtney's face. "Are you not being a little too high-handed? You seem so sure that it is in your power to make this girl fall in love with you. You have never been in love so you are not aware of the amount of pain you may be inflicting on her."

"I doubt very much if she *is* in love with me any more than any of the debutantes who languish each Season so prettily after my title and my fortune," said Lord Reckford with his long mouth set in an unpleasant sneer "I want you to call on her," he added abruptly.

Lady Courtney stared at him in surprise. "You are too arrogant by half. Why should I call on a presumptuous nobody from some vicarage?"

"*Now,* who is being arrogant!" laughed Lord Reckford. "Come now, sis, I hardly ever ask you to do anything for me. I do need your help."

She gave him a rueful smile. "I never could resist helping my little brother. I'll call. But just this once!"

Unaware that their social life was about to begin, Henrietta and Miss Mattie sat in the morningroom and looked dismally at each other.

"I don't think anyone is going to call . . . ever," said Miss Scattersworth sadly.

Miss Scattersworth was a vision in pink sprigged muslin with her grey hair cut in a smart Brutus crop. It was perhaps an embarrassingly youthful ensemble but since no one but herself seemed likely to see it, Henrietta had refrained from comment or criticism. She herself was looking very pretty in all the glory of a yellow silk morning gown with tiny puffed sleeves, its simple lines ending in three deep flounces.

"I would so love to go to a ball or party," sighed Henrietta. "We have seen enough of the unfashionable sights from the Tower to the wild animals at Exeter 'Change. What do you say, Mattie? Shall we count ourselves defeated?"

Miss Mattie's eyes filled with tears like a disappointed child. "I did so hope to meet the man of my dreams," she sobbed.

Henrietta looked at her in consternation. "You, Mattie!"

"Yes, me!" said Miss Mattie, tearfully and defiantly. "I do not *feel* old, you know, and I thought that there might be some elderly gentleman who would . . . well . . . feel the same as I."

"Oh, Mattie, I'm sure there is," said Henrietta soothingly.

She broke off in confusion as the butler announced, "Lady Courtney."

Both women jumped to their feet and had only a second to exchange surprised glances as Lady Courtney came into the room. Henrietta's heart missed a beat as she saw Lord Reckford's features set oddly on the small, plump figure of Lady Courtney.

Lady Courtney quickly took in the details of Henrietta's appearance and liked what she saw. The girl was no beauty but she looked a gentlewoman. "I believe you have met my brother, Lord Reckford. He told me you were in town for the Season and begged me to call. He will be calling himself on the morrow but I heard such good reports of you, I was anxious to make your acquaintance."

Henrietta would normally have been too shy to say more than "yes" or "no" but pity for Miss Mattie made her bold. She sat down beside her visitor and began to eagerly ply her with questions about the London Season.

"We shall be meeting at the opening ball at Almack's, no doubt," said Ann Courtney eventually.

Henrietta flushed. "I must confess that I have been too timid to apply for vouchers for fear of a rebuff."

Lady Courtney decided that Henrietta had been much maligned. She was obviously a pleasant girl with an open friendly manner.

"I think I can secure the necessary vouchers for you," said Lady Courtney, after a little hesitation. "I am acquainted with several of the patronesses."

"But Lady Belding has put it about that. . . ." Henrietta began to stammer.

Lady Courtney held up her hand. "My social power is infinitely greater than Lady Belding's," she said imperiously. Henrietta thanked her warmly and Lady Courtney rose to her feet thinking that her brother could do worse than marry such a charming, guileless girl. Unfortunately, before she reached the door of the morningroom, Miss Mattie woke from her happy dream.

"Oh, Henrietta," she cried. "It's just like a novel. He has rescued you from social ruin. You will be lifted up into his strong arms and carried to the altar."

Henrietta winced and blushed furiously. The warmth fled from Lady Courtney's face and she made a chilly *adieux.*

Ann Courtney went straight to her brother's house. "Well, I have done my duty. At first she seemed a pleasant, likeable girl and then, just after I had promised to get her vouchers for Almack's, that peculiar female she lives with blurted out something about you bearing Henrietta off in your strong arms to the altar."

"In that case, I'd better forget about the whole thing," said her brother.

Ann Courtney sat bolt upright. "Oh, no you don't. You shall call tomorrow as I promised. It would be shabby indeed to raise the girl's hopes and then dash them. Besides—I have been thinking. Perhaps all this business of her wanting to marry you is sheer fantasy on the part of that elderly companion of hers."

"Well, well," said her brother reluctantly. "We have set the wheels in motion and may as well go along with it. I shall see for myself."

For Henrietta, the day of surprises was not over. No sooner had Lady Courtney left and she had turned to remonstrate with Miss Mattie than another visitor arrived. "Mr. Edmund Ralston," the butler announced. Both ladies turned round as the most exquisite young man they had ever seen was ushered into the room. His slender figure was encased in a tight-waisted coat worn over skin-tight pantaloons and the whole embellished with a cravat which must at least have been a foot high. His golden curls were combed into a riot of fashionable disorder and topped a thin, white, painted face. His light green eyes had extremely thick curling lashes which gave his face a look of vicious femininity.

Mr. Ralston made a magnificent flourishing bow and stood leaning on his tall cane and surveying Henrietta with interest.

"So you are the young lady who took my fortune away from me." He glided forward with a slow dancing step and to her extreme embarrassment, pirouetted round her.

"Not at all bad," he murmured half to himself. "You could have been infinitely worse. I am decided. We shall be married."

Henrietta nervously stretched her hand towards the bell rope. "Come now," said Mr. Ralston, neatly depositing his elegant being into a small hard-backed chair, "you would not dismiss your own flesh and blood."

Finding her voice at last, Henrietta demanded, "You must immediately introduce yourself, sir, and explain your business."

He slowly took out a small Sèvres box and delicately inhaled a pinch of snuff, keeping his light green eyes steadily fixed on her. "I shall explain. Mrs. Hester Tankerton was a distant relative of mine—very distant. I will not bore you with the genealogy but up till her death I was sure I was her only relative—with the exception of your so dear brother whom I discounted. Mrs. Tankerton had long ago taken a dislike to him. I expected no competition from that quarter.

"I danced attendance on Mrs. Tankerton constantly on the understanding that I was to inherit her great fortune. Imagine my distress"—he waved a gossamer wisp of handkerchief in Henrietta's direction—"when I was apprised that Henry Sandford had a sister and that that sister inherited all."

He held up a thin, white hand with polished nails as Henrietta would have spoken.

"Now what did you do for the old lady? Nothing. While I ran and fetched and carried for her. So you must make restitution and that you can do by marrying me."

"Don't be absurd," said Henrietta roundly. "I am sorry that you have been disappointed in your expectations. Perhaps you are in need of immediate funds. . . ."

Mr. Ralston rose to his feet with a sinuous movement. "No. I am tolerably well in funds at present. I merely wish to claim that which is mine with the least possible fuss." He moved to the looking glass to inspect his cravat. "I am not ill-looking, you will allow," he said over his shoulder. "*You* should be flattered."

Henrietta felt an insane desire to giggle. Her practical common sense fortunately took over.

"I must answer 'no' to your absurd proposal and"—she tugged the bell rope violently—"bid you good day."

"So be it," said Mr. Ralston indifferently. "Obviously you are overwhelmed. I am, after all, something out of the common way."

He made a courtly bow and glided from the room, leaving both ladies to stare at each other in dismay.

Miss Mattie put her hands to her mouth and stared wide-eyed at Henrietta. "He is a villain, I declare. You must be on the watch. He will snatch you up and bear you off to some remote abbey where he will have you in his power."

Henrietta sat down, hardly listening to her friend's wild flight of fantasy. Her everyday world seemed to have slipped out of focus and everything in the room suddenly looked two dimensional. She felt as though she had just taken part in some bizarre play or that

Mr. Ralston had been the figment of a laudenam-induced dream. Suddenly she brought the ordinary world back into focus with a determined blink.

"Mattie, we must learn to deal with strange callers," she said with a worried frown. "Until this morning, no one *at all* has called on us so I simply gave Hobbard instructions to admit everyone. Now, I feel, I should perhaps tell him that we are not at home to Mr. Ralston."

"He frightens me," said Miss Mattie forthrightly. "He reminds me of a serpent."

Henrietta got to her feet. "Let us take the air, clear our brains and think of more cheerful topics. If Lady Courtney manages to arrange vouchers for Almack's, we shall indeed begin our debut in style. I know, we shall go to Gunter's for some splendid ices and forget about the whole confusing business."

"Including my Lord Reckford?" queried Miss Mattie with a sly look.

"Especially Lord Reckford," said Henrietta. "Perhaps he will forget to call. I do not mean to fret myself to flinders. I shall not trouble myself at all over his proposed visit."

But it was a very nervous and anxious Henrietta who woke the following morn. She had relegated the Beau to the back of her mind along with her other dream lovers. Now she was to see him again, and actually talk to him! Her heart beat fast as she removed her curl papers with trembling fingers and then realized with a sigh of relief that she had now a maid to cope with the tedious job of hairdressing. She could eat no breakfast and her nervousness communicated itself to Miss Mattie who trembled and twittered and knocked over the coffee pot.

By eleven o'clock, both ladies were still seated in the drawingroom where they had been waiting a good two hours. Henrietta's face was at its most expressionless, a sure sign of extreme nervousness. But Miss Mattie reflected that her friend had never looked better. Henrietta's fair curls were confined by a pretty ribbon tied in a bow over her left ear. Her sky-blue dress of jonquil muslin trimmed with lace accentuated her excellent shoulders and bosom and flattered her plump figure.

"Oh, Mattie, if only he would come," Henrietta burst out. "If something would only happen to break the monotony of our existence, then I swear I would become as slim as a sylph."

Miss Mattie looked down complacently at her own bony figure. "You must avoid eating potatoes," she advised. "They are served with *everything*, I declare, and not just with the roast as we had in Nethercote. I heard a lady at Gunter's yesterday holding forth on the matter. She declared that the potato made one *swell*."

"I'm not swelling, Mattie," said Henrietta. "I'm just the same round person I was in Nethercote."

Both heard the sound of a carriage coming to a stop outside the house. Although both had spent all morning running to the window at the least sound, by an unspoken consent, they remained seated, staring at each other anxiously.

There was a murmur of voices in the hall, Hobbard's familiar tread followed by a firm step. "Lord Reckford," announced Hobbard with the suspicion of a twinkle in his august eye. He was fond of his young mistress and had often confided below-stairs that it was a crying shame that a lady as amiable as Miss Henrietta should have no *beaux*.

Henrietta rose to meet Lord Reckford with a social smile fixed on her round face. He appeared even taller then before and very remote and elegant. He made a very correct bow.

"Pup—p—lease sit down," stammered Henrietta.

"I beg your pardon?" remarked the Beau politely.

"*I said, 'Sit down,'*" shouted Henrietta and then blushed miserably.

He still stood.

"Is anything the matter?" faltered Henrietta.

"You are supposed to sit down first you know," he said kindly, drawing forward a chair. Henrietta perched primly on the very edge and stared at her smart kid half boots as if they were her only consolation in a wicked world.

"My sister tells me she is to procure vouchers for Almack's for you," remarked Lord Reckford in his pleasant husky voice.

"Oh, *so* kind," bubbled Miss Mattie. "We are indeed saved from social ruin."

"Please, Mattie," begged Henrietta. "Do not be so dramatic."

"Oh, I think Miss Scattersworth has the right of it," said the Beau languidly but with a gleam of mischief in his eyes. "You must give credit where credit is due, Miss Sandford. Had I not ridden to the rescue, you would have been socially spurned."

"Sneered at by all and ground to social dust," breathed Miss Mattie, her curls bobbing energetically.

"Every elegant back in London turned against you," agreed Lord Reckford.

"We may have had to resort to the demi-monde," whispered Miss Mattie.

"And we would wear a lot of paint and talk in terribly loud voices to show that we did not mind in the least," said Henrietta with a laugh, beginning to enjoy the joke.

Lord Reckford began to believe that the rumor that Henrietta wished to marry him was part of her companion's imaginings and prepared to enjoy himself.

"You are looking very *tonnish* since I saw you last, Miss Sandford," he commented, admiring her dress appreciatively.

"I am glad I complement your lordship's elegance," said Henrietta with the mischievous twinkle in her eye that he remembered.

"And I notice your wrists are so *clean*. Alas! My heart is broken. You were only funning when you said you would never wash it again."

"Ah!" teased Henrietta with a boldness that amazed herself, "I had faith, you see, that I might perhaps soon have another."

He rose to his feet to bend over her hand, looking mockingly into her eyes. "Then such faith shall be rewarded," he teased.

Miss Mattie suddenly wagged a roguish finger at the pair of them. "Young love," she sighed. "Will it be a social wedding do you think? Or will you ride madly to Gretna Green one dark moonless night?"

Both stared at her in consternation.

"Lady Belding and Miss Belding," announced Hobbard.

Alice drifted up to Henrietta and kissed her sorrowfully on the cheek. "My poor dear friend," she sighed. "Oh! Lord Reckford!" All fluttering eyelashes and swirling skirts, she dropped Lord Reckford her best curtsy.

"I am surprised to see you here, Reckford," snapped Lady Belding. Her high patrician nose turned in Henrietta's direction. "As for you, miss, you are to cease this nonsense and return to Nethercote immediately. Your brother agrees with me that you have proved yourself unable to handle your fortune."

"I am not a child, Lady Belding," retorted Henrietta. "You may tell my brother from me that I shall *visit* him when the Season is over."

"Season! What Season?" snorted Lady Belding. "There will be no Season for you, my presumptuous miss. No lady of the ton would be seen in your company."

The Beau got lazily to his feet. "I really must protest, Lady Belding, but it is the first time that anyone has suggested that my sister does not belong to the first circles. Ann has already called on Miss Sandford and will be seeing a good deal of her in the coming weeks."

Lady Belding bit back the angry remark that rose to her lips. The Reckfords were socially powerful and she must be careful to do nothing to thwart her daughter's ambitions.

Alice Belding narrowed her pretty eyes. If the Beau and his sister meant to bring the dreary Henrietta into fashion, they were probably doing it out of sheer kindness. After all, Henrietta was positively *old*. But perhaps she had better establish her friendship with Henrietta if it meant that she could thereby see more of the Reckfords. Accordingly, she tripped forward and hugged the surprised Henrietta with great warmth.

"Why, mama, you are too severe on my dear friend! It is not as if Henrietta has had our social advantages," cried Alice, admiring her reflection in the looking glass over Henrietta's shoulder. "Henrietta shall stay in London and I will not let any of you say her nay!"

Henrietta started to mutter ungratefully that she was not in need of a champion but the Beau gave Alice a warm smile of appreciation. He must have been mistaken in her. She was a thoughtful and kind girl after all . . . and extremely beautiful.

Catching his admiring look at Alice, Henrietta felt all the warmth and light go out of her day. Then Lord Reckford bowed his handsome head over her hand. "I should be honored if you would drive with me in the park tomorrow afternoon, Miss Sandford." The sun shone out again behind Henrietta's clouds and she raised her head to accept when Alice rushed forward. "Why, we would be delighted! Would not we, my dear."

The Beau looked down at Henrietta's face and wondered why he had ever considered it expressionless.

One minute she had looked radiant and the next as if the world had come to an end. "My apologies to you Miss Belding," said Lord Reckford, "but there is only room in my curricle for one passenger."

"Oh, I am sure Henrietta will not mind us going without her," said Alice blithely, bringing her long eyelashes into play.

Lord Reckford rapidly revised his recent favorable

opinion of Alice. Why, the girl was as pushing and forward as a Cit.

"You misunderstood me, Miss Belding," he said with a steely note creeping into his voice. "The invitation was issued to Miss Sandford."

Alice flushed and her eyes began to glitter dangerously. Lady Belding realized that her daughter was about to throw one of her well-known temper tantrums and they hurriedly made their goodbyes.

"Until tomorrow then," said the Beau, bending to kiss Henrietta's hand. He raised his head and tawny eyes met hazel for a long moment. A thin tenuous thread of emotion seemed to momentarily join the pair. Then with another bow to Miss Scattersworth, the Beau was gone, leaving Henrietta to place the hand he had kissed against her cheek.

Miss Mattie looked at her anxiously. "Do not be overcome with passion, my dear. Passion is a very dangerous animal."

Henrietta gave her infectious giggle. "Really, Mattie, what will you say next? What a morning! Now, no one else can *possibly* call."

Suddenly the door was flung open and brother Henry bustled into the room in great haste followed by his curate, Mr. John Symes. Henry's elaborate garb made the drab clericals of Mr. Symes look positively poverty-stricken. He swept past the astonished Henrietta and ran about the room, picking up *objets d'art* one after the other and carrying them to the light.

Mr. Symes, an elderly white haired man with a stoop which betokened years of servitude, gave his vicar an embarrassed look and went to sit down beside Miss Mattie.

"What on earth are you *doing*, Henry," asked Henrietta at last.

"I am looking at all this waste of money on trivia . . . all this sheer extravagance," spluttered Henry.

"All this 'sheer extravagance' as you call it, is part of the estate left me by Mrs. Tankerton," said Henrietta, eyeing the silver buttons on her brother's coat with disdain.

He gave her a look of relieved surprise. Thoroughly annoyed, Henrietta went on, "But do remember, dear brother, it is *my* fortune and I shall dissipate it in any way I please."

"Of course, my dear, of course," said Henry soothingly. "But I am sure, for all your wealth, you will not forget the poor of your old parish. They are always in sore need of money."

Henrietta shrewdly decided that Henry's tailor was in sore need of money but wisely held her tongue. Instead she turned to Mr. Symes. "Since you have more to do with the poor of the parish than my brother, Mr. Symes, I shall give you a draft on my bank and you may use the money as you think fit."

Henry gave an almost audible moan. Once his curate had his hands on the money then he, Henry, would most assuredly never see a penny of it. Mr. Symes cheerfully did far more than his share of work but helping the poor was his one great enthusiasm. "If I take any of it, he would probably report me to the Bishop," thought Henry, giving his meek curate a venomous look.

"Of course, dear brother, I am quite prepared to keep you in funds. I realize you have certain pressing bills," said his sister.

Henry stared at her in amazement and gratitude. "Well, now, I call that very generous of you, Henrietta. Very generous indeed!"

"In return," she went on as if he had not spoken. "I expect you to leave me to enjoy my Season. I think your friends, the Beldings, will be formidable enough opposition as it is."

"Of course, of course," said Henry placing a chaste kiss on her cheek. "In fact I shall visit you often in order to escort you on occasion. I am said to be a very pretty dancer," he added complacently.

His sister thanked him in a faint voice and patiently

waited for him to take his leave. But to her surprise, her brother sat down and began to regale her with tales of various parish events. To her even greater surprise, these were often very witty. She felt more in charity with him than she had ever felt before and after a pleasant half an hour, it was with a certain reluctance that she watched him leave.

She turned to Miss Mattie to discuss the astonishing visit but found that her friend was sitting bolt upright on the sofa with a rapt expression on her face. "Do attend to me Mattie. Was not Henry in surprising good form?"

Miss Mattie came slowly back from some faraway country of the mind and focussed on Henrietta. "He is a saint. I can see him riding to some Crusade on his charger. I shall wait and weep of course, but how proud I shall be."

Henrietta patiently took her friend's hand in her own. "What has come over you, Mattie? Henry was surprising cordial but he is always too much of this world of society to *ever* be considered a saint."

"I was talking of Mr. Symes," sighed Miss Mattie. "Did you notice his noble forehead? Did you note the tinge of passion in his voice when he was conveying to me Mrs. Church's recipe for tansey-pudding?"

"I am afraid I was not attending. Why, Mattie! You are in love with the curate!"

Miss Mattie nodded and trailed from the room with her hand to her brow. Then she swept round on the threshold with a gesture worthy of Mrs. Siddons and declaimed, "I shall carry my secret to the grave and should they cut open my heart, engraved on it will be. . . . 'John Symes.'"

After she had gone, Henrietta sat down at a pretty escritoire, sharpened her quill and prepared to go over the household accounts. She could only hope that Miss Mattie's passion for the curate would modify her style of dress.

Mattie's behavior had been embarrassing and infuriating. Henrietta bit her lip in vexation. She really *must* tell Mattie not to behave so. But . . . but Mattie would cry and would really be crushed. "I will just have to make the best of things," sighed Henrietta.

But Henrietta wished heartily with a certain guilt that she did not "have to make this best of things. . . ."

By evening, Henrietta felt exhausted with the emotional strain of waiting for the next day to arrive and bring Lord Reckford. She had also spent a frenetic afternoon searching for the exact bonnet to charm the Beau. At last she had settled on a dashing shako—if it rained—and a charming chip straw—if the sun shone. Her neck quite ached from watching the sky, trying to foretell tomorrow's weather. She had considered everything but the wind. By the time her maid undressed her for bed, an unseasonal gale was reminding fashionable London of wilder, more unsheltered country. It shrieked through the canyons of the old buildings in the City and then raced in a hurly-burly, vulgar fashion up the reaches of the Strand to shriek and moan and form violent whirlwinds in the elegant squares and tree-lined streets of the West End.

Henrietta climbed into bed, blew out her candle and then tossed and turned sleeplessly as she listened to the tumult outside. Somewhere in the house a loose shutter banged and the whole building heaved and shook like a ship riding out a stormy sea. Suddenly, the wind dropped abruptly and in the ensuing silence, a disembodied whisper sounded in the room. "You are going mad, Henrietta. Mad! Mad! Ma . . . a . . . a . . . d!"

She sat bolt upright in bed and lit her candle with shaking fingers. The gale sprang up again and the candle flame danced and flickered sending sinister shadows running round the walls. But though she sat as still as a mouse, straining her ears against the noise of the storm, there was no reoccurence of the mysterious voice.

Chapter Six

THE NEXT DAY DAWNED bright and sunny and, as Henrietta prepared for her excursion to the park, she decided that she must have imagined the episode of the mysterious voice.

Miss Mattie fluttered after her, almost as nervous as Henrietta herself. "My dear," she exclaimed, clasping her hands together, "now that I am aware of the tender passions, I know how you must feel. The palpitating bosom, the trembling legs, the . . ."

Her effusions were mercifully interrupted by Hobbard who handed Henrietta a parcel. "This is for you, Miss Sandford," he said. "A messenger has just delivered it."

Henrietta opened the wrappings and found a square wooden box of Turkish Delight with a neat white card lying on top of the sweetmeats. It said simply, "Sweets to the sweet. Yr. devoted admirer."

"It must be from Lord Reckford," breathed Miss Mattie. "You must try one."

Henrietta hesitated, her hand hovering over the box. "I am sure his lordship would send a more original message, Mattie, and he would certainly put his name to it."

But she adored sweets and the succulent squares

with their powdering of sugar were the most tempting things she had ever seen. "Well, just one," she said, popping a large piece in her mouth and then swallowing it hurriedly as Lord Reckford was announced.

With a rising sense of excitement and anticipation, she had not felt since she was a child, Henrietta was handed up by Lord Reckford into his curricle. His team was fresh and restive and he gave them all his attention, guiding them down the street at a brisk trot, driving them well up to their bits. As they turned into Hyde Park, he finally addressed his companion. "What a dreadful storm we had last night. I was awakened by a terrible crash about three in the morning. One of the chimneys had crashed down through the attics. Mercifully, no one was hurt."

Receiving no reply from his fair companion, he reined in his teams of greys and turned to look down at her. She sat very still, very quiet, her face hidden by the brim of her hat. "Miss Sandford! Miss Sandford? Is anything amiss?" No reply. He removed his gloves of York tan and reaching out his long fingers, took Henrietta's chin in his hand and turned her face towards him.

Henrietta was far away on another plain, a dream country where the grass was made of green glass and the sunlight snaked through the trees in rivers of molten gold and she felt sure, if she sat very still, small beautiful wild creatures of ivory and silver would slowly appear.

Lord Reckford dropped her chin. Her eyes were unfocussed and the pupils like pinpoints. He swore under his breath and took a hurried look round. They were on the broad southern avenue that paralleled Rotten Row. Rotten Row—an English contraction of the French, *Route en Roi*—was an unsurfaced road of loose sand and gravel which would be jammed to capacity during the fashionable hour.

He had deliberately arrived a quarter of an hour early so that all the arriving fashionable throng could see him with Henrietta. He knew his worth as a leader of fashion to the last inch. Henrietta would be the envy of all the debutantes and a subject for speculation among the gentlemen. Now he was anxious to escape before anyone could catch so much as a glimpse of his companion. In the distance, he could see the heavy old family coach of the Beldings, its recently revarnished panels shining in the sun, come lumbering towards the Row.

He flicked his leader deftly with his whip and in less than ten minutes was carrying his companion into her house in Brook Street.

Miss Mattie shooed him into a small saloon where he laid Henrietta on a day bed. "I see it all," cried Miss Mattie tragically.

"You do!" exclaimed Lord Reckford in surprise. "I would not have thought that Miss Sandford was in the habit of . . ." But he was interrupted by the forceful Mattie.

"Yes, yes," she cried. "Your horses bolted with you. Henrietta tried to assist you. People screamed. The carriage swayed dangerously. A low branch stunned her. She collapsed in your arms. Oh, how terrible! Oh, how romantic!"

"The branches of the trees in Hyde Park are pruned so that they do not . . ." Lord Reckford began acidly and then stopped. "Really, Miss Scattersworth. You are getting me carried away by your nonsense." He glared at poor Miss Mattie who blushed and hung her head.

Lord Reckford was a notable whip and could drive to an inch. And now this damned female, instead of helping him, was babbling away about his horses bolting with him.

"I am sorry to deliver myself of such a mundane explanation, Miss Scattersworth, but Miss Sandford is suffering from having taken an amount of some drug, probably opium."

Miss Mattie looked at him in horror and came down

to earth with a bang. "What can I do?" she asked in a reassuringly practical voice. "Shall I send for the physician?"

He shook his head. "Miss Sandford is now in a heavy sleep from which she will emerge in an hour or two completely unharmed. Is she in the habit of taking drugs?"

Miss Mattie shook her head vehemently. "Never! Not even laudenam to help her sleep."

The Beau looked at the sleeping girl. "Perhaps the wicked sophisticated delights of the metropolis have changed her," he remarked dryly.

"Impossible," remarked Miss Mattie and the Beau was relieved to note that worry over her young friend had revealed her to be a sensible woman. "Why, Henrietta was in the best of spirits. She had too little to eat at luncheon, of course, and then nothing else except a piece of Turkish Delight . . . from her admirer," added Miss Mattie with a coy look at Lord Reckford. "An anonymous present."

"I am not in the habit of sending anonymous gifts," he remarked.

Miss Mattie looked at him for a minute and then scuttled out to return with the box. The Beau lifted a piece and tasted it with his tongue. "Opium," he said, fastidiously wiping his mouth with his handkerchief. "Someone wishes Miss Sandford ill."

"The villain," gasped Miss Mattie. "Her relation, a Mr. Ralston, he said the fortune should have been his and he wishes to marry Henrietta!"

"I am not acquainted with Mr. Ralston but I shall certainly make it my business to seek him out," said Lord Reckford grimly.

He turned again to look down on the sleeping girl. She was breathing evenly, her heavy lashes fanned out on her cheeks. The quiver of emotion that he had felt when he had looked into her eyes was gone. He felt old and protective. "Poor child," he said. "I shall call again tomorrow to find out how she is keeping. I think you and I shall have to keep a good watch on Miss Sandford from now on."

"Indeed, yes!" agreed Miss Mattie, looking intently into his eyes. "Friendship, concern, alas!" she exclaimed, much to Lord Reckford's bewilderment.

He made his best bow and took his leave. Miss Mattie sighed as she watched the strong athletic figure climbing into the curricle. "Friendship hardly ever leads to passion," she said, shaking her head and going to take her place beside her sleeping friend.

Henrietta was amazed and frightened when she eventually awoke to hear the story about the opium in the Turkish Delight. But as the days passed and the event of her first London ball drew near, she almost forgot about it. The sun shone on London Town and the Beau was in constant attendance. But Henrietta sighed disconsolately.

She had still not received cards to any social event. Lord Reckford escorted her on sedate walks as if she were a schoolgirl and he, the governess, and Miss Scattersworth always came along as well. He was a considerate and friendly companion . . . and nothing more.

Mr. Ralston had called several times but had been informed by Hobbard that "Miss Sandford was not at home to Mr. Ralston" so firmly that he had eventually given up.

At last, the evening of the ball at Almack's had arrived. It was to be the first event of the London Season. Lady Courtney had been successful in procuring vouchers for both Henrietta and Miss Scattersworth. Lord Reckford had promised to be early for once in order to lead Henrietta into the first dance and establish her social status. All that was left to do was to get dressed . . . and pray.

Henrietta had refused to dress in white. She was much older than the other debutantes and had no intention of looking like a quiz. Instead she wore a stately gown of green crêpe, tied under the bosom with long green silk ribbons. Her heavy fair hair was dressed *à la Sappho* and a magnificent topaz necklace flashed on her bosom.

Miss Scattersworth, attired in a gown of heavy burgundy silk, looked all that was proper in a chaperone. She was still pining for the curate and, as Henrietta had hoped, it had had a sobering effect on her mode of dress.

By the time the ladies were deposited outside the famous assembly rooms in King's Street, St. James's, Henrietta felt that everything would be all right. They had dressed their best, Lord Reckford would be waiting for them and the evening would be a success.

The rooms were not nearly so grand as Henrietta had expected and the only refreshments were orgeat and lemonade. But society came here to see and be seen. Henrietta glanced round the glittering throng but could see no sign of the tall figure of Lord Reckford. Lady Belding and Alice were already there, whispering and gossiping and waving their long fans in Henrietta's direction. Heads began to turn, quizzing glasses were raised.

Dance followed dance and Henrietta sat as if turned to stone. Glittering and chattering and flashing pitying looks, Alice Belding floated past, the sight of the disconsolate Henrietta lending her feet wings.

Henrietta began to feel immeasurably tired. Her eyes glistened with unshed tears. The painted faces of the Dandy set swirled before her like some exotic dream. The dancers advanced, retreated, curtsyed and bowed. And still he did not come.

Lord Reckford sat on the edge of his bed, nursing his bruised shoulder. He had just been trying, without success, to break down his bedroom door. He had been on the point of leaving for Almack's when he had heard the click of the key in his door and stealthy footsteps hurrying down the corridor. Startled, but not very worried, he had pulled vehemently on the bell rope and after several minutes stood staring at the door in surprise. There had been no answer to his summons. The windows were heavily barred and the door was of solid mahogany.

A sudden jab of concern for Henrietta stabbed him. He could think of no other reason for this insane practical joke. He looked thoughtfully at the fireplace. It was a capacious one and the chimney had been recently cleaned. Then he shook his head. Something had happened to the servants and if he got stuck in the flu then God alone knew how long he would be forced to stay there.

But his temper was rising. Henrietta would now be at Almack's thinking that he had deserted her. His sister, Ann, was ill so Henrietta and Miss Scattersworth would know no one. He came to a sudden decision. He hauled out a game bag and stripping off his evening clothes, he folded them carefully into it along with his diamond jewellery. He rummaged in his wardrobe and found an old hacking jacket, a venerable pair of buckskins and an old pair of shoes.

Tying his shoes and the game bag round his neck, he crossed to the fireplace, got down on all fours and stared up the chimney. One mocking star stared back down at him. It seemed very far away at the other end of an eternity of sooty blackness.

But the roof could not be so very far away. Only the attics were above his room. He tried shouting for help several times but there was no reply. His bedroom windows faced the garden at the back of the house.

With a sigh of resignation, he crawled into the fireplace, stood upright and started to climb. Several times his broad shoulders jammed and he had to pause with cold sweat trickling down his soot-stained face until with a massive wrench, he managed to free himself. He was nearly at the top when he suddenly realized he would never, ever get himself through the chimney pot. He was no climbing boy. He wedged himself against the walls of the chimney and fought against an overwhelming attack of claustrophobia which threatened to unman him. He rested, gulping for air and trying to calm his trembling body. Then the thought that someone had deliberately locked him in his own bedroom like a naughty schoolboy hit him with violent force. His attack of claustrophobia fled before a wave of healthy anger. Chimney pots could be broken. He scrabbled upwards, envisaged the chimney pot as the fool who had got him into this situation and struck it with all his might.

Fortunately for Lord Reckford, its hold on the building had been weakened by the recent storm and with an almighty crash, it plunged over the slates and into the gardens below. A slate whizzed down into the great gaping hole left in the roof, missing him by inches. He hauled himself out onto the roof and slithered down the slates and, with the agility of an acrobat, made his way down the drainpipe to the street.

He planned to make his way down to the kitchen area to see what on earth had happened to his servants when there was a cry of "Hold there" and a waving lantern.

"The watch!" Lord Reckford cursed under his breath. It would take hours to establish his credentials. Who would believe that the famous Beau Reckford had been climbing around the roof of his town house in torn clothes and covered in soot? He felt a heavy hand on his shoulder and turned and drove his fist into the watch's kidneys. The man gave a scream of pain and doubled up. There was another bobbing light at the end of the street. Lord Reckford fled.

He zig-zagged through the night-time streets until all sounds of pursuit faded behind him. He tried to hail a hack but the driver told him in no uncertain terms that he only allowed *clean* gentlemen in his carriage. His lordship became aware of the filth of his appearance and took himself off to the Hummums on foot for a Turkish bath.

Henrietta's heart felt like lead. The clock stood at two minutes to eleven and no one, not even the Prince Regent himself, was allowed in after eleven o'clock. She would not be humiliated any more. She turned to Miss Mattie to suggest that they leave. Lord Reckford entered the room and Henrietta looked across at him with her heart in her eyes. Oh, horror! He was not going to join her. He was talking to one of the patronesses, the ultra-snobbish Mrs. Drummond-Burrell. Mrs. Drummond-Burrell frowned, his lordship insisted and bent to whisper something in that august ear. Mrs. Drummond-Burrell smiled like the sun on a winter's day and got to her feet. Oh, God, he was leaving! No, he was looking at her and leading the formidable patroness across the floor.

Mrs. Drummond-Burrell looked down at Henrietta as if she were some peculiar kind of insect. "Lord Reckford has prevailed upon me to allow you to waltz," she said haughtily, and having felt she had done more than enough, turned on her heel, leaving Henrietta to look up at Lord Reckford with a question in her eyes.

"Later," he said in his attractive, husky voice. He drew her into the steps of the waltz and Miss Mattie watched them, her eyes filling with sentimental tears.

Myriads of fans fluttered and turned, turbans and feathered headdresses bowed and bobbed, jewels blazed and sparkled on men and women alike as all turned to watch Henrietta in the arms of Lord Reckford. He was smiling, he was laughing, what were they saying? Alice Belding led her mama behind a potted palm and kicked her viciously in the ankle.

All this passed the bedazzled Henrietta unnoticed. She gazed adoringly up at her saviour and he smiled back at her in a kindly way. Lord Reckford was so used to adoring glances that he only felt very protective and thought what a pleasant, *comfortable* sort of girl Henrietta was.

"You will not lack dancing partners now," he said when the waltz came to an end.

"I do not feel like dancing any more tonight," replied Henrietta who felt exhausted with all her seesawing emotions.

"I confess I am feeling very tired myself," laughed the Beau, "and I have not yet told you what delayed me. We shall make a grand exit."

They collected Miss Scattersworth and strolled from the ballroom arm in arm, the dagger-like stares of all the match-making mamas boring into his lordship's exquisitely tailored back.

As the carriage clattered over the cobblestones on the road to Brook Street, Lord Reckford told his companions of his adventures. Henrietta felt a sudden clutch of fear at her heart. Her spiteful enemy seemed to be everywhere. Assuring the ladies that he would call in the morning, the Beau hastened off.

To his relief, his door was answered by his butler, Gibbs, who was looking anxious and flustered. He explained that a travelling wine merchant had called early in the evening at the kitchen door while his lordship was dressing. He had explained that all his lordship's wines were ordered from Bullock's in the City but the merchant had some excellent vintage madeira at extremely low prices. The merchant had said that his wife had just given birth to twins and he would esteem it an honor if the staff would join him in a celebration glass. Well, put like that, said the contrite Gibbs, it seemed only decent to 'wet the babie's head.' As it happened, all the staff had been gathered below stairs, their duties for the day finished since my lord had told them not to wait up for him. Next thing they knew, they had awakened some hours later and of the wine merchant there was no sign. The watch was banging at the door, crying out that a man had descended from the roof. His lordship's bedroom door had been broken down with an axe by himself and the watch but nothing of value was found to have been taken.

Lord Reckford dismissed the trembling Gibbs, assuring him that no blame should fall on the staff, and sat in his study, staring at the empty fireplace, deep in thought. In the middle of all his concern for Henrietta, he realized, with a slight shock, that he was worried and anxious—but not bored.

And it was a long time since his lordship could remember having been so intrigued about anything.

He would call on her in the morning. Lord Reckford went to bed with a pleasurable feeling of anticipation.

Henrietta was in a thoughtful mood. She reviewed her triumph at the ball with mixed feelings. Beau Reckford liked her very much indeed but that in itself seemed to raise a barrier against his feelings becoming anything stronger. She suddenly felt weak and very feminine and wished she had a pair of strong masculine arms wrapped round her to make the uncertainties and worries of the world go away.

Chapter Seven

Two weeks of the Season had passed and Henrietta was still alive. That was a comfort, she reflected, although little else was. Lord Reckford was more fascinated by the mystery than by Miss Henrietta Sandford. At his earnest request, she had been obliged to endure the company of the people she liked least. In that way, said his lordship, he would have an opportunity to study the characters concerned and keep watch for anyone with murderous intentions.

The only person here today with murderous intentions, thought Henrietta, is myself. Lord Reckford had made up a party to visit his aunt, Lady Haddington, who lived in Streatham. Lady Belding and Alice had headed the guest list followed by none other than the elegant Mr. Ralston and his mother, a thin, faded lady who said the nastiest things in the sweetest voice and with such a charming smile that people were inclined to charitably believe that she had said something or other entirely different. Brother Henry came too, vastly honored by the Beau's invitation. Lord Reckford's friend, Mr. Jeremy Holmes was there, paying ardent court to Alice Belding. Miss Scattersworth enlivened the party by disposing of her wraps when it was too late for anyone to order her to go and change to show her scrawny figure coyly revealed through the near-transparent muslin of a clinging summer gown. Miss Scattersworth had transferred her affections from the curate to the rotund and overdressed person of a retired admiral, Sir Percival Jenkins.

Sir Percival was a very roguish man, fond of saying that he liked a gal with a bit of spirit, what! . . . dresses up to the mark, what! He ogled the bedazzled Miss Scattersworth shamelessly and Henrietta was the one who blushed.

For the hundredth time, Henrietta feverently and disloyally wished she were chaperored by a less . . . well, *eccentric* and embarrassing lady than this late-blossoming flower of spinsterhood.

Lady Haddington had retired after luncheon for an afternoon nap, being a frail elderly lady, but she urged her guests to explore the gardens. Henrietta had taken the opportunity to escape from the company. Alice Belding had once again changed her tactics and had adopted a frank, open and friendly manner. Mr. Holmes was quite besotted and even the Beau, thought Henrietta bitterly, smiled his approval.

Henrietta saw the willowy form of Mr. Ralston approaching and glided quickly behind a yew hedge. The sun was very hot and she sank down gratefully onto a stone seat and surveyed her surroundings.

The lawns sloped down to a ha-ha and beyond the ha-ha lay an uncultivated stretch of woodland. The shade under the trees looked cool and inviting. Hearing approaching voices, Henrietta got to her feet and ran lightly over the lawns. She nimbly jumped over the ha-ha and plunged recklessly into the woods.

It was suddenly very quiet. Bars of sunlight struck down through the trees onto the mossy carpet underneath. The air was heavy with the damp woodland scents of herbs and flowers. It was pleasant to relax and leave the social world behind. Lord Reckford had indeed brought Miss Henrietta Sandford into fashion. The past fortnight had been crowded with social events and the house in Brook Street seemed to be filled from morning to night with callers.

All London talked about was of the 'romance' between Henrietta and Beau Reckford. He was constantly in her company and assiduous in his attentions. But always, the eyes that met hers were open and friendly. In desperation Henrietta had tried to flirt in an awkward amateurish way but all her sallies were immediately countered by Lord Reckford's practised gallantry. He even applauded her efforts, seeming to assume that she was using him to cultivate a flirtatious social manner.

Henrietta's appetite was beginning to fail and most of her dresses had had to be returned to the dressmaker to be taken in. The willowy figure she had long dreamed of was slowly taking shape.

Troubled by her thoughts, she wandered on through the woods, until she came to a small glade, carpeted thickly with bluebells. They spread away from her feet across the little glade and through the trees on the other side like some enchanted blue mist. She gave a sigh of sheer delight and sat down on a fallen tree trunk to enjoy the view.

Somewhere up in the dark green of the branches, a thrush began to pour out his liquid, tumbling rhapsody and Henrietta sat very still. Then under and over the glory of the bird's song came a thin, unearthly voice, sexless and eerie. "You are going mad, Henrietta, mad, mad ma . . . a . . . d." Henrietta gave a sob of fright and jumped to her feet looking round wildly.

The bird fell silent. "Who is there!" shouted Henrietta. A thin voice like the wind whispered in reply, "If you want to see me, look up. Look up!"

Henrietta stared up into the branches of the tree above her head and gave a scream of horror. A thin greenish mist was coiling round the upper limbs of the tree and red-eyed and horned, the face of Satan himself stared down at her with an awful smile.

As in a nightmare, Henrietta opened and shut her mouth but no sound came out. She could feel her heart beating faster and faster against her ribs and a suffocating constriction in her throat. She suddenly found her voice and the use of her legs at the same time. Screaming and sobbing, her dress torn with briars, she hurtled from the wood, leapt over the ha-ha and headlong up the lawns to the house. She threw herself into Lord Reckford's arms, gasping and crying, "Satan! The devil is in the woods. He . . . he . . . *spoke* to me!"

Lord Reckford handed her over to Miss Scattersworth and he and Mr. Holmes raced off in the direction of the woods leaving Henrietta to face a circle of disbelieving eyes. "Devil, indeed!" snorted Lady Belding.

"Probably lads playing tricks." (Sir Percival)

"Too much sun on top of all that wine." (Alice)

"Hysterical women are always . . . how shall I say . . . exhausting." (Mrs. Ralston)

"My dear Henrietta . . . such want of conduct." (Henry)

Only Miss Scattersworth was sympathetic and, for once, Henrietta could have done without her voluble defence.

The frail figure of Lady Haddington appeared and was helped to a chaise-longue by the window. Several voices told her of Henrietta's adventure. "How very odd," commented her ladyship in a thin, faint voice. "I had a housemaid once who thought she saw a monk walking round the house and had us all quite frightened. But it turned out that the girl had been helping herself liberally from the cellars. She saw snakes . . . finally, that is. . . ."

Lady Haddington, like many lonely elderly people had developed a habit of talking to herself and she went on as if she were alone.

"Yes, yes, that must be it," she murmured, her head nodding under the weight of an elaborate starched and embroidered cap. "The girl drinks. Obviously, obviously. I must tell the servants to lock the cellars."

There was an embarrassed silence and Lord Reckford arrived back with Jeremy Holmes and Mr. Ralston. The latter had helped them to search, explained Lord Reckford in a sardonic voice. Mr. Ralston had in fact stood at the edge of the woods composing a sonnet entitled "To Henrietta in Her Hour of Peril." He had got as far as "Behold! She stands like some frightened fawn!" but had not been able to find a suitable rhyme for fawn.

"My dear, dear Henrietta," gasped Miss Mattie, trying to pull Henrietta's head down to her withered bosom in an attempt to copy the "Mother and Daughter" pose in a very affecting picture in the Academy. "How terrified you must have been. To be pursued by the Evil One himself. Did you smell brimstone?"

Her nonsense, however, had the effect of calming Henrietta's fears. "I am sure it was not the Devil. But in the first shock, you know . . ." She broke off in some confusion as she caught the admiral looking at her and slowly tapping his head. "Too much sun, Miss Sandford. Too much sun. Bosun got that way off Gibraltar and jumped over the side, poor fellow. 'Course, it could have been the rum."

"Do you *drink,* my dear?" asked Mrs. Ralston with such a warm look of sympathy that no one could possibly believe she meant to be malicious. "I saw you empty several glasses at luncheon." She wagged a finger at Henrietta and the admiral wagged a finger as well and Henrietta felt as if she were taking part in some strange play.

"Nothing there! Nothing at all," sighed the Beau.

"Sure it wasn't the heat?" asked Mr. Holmes, "or . . . or . . . you know . . ."

"Yes, I *do* know and no, I was not *foxed,*" said the much tried Henrietta, bursting into tears and escaping to the rooms assigned to her.

Lady Belding sniffed, "I am sure my dear Alice would never use such a *cant* expression."

Alice smiled and lowered her eyelashes. "You are too hard on Henrietta, mother. I find her a truly ladylike girl." This had the effect of making the Beau smile on her and Mr. Holmes to fall even deeper in love . . . which was exactly what Alice intended.

Henrietta sat at her bedroom window feeling bewildered and miserable. Everyone thought she was mad or bosky or both. She had had as much wine as the other ladies at luncheon, no more, no less. Here, in the safety of the house, with the reassuring murmur of voices rising up the stairwell, it began to seem as if she had imagined the whole thing. The face hanging, disembodied in the trees, the wreaths of smoke, seemed more like a dream than something that had actually happened. She wished they did not have to stay the night.

There was a gentle knock at her door and she wearily got to her feet to answer it. It was Lord Reckford, smiling down at her. As usual, Henrietta's poor heart gave a painful lurch. "If I did not know I was in love," thought Henrietta, "I would swear I had the symptoms of some terrible illness." Well, Donne had thought it a severe malady. "Who'll believe me if I swear, that I have had the plague a year."

Lord Reckford followed her into the room, punctiliously leaving the door ajar.

"Perhaps it would be a good idea if I slept in your bed tonight, Miss Sandford." As Henrietta blushed furiously, he hastened to explain. "I do believe your story of the face in the woods, Miss Sandford. But I think you have been the victim of a nasty, practical joke. Now, if you could remove to Miss Scattersworth's room, say, at midnight, I will take your place. Then the joker will have *me* to deal with."

Henrietta looked at him shyly from under her lashes. They were alone in her bedroom after all. But his lordship's handsome face only showed interest in catching her tormenter. "Are you sure you will be awake at midnight in order to change your room?" he asked.

"Of course," replied Henrietta. "I shall not sleep a wink in any case, I can assure you!"

"That's my girl!" said the elegant Beau with a fond

smile and, to her dismay, he gave her an affectionate slap on the back before he left the room.

"It's too bad," thought the much mortified Henrietta. "He would *never* dare slap Alice on the back. I feel like his pet hound!"

She planned to eat very little at dinner but her beloved seemed to be drinking rather a great deal and was flirting lightly with Alice. Dismally Henrietta threw her churning stomach down great lumps of food as if trying to quiet a savage dog. By the time the ladies retired to leave the gentlemen to their wine, Henrietta's dress, which had recently been taken in, was uncomfortably tight at the seams. She felt round and placid and dull like . . . a . . . suet dumpling beside the glittering Alice. Certainly Alice switched off the glitter when the gentlemen were not present but on the other hand neither did she feel it necessary to be sweet to Henrietta.

"I hear your son means to wed Miss Sandford," remarked Alice to Mrs. Ralston in a conversational voice.

"So he tells me," snapped Mrs. Ralston and then suddenly a smile of great beauty illuminated her thin features. "But I think that he should carefully reconsider. Money can be little comfort when one's wife is mad."

"Are you, by any chance, referring to me?" gasped Henrietta. Mrs. Ralston's smile had been worthy of a madonna and it seemed incredible that she had actually meant what she had just said.

Mrs. Ralston did not reply. She merely gave another of her beautiful smiles and then shook her head sadly.

"Who is mad?" queried the faint voice of their hostess. "Is it that gel who drinks too much?"

There was a silence broken by an audible snigger from Alice. Lady Belding felt that Henrietta had had enough attention and launched forth at great length on the presumption of a young man who had called at the

Belding town house and claimed to be a distant relation.

"But he could not possibly be," said Lady Belding. "You see, he had *not* the Nose. And so I told him. He had a nose like a squashed cabbage leaf. Now, the Nose . . ." here Lady Belding turned her profile to the company . . . "The Nose has visited the field at Crecy. The Nose was wounded at Agincourt. The Nose . . ." her voice dropped dramatically . . . "rode to England in Norman the Conqueror's rearguard."

Please God, let me not laugh, prayed Henrietta desperately. Her throat hurt with the effort and the tears stood out in her eyes. The gentlemen were arriving to join them. She must *not* laugh.

"How wonderful," breathed Miss Scattersworth . . . "to think of such an aristocratic piece of anatomy woven into history's tapestry. The nose at the signing of the Magna Carta. The nose with Richard the Third when he cried, 'A horse, a horse, my kingdom for a horse,' " roared Miss Mattie.

It was too much. Henrietta howled with laughter till the tears rolled down her cheeks. Everyone stared at her and then exchanged significant looks. The gentlemen had entered the room and Henry moved forward to take his sister's arm. "Go to your room, Henrietta," he ordered. "You are completely overwrought. Go and lie down, my dear."

Henrietta began to feel as if she might be a little mad. Had none of the other ladies found Lady Belding's discourse funny? But there they all sat, as solemnly as owls.

She sighed and moved to leave the room. A soft whisper of "midnight" from Lord Reckford caught her ear and she nodded briefly to show him that she had heard.

She undressed and climbed into the huge fourposter bed and blew out the candle. It was only two hours to wait until midnight. She would creep into Mattie's room and leave the coast clear for his lordship. She doubted if she would manage to sleep at all.

But the great amount of food she had consumed at dinner hit her like a drug and she fell instantly asleep.

At precisely midnight, Lord Reckford crept into Henrietta's room. He was fully dressed, not having wanted to encounter anyone in the passage dressed in his night shirt. He settled himself in a chair by the window and prepared to wait. But the chair was hard and uncomfortable. There could be no harm in going to bed and stretching out. He might fall asleep but he would certainly awaken before the servants. And if anyone wanted to frighten or attack Henrietta, they would certainly have something planned that would awaken her.

Accordingly, he stripped off his clothes, placed them neatly on the chair, and with a sigh of relief, climbed into bed.

The sheets smelled faintly of lavender and he stretched himself out and prepared to wait. Suddenly, a small answering sigh caught his ear. He abruptly sat up and, fumbling around for the tinder box, lit the candle beside the bed. He turned and looked down at the sleeping figure of Miss Henrietta Sandford and swore roundly.

For one dreadful minute, he thought that she might have stayed in her bed deliberately in order to coerce him into marriage. He decided to give her the benefit of the doubt.

"Miss Sandford!" he whispered, shaking her shoulder.

Grumbling like a sleepy child, Henrietta slowly came awake . . . and then sat bolt upright with a gasp of alarm. She stared into Lord Reckford's enigmatic face. The tawny eyes were inscrutable. Her bewildered gaze finally registered that, as much as she could see of his lordship, was stark naked and she gave another gasp and cowered back against the pillows.

"There is no need to be so shocked, Miss Sandford,"

said the Beau dryly. "This has only come about because you fell asleep instead of removing to Miss Scattersworth's room."

Henrietta blinked to drive the last remnants of sleep from her wide eyes and then began to blush. She could feel herself blush from the top of her head to the tip of her toes. "I . . . I . . . am t-truly s-sorry, my lord," she stammered. "I will leave immediately."

"Wait a bit," said Lord Reckford. "Since we *are* alone, we can take this opportunity to discuss the business and see if we can imagine which of the guests would wish to harm you."

Henrietta nodded weakly. The Beau put his hands behind his head and settled himself comfortably against the pillows. "I am inclined to favor Ralston. What do you think?"

His companion was practically incapable of thought. Waves of violent emotion roused by the close proximity of this naked man were threatening to tear her apart. And underneath it all, was a faint cold feeling of pique that his lordship should be so absolutely and completely unaware of her as a woman.

Incurably honest, Henrietta replied with a certain edge to her trembling voice. "You must forgive me, my lord, if I seem somewhat distraught but I am not in the habit of sharing my bed with a member of the opposite sex. It may be an everyday matter for you. . . ."

Lord Reckford burst out laughing and a mocking light began to dance in his eyes. "Poor Henrietta, how I must be shocking you! I declare I am so intrigued by the mystery of your tormentor that I had quite forgot the conventions. I suppose you feel compromised and wonder why I do not propose."

"Fustian!" said Henrietta, anger driving away her embarrassment. "If and when I get married, it will be to some gentleman who is in love with me." Henrietta's hand started to pluck nervously at the bedspread and then she found it covered by Lord Reckford's long fingers.

"So little Henrietta will marry for love," he teased, while Henrietta stared mesmerised at their joined hands and felt about to faint from an excess of emotion. "Well, some fellow will indeed be lucky. I declare you grow prettier each day."

He twisted his head to look at her. In the flickering light of the candle, Henrietta's eyes looked enormous and her heavy hair spilled over her shoulders in a shining, golden cloud.

Their eyes met and held, tawny eyes staring into hazel ones with an intent, troubled, searching stare. Lord Reckford gave himself a slight shake and asked, "What on earth were you laughing about this evening?"

Henrietta told him all about the Belding nose and, to her relief, the Beau began to laugh. Then they both began to laugh wholeheartedly, the elegant Beau and the vicar's sister, till the tears ran down their cheeks.

"This is ridiculous," finally gasped Lord Reckford. "I must leave. I have a feeling that nothing will happen to disturb you tonight." Poor Henrietta decided that she had never felt so disturbed in all her life. Lord Reckford blew out the candle, left the bed and slipped noiselessly into his clothes. Henrietta lay rigid, with her eyes closed tight. She felt a shape looming over her, a light kiss was dropped on her cheek. . . . and he was gone. Long into the night, Henrietta lay awake, thinking how hopeless was the idea of Lord Reckford falling in love with her. For all Lord Reckford cared, thought Henrietta, he could have been sharing a bed with . . . with . . . a young brother!

She would have been reassured had she known that Lord Reckford had passed an equally troubled night. Only when he had reached his own bedchamber and felt his head swimming did he realize he had drunk far too much at dinner. He poured a pitcher of cold water over his head and felt worse. He could not explain his strange behavior, even to himself. He should have quit the girl's chamber as soon as he had found her in bed.

But he had never been on such easy, friendly terms with a young lady . . . a *respectable* young lady . . . before and at the time, he had not felt at all strange or embarrassed.

To his relief, when he met Henrietta at the breakfast table, she had merely given him a placid smile and commented that it was a fine day for their return to London.

Miss Scattersworth fluttered in still in all the glory of transparent muslin. She was wearing one of the new scanty petticoats beneath it. Everyone, with the exception of Sir Percival, hurriedly stared at their plates. Henrietta sighed. She really must tell Miss Mattie that her mode of dress was unsuitable and do it in such a way as not to hurt the elderly spinster's feelings. Fortunately for her and unfortunately for Miss Mattie, Henrietta was spared that distasteful task.

Sir Percival was conveying Miss Mattie in his open carriage to the house in Brook Street. As his horses picked their way disdainfully through a poorer quarter of the city, some street urchins began to point and stare at Miss Mattie. "Cor . . . look at 'er. Hey, missus, we kin see everythin' wot you 'as got." This was followed by a stream of insult, mercifully for Miss Mattie in too broad a cant for her to understand, but Sir Percival went red to the ears and told her in a brusk voice to "cover herself up."

Miss Mattie descended from the carriage and went in to the house in Brook Street after a subdued farewell to Sir Percival. But her ordeal was not over. She threw down her wraps in the hall and went in to the drawingroom . . . and presented herself in her full glory to the scandalized gaze of the curate, Mr. John Symes. The curate got to his feet and addressed a Buhl cabinet in the corner of the room.

"I did not realize it was so late, Miss Scattersworth. I only stayed to have a word with the vicar."

"He will be here directly," pleaded Miss Mattie. "Do allow me to offer you some refreshment. Some tea . . ."

She broke off in confusion as the curate sidled to the door, his eyes still fixed on the cabinet. "No, indeed. So kind . . . must leave . . . so kind." His groping hand found the door knob and with an audible gasp of relief, he flung open the door and scuttled off across the hall and out into the safety of the street.

Henrietta found Miss Mattie in floods of tears. "I am a shameless woman," she sobbed, flinging herself down on a hard unyielding sofa. "Mr. Symes would not even look at me."

"Well, my dear, it is perhaps too *outré* a mode for you."

"I know, I know," sobbed the broken-hearted Mattie. "But . . . but Sir Percival seemed to like dashing women. Alas, I have thrown myself away on a man who is nothing more than an elderly roué."

Henrietta sighed. "Believe me, when Mr. Symes next sees you looking your usual self, he will forget all about it. Or better still, tell him there was an accident to your trunk and your clothes were ruined and that one of the ladies of the party who was of your size lent you that dress."

Mattie's tears fled like magic. "I never did really care for Sir Percival," she said shyly. "I was merely dazzled by his worldly manner."

"Let us both forget the visit to Lady Haddington's. Too many unpleasant things happened there."

But try as she would, Henrietta could not banish the memory of that awful face among the trees or Lord Reckford's bewildering lack of embarrassment when he had shared her bed.

The other members of the late house party were also chewing over their visit to Lady Haddington in their respective homes.

Mr. Edmund Ralston and his mother were sitting in their elegant drawing room. Mrs. Ralston eyed her exquisite son with a shrewd, hard and calculating look which changed like quicksilver to one of pure maternal affection when her son looked across at her. Her body, which had appeared rigid and masculine a moment before, seemed to lose its muscles and bones and become soft and vulnerable.

"You owe it to me, Edmund, you really do," sniffed Mrs. Ralston. "Are you to be wed or no? Have you considered my delicate nerves—my sensibilities. To have to live with a madwoman?"

The pale green eyes of her son opened wide in surprise. "But I *must* marry, Henrietta, mama. She has my money. And I want my *money*."

Mrs. Ralston shifted uncomfortably on her seat. Sometimes, she found herself wondering if her precious son were quite sane. At that moment, a stray beam of sunlight shone like a halo on Edmund's golden curls as he still stared wide-eyed at his mother. The look of maternal love became genuine. Mrs. Ralston sighed. She could never resist her son's wide-eyed appeal. "If you want her . . . why, then you shall have her," she promised. Edmund gave her a seraphic smile. Mama would see that everything was all right. She always had, from his first rocking horse to his membership of the exclusive White's Club in St. James.

Alice Belding's admirers would have been hard put to recognize her. Her pretty face was contorted with fury, her hair was dishevelled and her voice was strident as she berated her mother. Few but her servants would have recognized the proud and domineering Lady Belding as she cringed like a schoolgirl before her irate daughter.

"Can't you do *anything*," screamed Alice, pacing up and down the saloon of their town house. "Lord Reckford is going to marry that fat nobody from the vicarage unless you put a stop to it. I thought I had made myself plain. I want to be my Lady Reckford and if you do not do something about it quickly, I shall . . . I shall *kill* myself."

"My dear," said her mother in a faltering voice. "My

dear, dear child. You know I am only doing my best. . . ."

"Your best is not good enough, ma'am," snapped her angry daughter, stopping her pacing and coming to a stop before her agitated parent. "You never do anything, you silly old frump. You . . ." Suddenly Alice's stormy furious face changed in the twinkling of an eye and she sank to the floor beside her mother's chair and twined her arms around the anxious woman's waist. With a melting expression. she looked up at her mother. "Please, mama," she said in a little-girl voice. "You must get Lord Reckford for me. You really must. Don't let howwid Henrietta take him away from your Alice."

Lady Belding clasped her daughter tightly, her severe patrician features softened with love. "Leave everything to mama," she said grimly. "I shall do everything in my power to put a curb on Henrietta Sandford's ambitions."

Henry Sandford was tooling his curricle at a smart pace along the Nethercote Road. Beside him sat his curate, Mr. John Symes, who seemed more than ever cowed and subdued.

"Well, have you nothing to say for yourself?" snapped Henry, finally becoming annoyed by his partner's silence. "I declare I have worries enough about my sister's state of mind without having you go into the sulks." The curate raised a faint murmur of protest but was drowned out by his more voluble superior. "She must get rid of that peculiar companion of hers for a start. You should have seen her dress. Disgraceful! Utterly disgraceful! Miss Mattie Scattersworth indeed!"

"I don't think Miss Scattersworth meant any harm by it," ventured Mr. Symes timidly. "It was extreme perhaps but I think poor Miss Scattersworth was only trying to follow current fashion. When she comes to her senses. . . ."

"Pah! That one will never come to her senses. Nor

83

my poor sister either. You should have heard her laughing last night. Wild maniacal laughter for no reason at all! I am all concern for my sister as you know, John. She has not the stability of mind to be in charge of such a great fortune. Not that she has been ungenerous. By no means!"

"No, indeed," said Mr. Symes feverently. "Her munificence . . . her donations to the poor are all that is marvellous."

"Well, well . . . there is much in what you say, my dear John, but you know we do hold opposing points of view. I do not consider it anyone's duty to help the poor. Poverty is a disease. They're simply lazy, mark my words. Poverty, indeed! Nothing up with them that a good day's work wouldn't cure," said the vicar forgetting that most of his tennants worked long and hard hours each day and still did not have enough to keep body and soul together.

"But to return to the more interesting subject of my sister. When I return to town, I shall try to persuade her to see a doctor. I am sorry to leave you with so much of the parish work but blood is thicker than water." Mr. Symes fought down a nasty, uncharitable thought that Henrietta's blood must have been very thin indeed when she had no money.

Mr. Jeremy Holmes and Lord Reckford had repaired to the Cocoa Tree. That famous coffee house seemed to be packed to capacity but, for the moment, both were content to survey the scene around them. Suddenly Lord Reckford felt a hand tugging at his sleeve and turned round. A small, thin man was bending over him. He was tricked out in tarnished finery from the enormous silver buttons on his soup-stained velvet coat to the glittering rings of paste and pinchbeck which embellished his long, dirty, tapering fingers. "What is it?" demanded Lord Reckford, recoiling slightly from the sour-wine breath of the man.

"Would your lordship be prepared for to buy information relating to a certain young lady?"

"What young lady?" demanded the Beau, twisting round in his chair.

His friend, Mr. Holmes, unfortunately decided that Lord Reckford was being annoyed. "What's going on? What's your business, fellow?"

Heads began to turn for Mr. Holmes' voice had carried to every corner of the room. The man gave a wild look round and then darted like an eel through the crowd and disappeared.

Lord Reckford swore. "Damme, Jeremy, the fellow had some information for me and you scared him off."

Mr. Holmes looked contrite. "I'm truly sorry, Guy. Thought he was bothering you."

"Now, I'll never know what he had to tell me," sighed the Beau. "Someone is playing dangerous and malicious tricks on Miss Sandford and I mean to find out who it is. Everyone looks suspicious . . . that terrible Mrs. Ralston and her peculiar son . . . Alice and her mother. . . ."

"I would have you know that I shortly hope to have the honor of making Miss Belding my wife," said Mr. Holmes stiffly.

"Never say she has accepted you?"

"And why not?" demanded Mr. Holmes. "Truth to say I have not yet had the courage to approach Lady Belding for her permission. But I am by no means a pauper and my line is as old as theirs."

"Ah, but do you have the nose," teased his lordship and then regaled his friend with the story of the Belding Nose.

Mr. Holmes laughed reluctantly. "All these old families have their idiosyncracies. But none of that makes my Alice any less fair."

"She is an extremely beautiful girl," agreed the Beau. "When I first met her, I must admit that I suspected she was spoiled and demanding. But her behaviour has been all that is nice of late and she has been an exceeding good friend to Henrietta."

"There you are then," exclaimed Mr. Holmes. "She would not harm Miss Sandford in any way. By the way, is the vicar's sister shortly to realize her ambition?"

"Fustian!" drawled his lordship. "I am sure Miss Sandford had no such ambition. The idea that she wished to marry me was put about, I am sure, by that romantic companion of hers. Miss Sandford is like a sister to me. I think highly of her and enjoy her companionship and am intrigued by the mystery that surrounds her. That is all."

Mr. Holmes was silent. With a delicacy and tact foreign to his usual forthright nature, he did not point out to his friend that the look in Henrietta's eyes betokened anything but simple friendship.

He was roused from his reverie by his lordship's asking, "Well, and when do you plan to propose to the fair Alice?"

"I am to call on Lady Belding at five o'clock. I hope my courage will not fail. I did not state my reasons for calling."

The Beau's harsh features softened as he surveyed the anxious expression on his friend's cherubic countenance. "You look as fine as fivepence, Jeremy. I am sure you will soften even Lady Belding's flinty heart."

"My appearance won't," said his friend dryly. "But mayhap my fortune will."

Nonetheless it was an unusually dithering and anxious Jeremy Holmes who presented himself at the Belding household. To his relief, the butler informed him that Lord Belding had come to town and was at present in the study.

This was better, thought Jeremy. He should not have to face the terrifying mother after all. Accordingly, he followed the butler to the study where he found Lord Belding fortifying himself from the brandy decanter.

Lord Belding did not share his wife's aristocratic looks. Lady Belding was also his second cousin and had all the Belding aristocratic hauteur. Lord Belding looked, on the other hand, for all the world like a farmer. He had a round red face with white bushy eyebrows and a short stubby nose. He wore an old-fashioned bagwig and knee breeches. His pale, bulbous blood-shot eyes surveyed Mr. Holmes with surprise, taking in all the glory of his appearance from his pomaded curls to his shiny hessians and the lacings on his breeches.

"Well," demanded Lord Belding finally. "What brings you here, Holmes?"

Jeremy eased a finger into his cravat. "I am come to ask your permission to pay my addresses to your daughter."

"Oh, is that all," said his lordship. "Thought you was goin' to ask for money. Sit down, m'boy and take a glass with me." Jeremy raised his hand to protest but Lord Belding had already seized the decanter and was pouring a liberal measure into a goblet. "Drink up, m'boy. I'll send for Alice." He gave the bellrope a massive tug and, when the butler appeared, instructed him to fetch Miss Alice directly, with so many nods and winks that the butler only gave one significant look at the decanter before departing on his errand.

"Well," said Lord Belding raising his glass. "What yer waitin' for. No heel taps."

"No heel taps," said Jeremy faintly, draining the massive goblet and feeling his head beginning to reel. Why, it must have held at least a pint! And he had had several glasses of madeira to fortify himself for his ordeal before he had even left his house.

He blinked to clear his head and then stumbled to his feet and he found himself confronted with the beautiful vision that was Alice Belding.

"Leave you two young things alone," said Lord Belding with an awful leer, and lumbered towards the door. He nearly collided with his wife who stood majestically on the threshold, her bosom thrust forward like the figurehead on a frigate.

"Alice! What is going on here!" demanded Lady Belding.

"Why, mama, I know not," said Alice, dimpling adorably.

"Holmes's come to propose," said Lord Belding.

"Nonsense!" said Lady Belding, seizing Alice by the arm. "I've never heard of anything so ridiculous. My Alice marry a plain Mister! Come child. They have been been . . . *drinking*."

She thrust her reluctant daughter from the room, leaving both men feeling extremely foolish. To her surprise, Lady Belding was subjected to one of her daughter's worst fits of tantrums. Alice did not want to marry Mr. Holmes. But she felt that her mama could at least have given her an opportunity of breaking the young man's heart.

Jeremy and Lord Belding found refuge from the weary world of women in the bottom of the decanter and two hours later, with unsteady gait and a head that felt as if it were stuffed full of gun cotton, Jeremy remembered that he was to attend a ball at the Duke of Westerland's. With a groan, he weaved homewards to change.

Henrietta stood at the top of the staircase leading down into the ballroom at the Duke of Westerland's magnificent town house . . . and blinked. She found herself looking down on a sea of silks and satins, feathers and jewels. Diamonds, rubies, emeralds and sapphires dazzled and sparkled in the light. The smell of the ballroom compounded of flowers, scent, snuff, pomades and bear grease rose around her like incense. One of the lengthy, exhausting country dances had just come to an end as Henrietta descended the staircase with a much subdued and severely dressed Miss Mattie in her wake.

Heads began to turn in their direction and Henrietta

felt a sinking feeling in the pit of her stomach. Was there something odd about her appearance? She was dressed in a slim gown of burgundy crêpe cut low over the bosom. The full puffed sleeves were slashed to reveal silk insets and the gown fell in straight Empire lines to six deep flounces from knee to hem. Her fair hair was dressed *à la Sappho*, lending height to her slim figure. For Henrietta had finally achieved the sylph-like figure of her dreams. Her wide eyes sparkled with animation and, in all, she had never looked better. Heads nodded and voices whispered. The vicar's sister had style!

Her seemingly placid good nature had made her a popular dance partner and her friendship with the famous Beau Reckford and then her enormous fortune assured her social success. She was soon surrounded by a knot of admirers and her dance card was rapidly being filled when a familiar husky voice said, "But the waltz is promised to me."

Lord Reckford led her onto the floor and clasped her lightly round the waist. He smiled down into her eyes. "You must always save the waltzes for me Miss Sandford."

Heart beating fast, Henrietta bowed her head and wished that he would not flirt so easily, so lightly and so . . . so . . . meaninglessly.

After they had finished waltzing—companionably on the Beau's side and emotion-torn on Henrietta's—she shyly promised to save him the supper dance and returned to her place beside Miss Scattersworth. She paused in surprise and looked around. Of Miss Mattie, there was no sign. Feeling perturbed and anxious, she began to search the ballroom, forgetting in her anxiety that her next dance partner was waiting for her.

Increasingly anxious, Henrietta was about to enlist the aid of Lord Reckford when she heard a familiar giggle from behind one of the long curtains. She jerked it open and stood with her mouth open in amazement. Miss Mattie and a military gentleman with fierce moustaches were seated side by side on a wrought iron bench on the balcony. The gentleman had an arm round Miss Mattie's waist and that lady was clutching a glass of champagne and giggling uncontrollably.

"Mattie!" cried Henrietta, outraged. "Why, you are *foxed!*"

Mattie's escort lumbered to his feet and, with a great creaking of corsets, made a magnificent bow. "Your servant, ma'am. 'low me to introduce myself, Colonel Witherspoon at your service. The lady here is safe with me, ma'am. Shall protect her, ma'am. Shall fight all comers, ma'am. Gawd, herrumph, yes, what!"

He was obviously as intoxicated as Miss Mattie and Henrietta was just wondering what on earth to do, when she felt an urgent tug at her arm. "Please, Miss Sandford, I must speak with you."

It was Mr. Jeremy Holmes, the hectic glitter in his eyes making him look like a fallen cherub. "Must speak with you!" he insisted.

Henrietta was in a quandary. Concern for Miss Mattie and worry about the Beau's best friend tore her in opposite directions. She finally decided to attend to Mr. Holmes. Miss Mattie was hidden from the public gaze for the present. Mr. Holmes drew Henrietta ungently on to the adjoining balcony and insisted she sit down beside him. Mr. Holmes had nearly drunk himself sober but he was in an anxious sentimental mood and his eyes kept filling with ready tears. "I know you love Miss Belding dearly," was his inauspicious beginning. He then blurted out the tale of his attempted proposal, his rejection by Lady Belding, his undying love for Alice.

Henrietta, as many of the poorer parishioners of Nethercote knew, was an excellent listener. Mr. Holmes blossomed under her sympathy and calm maternal air.

He was not aware how poor Henrietta was identifying with his feelings of rejected love. How under her serene mask there burned all the strong emotions of a fiery, passionate woman.

Although Henrietta had not uttered one word of advice, Mr. Holmes felt immeasurably soothed and calmed by the time he had reached the end of his impassioned speech. The pink clouds of drunkeness, which had retreated to the horizons of his mind, closed in again. In an excess of affection, he seized the astonished Henrietta in a warm clasp and placed an affectionate kiss on her cheek.

"Pray . . . what is going on here?" said a voice as cold as ice. Both rose to their feet in confusion. Lord Reckford stared down at them, his tawny eyes under their hooded lids glaring at the unfortunate Jeremy. Henrietta did not know what to do. If she explained, then she would be betraying Mr. Holmes' trust. She looked appealingly at that young man. But Jeremy merely stared at his aristocratic friend with a mischievous glint in his eyes.

"Well, what?" he mocked. "You turned Methodist, Reckford? Can't I kiss a pretty girl on this beautiful moonlit night?"

"It is beginning to rain," snapped Lord Reckford. "But perhaps you two lovers did not notice a little matter like that," he added with a sneer.

Jeremy Holmes caught the look of real distress on Henrietta's face and grabbed the Beau by the arm. "Now, look here Guy. Fact of the matter is . . . I was burdening her with all my troubles. And Henrietta's such a kind girl. Well, you know how it is. You said she was like a sister to you yourself, now didn't you?"

Now Lord Reckford had indeed said just that. So why, he wondered, did he have a sudden urge to land his oldest and dearest friend a facer? With a grim smile, he offered his arm to Henrietta and held back the curtain and ushered her into the ballroom. Alice Belding stood waiting with her mother in attendance. "My dance, my lord," she said with an enchanting smile. "Of course," he bowed to Henrietta, gave Jeremy a venomous look and led Alice off to where a set was being formed for the Cotillion. Jeremy had sobered completely. From the distress on Henrietta's face and the fury on his friend's, he realized that he had said something badly wrong. "Can I be of any assistance to you?" he asked Henrietta. "Fetch you a glass of ratafia or something?"

Henrietta refused and was about to turn away when she remembered Miss Mattie. "Oh, yes. Please do help me. I must get Miss Scattersworth home." Henrietta blushed. "She is with a gentleman and . . . and . . . oh dear."

"Lead the way," said Mr. Holmes gallantly, glad that he could be of service. There was something about Henrietta that really brought the Knight Errant out in a man, he reflected.

Henrietta was heartily grateful for his assistance. Nothing she could say could prise Miss Mattie from her gallant's side. It was left to Jeremy to put a quiet word in the Colonel's ear. What he said, Henrietta never knew, but Colonel Witherspoon shot to his feet with his face scarlet, made his adieux then staggered off. Miss Mattie dissolved into drunken tears, then she started laughing hysterically. Again Jeremy Holmes came to the rescue. He slapped Miss Mattie hard across her withered cheek. The transformation was instant. One minute there was a raucous, hysterical beldame and the next a contrite, if tipsy, elderly spinster.

Jeremy and Henrietta led Miss Mattie from the ballroom. Henrietta gave Mr. Holmes a glance of pure gratitude across Miss Scattersworth's bowed head. Lord Reckford caught the glance and suddenly felt that the ball was insipid and flat. He looked down into Alice Belding's beautiful face and decided that there must be something up with his liver. London, with its routs, balls, and parties was wearisome. He should visit his estates. He did not wish to be considered an absentee landlord. He would arrange a house party for the week-end. Unusual in the middle of the Season but then his estates were only a day's easy ride from London. And he would ask all the suspects in Henrietta's mystery and perhaps discover the culprit.

Feeling slightly consoled . . . though why he should wish to be consoled, he was at a loss to say . . . he turned his full charm on Alice Belding and raised that young lady's hopes of matrimony by leaps and bounds.

Chapter Eight

CHERWOOD ABBEY, HOME OF the Reckfords, was impressive enough to bring gasps of admiration from the arriving house guests.

It was a huge pile built on a long ridge of hills in the center of a crescent of woods. Following the medieval pattern, the principal rooms were on the first floor with broad double flights of stone steps from the windows giving access to the gardens. The ground floor was mainly taken up by a vast hall which was hung round with family portraits, armoury, and medieval banners. The Reckfords, unlike the Beldings, went to war.

The formal gardens in front of the Abbey were separated from an extensive park by tall iron gates, on each of the pillars of which was a griffin rampant supporting the escutcheon of the family. A long avenue of limes stretched from these gates in a direct line to the lodge house.

Through the woods of the park, Henrietta could see the sun shining on a pretty ornamental lake. Behind the crescent of trees at the back of the house, stood a tall sandstone cliff.

Since the house party was small—by Reckford standards—the guests had been allotted apartments instead of the customary bedroom and dressingroom each.

Miss Mattie, flitted about examining Henrietta's quarters and clapping her hands like a child. "Nothing eez lacking, *ma chérie*. It eez all, 'ow you say, *complét*. You even have a Bramah water closet," ended Miss Mattie, reverting to her normal voice.

Henrietta sighed. "Who is he, Mattie?" she asked.

"He? Who?" replied Miss Mattie rather incoherently.

Henrietta eyed the black velvet ribbon round Miss Mattie's throat. "The French *emigré*," she remarked dryly. "Really Mattie, why must you affect that nonsensical fashion. None of your family ever went to the guillotine."

"But . . . but . . ." stammered Miss Mattie, for once at a loss. Then her eyes lit up. "Why, my dear, perhaps in a *previous* life. . . ."

"Fiddlesticks!" said Henrietta roundly, but kindly forebore to remark that Miss Scattersworth had been very much alive herself during the French Revolution. "Anyway, who is the gentleman?"

"Well, he is a Monsieur Dubois," twittered Miss Mattie, "And he eez mos' *charmant*."

"But Mattie—why do you have to speak in that strange French accent? And who is Monsieur Dubois?"

"He is Lord Reckford's personal secretary and I think my accent is rather pretty. I adopt it to make him feel at home, you know. Ah! I can hear the noise of the *sans culottes*. But I shall not flinch. I shall be wearing virginal white and I shall stare down at the *canaille* with disdain. The tumbril moves on. To the guillotine! I refuse to have my eyes bound. Long live His Majesty. The blade falls. I die!" Miss Mattie collapsed artistically onto the oriental rug. Henrietta sighed again. Miss Scattersworth was indeed susceptible.

The light was fading behind the trees and, after Miss Mattie had left, Henrietta started to prepare for dinner. The party had spent Friday travelling to Cherwood Abbey in Surrey. The whole week-end stretched out in front of Henrietta. If only his lordship had not decided to once more invite all her antagonists. Mrs. Ralston had set the tone of the visit by remarking sweetly, "I realize you are not accustomed to this level of society, my dear Henrietta. Do consult me as to how you should act. I am quite sure you will be most dreadfully in need of help."

Dinner was served in one of the small dining rooms on the first floor. Alice Belding had cleverly chosen a dinner gown of a medieval cut in heavy cloth of gold. She looked like a heroine out of the pages of a romance about Camelot. She was seated on Lord Reckford's right hand—Lady Belding had bribed the butler to arrange the place settings—and they made a handsome couple. Henrietta had Mr. Holmes on her right and brother Henry on her left. Miss Scattersworth was seated next to Monsieur Dubois and spoke to him in such a broken French accent that the poor secretary, who spoke impeccable English, was under the misapprehension that Miss Scattersworth was speaking a patois from the West Indies and kept appealing to his neighbors for translations.

Jeremy Holmes realized that Alice was going to devote all her attention to her host so he spent the dinner chatting happily with Henrietta of whom he was becoming increasingly fond. He succeeded in amusing her so well that he managed to forget Alice and Henrietta managed to forget the Beau. Neither knew that they had finally gained the attention they craved. Alice was jealous that Henrietta seemed to be mending the broken heart of her suitor very quickly and Lord Reckford decided that his friend Jeremy was a heartless flirt.

An *al fresco* luncheon had been planned for the Saturday and Lord Reckford reminded the party to wear serviceable clothes because they were going to climb to the top of the cliff.

No ghosts haunted Henrietta that night, and all the previous happenings to scare her seemed like so many far away dreams.

Saturday dawned bright and fair—an English summer's day in full bloom. Henrietta was wearing a sensible pair of half boots, prepared for the walk ahead. Alice on the other hand was wearing frail slippers of sky-blue kid with the idea of stumbling on to the nearest supporting male arm, preferably the Beau's. Great was her disappointment to find that the party were to ascend the cliffs on donkeys. Everyone set off, riding comfortably, with the exception of Henry. His riding dress, although correct to an inch, complete with white tops to his boots, was far too tight and he wheezed and struggled as much as the poor animal that had to carry him.

The party came to a stop beside a rushing stream under the shadow of the top of the cliff. Henrietta sat down on a boulder and looked about her with a sigh of satisfaction. Oak trees, birch and larch crowded to the water's edge of this small plateau. The water foamed green and white over large boulders which sparkled and flashed with specks of marcasite in the morning sun. Thick clumps of long grass stood to attention in the breathless morning air, their translucsent green setting off the tremulous blue of the hairbells which nestled in their shade. All the birds of the wood serenaded them with song accompanied by the cheerful domestic sounds of the servants unpacking the lunch. There was a lazy hot smell of pine and brewing tea and methylated spirits.

Mr. Ralston struck a romantic pose on top of a rock at the edge of the glade. At any minute, thought Henrietta, he is going to shade his brow and stare off into the middle distance. Which he did.

Mrs. Ralston was telling anyone who cared to listen about the dangers of bee venom and above and under her voice in a sort of mad counterpoint came the chattering of Miss Scattersworth as she flirted desperately with Lord Reckford's secretary in broken English and broken French.

Beau Reckford was chatting idly with Alice while Lady Belding stood slightly apart from them, apparently defying anyone to break up her daughter's courtship. Henrietta watched them covertly. Alice, for all her beauty, did not belong in this sylvan setting. She appeared too well-coiffed, too brittle, whereas the Beau looked surprisingly at home although his morningdress would not have been out of place in the Regent's drawingroom. Henrietta moved into the shade of a stand of trees and began to search in her reticule for some *papier poudré* to dull the shine on her nose. To her surprise, a long letter had been thrust into her reticule. She drew it out and crackled open the paper. It contained one sentence, "If you wish to find all the answers to the mystery, lift the green rock at the top of the cliff, and do not tell anyone."

Henrietta crumpled the letter angrily in her small hand. Of all the gothic nonsense. She would not attend. She would join the picnic as if nothing had happened. But what if it were true? What if she could solve this riddle? She looked hurriedly around. No one was paying any attention to her. She looked up. The top of the cliff seemed only a few steps away. Quickly making up her mind, she slipped away from the house party and began to climb up a narrow sandstone path. She soon began to regret her impulse. By the time she gained the top of the cliff, she was sweating freely, and her pretty sprigged muslin was stained with sandstone dust. Her hair had been pulled and tangled by the low overhanging branches of the trees and her ankles stung from the whiplash of tall nettles.

She sank down onto the rough grass at the top of the cliff and then, lying forward on her stomach, peered over the edge.

The picnic party was spread out on the plateau thirty feet below her. Directly underneath where she lay stood Lady Belding and Alice with their heads together. A snatch of Alice's conversation rose in the clear air . . . "It is only a matter of time, mama. Reckford will ask. . . ." The rest of her conversation was lost as she and her mother turned to move away

"Ask?" thought Henrietta. "Ask what? Her hand?" She experienced such a pang of jealousy that for one awful minute she thought she was going to be ill.

Well, she may as well look for the green stone. That was what she had come up here for. She looked round. Next to her and under an outcrop of rock, lay a long narrow stone painted green. How melodramatic, thought Henrietta grimly. The whole affair was becoming reassuringly childish. Now for the mystery. She seized the green rock and lifted. It took all her strength. To her horror, the huge outcrop seemed to come slowly to life and she realized that the long green stone had been cunningly placed under it as a lever. The outcrop had been camoflaged with great tufts of grass to make it look secure. Henrietta opened her mouth to scream a warning but no sound came out. She flung herself down on her stomach and looked over, still gasping and trying to find her voice. The huge rock, dislodged from its moorings, seemed to hang motionless for a second in the still summer air while the figures of the house party moved gracefully below like actors in a pastoral play.

Then it hit the ground with a great *Crrummp* and clouds of sandstone dust swirled around, obscuring the house party from Henrietta's terrified stare. There were screams and cries, women shrieking, men cursing. Finally the dust cleared and an accusing ring of white faces stared upwards at Henrietta. Not one ran up to help her. All waited in silence as she descended the path with trembling limbs.

Everyone began to speak at once.

"Murderess!" (Mrs. Ralston)

"My dear sister, I fear for your reason." (Henry Sandford)

"Lean on me, Henrietta. I will protect you no matter what you have done!" (Edmund Ralston)

"Henrietta, a word with you." (Lord Reckford)

"An accident. *Of course* it was an accident." (Miss Scattersworth)

"From where I stood, it appeared to be a deliberate attempt to murder Alice." (Lady Belding)

Henrietta had found her voice and began stammering and crying at one and the same time. Lord Reckford held his hand up for silence and drew Henrietta aside.

"What on earth happened, Miss Sanford?"

Henrietta looked up at him piteously, "I . . . I . . . found a note in my reticule which told me that if I raised the green rock at the top of the cliff, I would find an explanation to the mystery. There . . . there . . . was a rock—a sort of long stone . . . but it only acted as a level to dislodge that large rock. I . . . I . . . can show you the letter . . . my reticule. I must have left it on top of the cliff."

"Wait here," said Lord Reckford and loped off with his easy athletic stride to the cliff path. Henrietta sat down on the edge of a rock. Everyone else waited in silence. She felt like a prisoner at the bar, waiting for the jury to reach their decision. After what seemed an age, he came back and announced smoothly, "Miss Sandford and all of us have been victims of a very dangerous and stupid practical joke. I suggest we compose ourselves and enjoy our luncheon as if nothing had happened. Come Miss Belding, so fair a face needs to have the roses brought back to it. My arm? Let me escort you to the table." He led Alice off, casting a curiously questioning and troubled look at Henrietta over his shoulder.

Mrs. Ralston and Lady Belding showed their annoyance on hearing Henrietta pronounced innocent. Henry Sandford puffed and hawed and hummed and begged forgiveness for his hasty remark. Henrietta had the doubtful pleasure of being escorted to table by Edmund Ralston.

She sat down with her knees trembling, picking at her food and trying to catch Lord Reckford's eye. He seemed too absorbed in flirting with Alice Belding with a carefree expertise honed to perfection in about every fashionable saloon in London. Alice blossomed like the rose. No one, thought Henrietta viciously, studying the beautiful, animated face would guess when she is like this that she is as petty, domineering and spiteful as her mother.

Mr. Holmes was seated on Henrietta's other side. He had been unusually quiet during the whole adventure but when Edmund's attention was wholly taken up by his mother, he asked her in a low voice what had happened. For the second time, Henrietta told her story. "But I don't think Lord Reckford found anything. He did not return my reticule to me and somehow I think the green stone has been removed."

"Tell you what," said Mr. Holmes. "I don't much feel like eating either." He gave a significant look towards Alice Belding and the Beau. "Perhaps we could go back to the top of the cliff and see if we can find your reticule."

Henrietta readily assented. Anything was better than sitting nursing her frightened thoughts. Jeremy got to his feet. "Going to take a stroll," he remarked to everyone in general and no one in particular, and, offering Henrietta his arm, strolled off.

The day had turned unusually warm and the pair were panting slightly with their exertions by the time they reached the top of the cliff. As Henrietta had feared, the green stone had disappeared along with her reticule. There was nothing to see but a huge gash in the cliff-side where the outcrop had stood.

"Don't despair," teased Mr. Holmes, feeling more light-hearted now that he was out of the bewitching presence of Alice Belding. "Let's search about. Come along," he added, giving the listless Henrietta a playful push. "Look about you!"

They started to search through the thick tuffets of grass and outcrops of sandstone. "Look here!" he suddenly shouted, making Henrietta jump. "See where the outcrop was. Well, it's been chiselled loose. There, see the marks. Done deliberately and taken a long time by the look of it. See, you ain't got windmills in your head after all! Keep looking. This is fun!"

Despite the fact that the hot sun seemed to be scorching through the thin muslin of her dress, Henrietta searched diligently around. "I've found something," she cried. "Why, it's a silver button." She held it up. Jeremy looked at the enormous silver button in her hand and his eyes narrowed.

"Now just where have I seen that before?" he murmured.

"There's another one," cried Henrietta, a glint of silver catching her eye. "Under that bush over there." Unmindful of the conventions, she crawled on her hands and knees under the bush. Her voice came back to Jeremy faintly. "I've got it . . . it's not a button. It . . . it's my reticule."

She backed out from the bush and triumphantly held up her reticule. Mr. Holmes was doubled up with laughter. "What are you giggling at?" demanded Henrietta severely.

"Honestly, Henrietta . . . I mean Miss Sandford, you're such a serene, correct sort of girl. But you should see the crazy mess you're in."

Henrietta fished in her reticule and, producing a small mirror, looked at her dishevelled hair with horror. "Oh dear! No wonder everyone thought I was mad. Perhaps if you would hold the mirror for me . . .? Thank you." She took a comb and began to deftly straighten out her tangled curls.

"You know, you're really a very attractive sort of girl, Miss Sandford, that is, when you're not being so quiet and correct."

Henrietta put down the comb with a sigh. "Come now, Mr. Holmes, I cannot act like a hoyden in the drawingrooms of London."

"No," agreed Mr. Holmes, stretching himself lazily out on the grass beside her. "But if you'll forgive me for speaking plain, you could do with a tiny bit more animation."

"Like Miss Belding perhaps?"

"Well, yes, that is . . . I mean," began Jeremy blushing scarlet. "Dash it all, Henrietta. I was just trying to give you some brotherly advice."

"I'm tired of brothers," snapped Henrietta, and then added in a kinder voice. "Oh, I know you're trying to help, Mr. Holmes. But you must realize, I have not been used to going about in society much. I went to various balls and parties in Nethercote, but then I was not an heiress, so I could sit against the wall all night, unnoticed."

Henrietta settled her shoulders against a sun-warmed rock. "You know, Mr. Holmes. The trouble I suppose is that I can't remember having any sort of carefree life as a child. All I can remember is having to be correct and watch my tongue. All the natural impulsiveness of youth was curbed by my brother's riding crop."

"Oh, come now," protested Mr. Holmes, sitting up straight and staring at her. But Henrietta went on, talking almost to herself.

"Oh, yes. But of course, it was never my brother striking me. He was but an instrument of God, or so he said. I thought when I grew up and became a young lady that I would be too old for such treatment but Henry listened to Lady Belding, you see. 'That sister of yours is too bold, Sandford,' she would say. 'A few lashes with the crop is just the thing to keep her in line.'"

"But Alice. . . ." began Mr. Holmes, much shocked.

"Oh, no Alice was never whipped. But she was sometimes allowed to attend my whippings as a special treat."

Jeremy stared at Henrietta. She was patently telling the truth.

Henrietta went on. "Even very correct young ladies seemed to be allowed to romp a bit, but never me. I do not expect pity, Mr. Holmes, I am merely trying to explain to you why it was necessary for me to develop a placid mask to hide my feelings."

Jeremy looked at her speculatively. "And now someone is trying to prove that you are mad or a murderess or both."

Henrietta sighed. "Sometimes I get so frightened, I can hardly breath. But until today, Lord Reckford has always been around to believe me and protect me. Today . . . well, he looked for the first time as if he thought there might be something strange about me. In any case, we are not observing the conventions at the moment. We should go back."

"Blow the conventions!" remarked Mr. Holmes with an airy cheerfulness, he did not feel. He could not help remembering Henrietta's remark about Alice being invited to view the whippings. He needed time to think. He heard a faint sound of voices ascending the cliff path.

"Let's escape!" he said, getting to his feet and holding out his hand to Henrietta. "Here they come."

Feeling like naughty schoolchildren, they ran lightly over the springy turf on the top of the cliff until they came to a narrow overgrown track on the far side. "Down we go!" said Jeremy blithely, leading the way. They stumbled headlong down, laughing and giggling, and the parishoners of Nethercote would have been hard put to recognize the vicar's staid sister, with her hair once more in a tangle and her skirts torn by briars. They arrived at the woods at the far side of the glade where the stream bubbled down in a series of miniature falls. They sank down on the turf beside it, breathless and laughing.

"Really, we are behaving abominably," gasped Henrietta. "What a wild schoolboy *you* must have been."

"Well, I was," admitted Jeremy, grinning unrepentantly. "Guy Reckford was the scholar. He didn't have much fun as a child either. His parents died when he was young and by the time he came down from Oxford he certainly had a job to sort out the muddle here. His uncle, Sir Marcus Hemmington had been regent of the estate, so to speak, and a right mull he'd made of it. Land lying fallow, tenants' roofs falling about their ears, and the whole of the Abbey turned into a sort of gambling hell. Reckford sent him packing and then by the time he had got everything running smoothly, he decided it was time he enjoyed himself. And he did. Wildest rake about town was Guy." Jeremy flushed. "Sorry, forgot who I was talking to."

They both sat for a few minutes in a companionable silence, listening to the stream rushing and chuckling between the stones. Far above them, the tops of the trees began to sway and whisper as a breeze sprang up.

"When I was a boy," Jeremy went on lazily, "we used to spend our vacations on my uncle's estate in Scotland. Right up in the Highlands it was, miles from anywhere. I used to run wild with the boys on the estate and, looking at this stream reminds me, they taught me how to catch trout without using a line."

"How did you do that?" asked Henrietta. "By magic?"

"No. Nothing to it. I'll show you." The elegant Jeremy carefully removed his coat and hung it on a branch. Then he took off his boots and stockings and unfastened the lacings at the knees of his buckskins and rolled them up with no little effort. They were skin tight.

"Now," he explained to the fascinated Henrietta. "You must be very, very quiet. Ouch, the water's icy." He stood in the stream, and bent his pomaded curls over the water. "Now we wait."

Both fell silent. Far away came the muted voices of the rest of the party. Henrietta's eyelids began to droop. They jerked open at a yell from Jeremy as he hurled a fat speckled trout onto the bank and then began dancing after it, cheering in triumph. "There you are!" he cried. "First one. What was it those Scotch boys called it? I have it ... guddling for trout."

"Could I try?" asked Henrietta.

"I don't see why not," he answered, looking doubtfully at her dress.

"My gown is ruined in any case and . . . and . . . if I hitch it up, you won't tell anyone. *Please*, Jeremy."

He shook his head and stared at Henrietta. With her huge eyes sparkling with fun and her heavy fair hair tumbling about her shoulders, she looked extremely attractive. Henrietta modestly pinned up her skirts a little above the ankle and waded into the stream. "Now," said Jeremy's voice behind her. "Bend over the water and keep very quiet. Hang your hands down just so. That's it. Now, all you have to do is grab one when he comes along."

Henrietta stared intently at the water and, after what seemed like an age, a fish flashed towards her. She stooped, she grabbed . . . and the fish slid neatly between her fingers and swam off downstream.

"Try again," called Jeremy.

She stared down into the water again. The afternoon began to drift lazily past. Just as Henrietta thought she would never have any feeling in her feet again, a trout flashed below her. She grabbed onto it and dragged it from the water, leaping about and crying for help. "Throw it on the bank," yelled Jeremy, nearly helpless with laughter. Henrietta was flushed with triumph. Unaware that the sun was beginning to sink in the sky, she bent her head again to the stream. In the next hour, Jeremy caught two and Henrietta, another one.

It was Jeremy who first became aware of the lengthening shadows. "Henrietta. We really must get back." He offered her his pocket handkerchief to dry her feet. Both had become fast friends and were on first name terms without being aware of it.

"Oh, dear. The others have left," said Henrietta, conscience-stricken. "What shall we do?"

"We'll leave the fish in the kitchen and creep up the backstairs to our rooms," said Jeremy. "Guy should know that you're all right with me."

But as they scrambled back down the hill on foot—

their donkeys had gone—they were met by the head gamekeeper who delivered himself of the grim message that he and the other servants had been searching for them for the past hour or more and that his lordship wished to see Miss Sandford in the library immediately on her return.

Feeling like chastened schoolchildren, they returned to the Abbey under the stern eye of the gamekeeper. Jeremy handed over his catch, and took Henrietta's arm. "Guy has a bit of a temper, especially when he's worried. Do you want me to come with you?"

Henrietta mutely shook her head. The gamekeeper escorted her to the library and shut the door firmly behind her.

Lord Reckford had been writing at a Chippendale desk over by the huge French windows which opened on to the first floor terrace. He rose to his feet and turned to face Henrietta. He was dressed for dinner in a rose coloured silk evening coat and breeches. There were diamonds in his snowy cravat, diamonds flashed on his long white fingers and on the buckles of his slippers. He wore his black hair unpowdered and his tawny eyes surveyed the trembling Henrietta with a fashionable air of boredom.

In actual fact, he was in a towering rage. He had been worried to death and then, to receive the news from a footman that Miss and Mister were returning with the gamekeeper and had been fishing. *Fishing!*

He stood over the shaking Henrietta and levelled his quizzing glass over her torn gown. "Well, madam?" he drawled.

Henrietta was about to burst out with all sorts of justifications and apologies when she remembered that she was a woman of twenty-six, an heiress and Lord Reckford's guest and bit her lip.

Guy Reckford walked slowly round her examining her muddy shoes and tangled hair.

"Well, madam?" he asked again, with an edge to his voice.

"Well, what?" demanded Henrietta rudely.

"I have been out of my mind with worry about you, madam," said his lordship. "Out of my mind worrying whether you are out of yours. You are part of an incident which could have meant the death of one of my guests and instead of waiting to discuss the matter with me, you go . . . *fishing*."

"I was enjoying myself and forgot the time," said Henrietta. "Furthermore, I *found* my reticule so that proves it was not me who was responsible for dislodging the rock. Mr. Holmes believes me."

"He does, does he. Very pretty. Well, madam, while you and Mr. Holmes were dancing about in your Arcadia, I had returned and marshalled the servants to search the estate for evidence of any stranger and also to ensure your safe return. I am extremely displeased with you, madam."

"Oh, fiddle," snapped Henrietta. "Mr. Holmes was protection enough, I assure you."

"You are distressingly innocent for a lady of your years," sneered Lord Reckford, making Henrietta feel like forty. "Surely, in that provincial backwater you hail from, they had enough sense to tell you that a lady does not play about the woods with a gentleman, unescorted."

"Pooh!" said Henrietta rudely. "I was perfectly safe. What could happen to me, my lord?"

"This," he said savagely. He dragged the surprised girl into his arms and began to kiss her, long, hard ruthless, insulting kisses. Henrietta gave a faint moan of protest. The room began to spin about her. The inner Henrietta took over. With a little sigh, she wound her arms about his neck and returned his kisses as wave after wave of pent-up passion swept through her body. The Beau suddenly forgot who he was, who Henrietta was, where he was. His kisses became longer, deeper, more exploring. His long fingers began to move over her body, easing her gown away from her shoulders to bare her breast. Henrietta let out a high, thin cry of passion and he bit her neck and then bent his head to her bosom. "Oh, my dear Lucinda," he sighed.

Henrietta felt exactly as if a bucket of ice-cold water had been thrown over her. She dragged herself away and struck Lord Reckford with her clenched fist as hard as she could and ran sobbing from the room.

Miss Mattie was waiting for her in her bedroom and jumped up in amazement as Henrietta ran past her and flung herself on the bed. "Oh, what is the matter?" gasped Miss Mattie.

"He . . . he . . . called me . . . *Lucinda*," wailed Henrietta between sobs.

"Oh, dear," Miss Mattie sat down beside the bed and reached for Henrietta's hand. "I had the whole story of Lucinda from Monsieur Dubois."

With none of her usual silliness, Miss Mattie told her story in a low voice. Lord Reckford was a young man of twenty-one when he had his first Season in London. Ignoring the charms of all the debutantes, he had fallen in love with a very beautiful widow, Lucinda Braintree. Their stormy affair lasted six months. Lucinda had been charming, enchanting . . . and heartless. At the end of the six months, she had left Lord Reckford to live under the protection of the elderly Marquis of Glenmorrison. In despair, the young Lord promised marriage but Lucinda only laughed and patted his cheek and went off with her Marquis.

Since that time, Lord Reckford had shown no interest in women apart from a series of opera dancers. He had stated his intention of eventually getting married to a lady of suitable birth.

Miss Mattie ended her tale and looked sadly down at Henrietta who lay on the bed, wide-eyed, her face tear-stained. She suddenly felt very old and had no romantic fantasies to comfort her young, heart-broken friend.

Henrietta rose wearily from the bed and began to prepare an especially elaborate toilette for dinner. She rang for her maid who raised her hands in horror at the sight of her mistress's tangled locks. An hour later, and Henrietta was once again an elegant young lady in all the glory of a smart silk gown, pale green like young spring leaves, and with a heavy set of garnets clasped round her neck. She was carefully choosing a suitable fan when a servant scratched at the door to inform Miss Sandford that his lordship wished to see her urgently.

Well, she may as well get any embarrassment over before facing the beady eyes of the Beldings at dinner.

Lord Reckford was pacing up and down the library as she was ushered in. "Please sit down, Miss Sandford," he said in a chilly voice.

Henrietta sat down primly on the edge of a small upright chair and stared with intense interest at the carpet. Lord Reckford stood for a few seconds looking down at her. Then he drew up a chair and sat down opposite.

He cleared his throat. "Miss Sandford, I do not know how to begin to apologise for my behavior. Please believe me when I say that I was ill with worry about you. I am at a loss to explain my conduct even to myself. I added insult to injury by mentioning another lady's name. That lady has been long forgotten, I assure you.

"The fact is," he went on more briskly, "that although there were no witnesses, I feel I have compromised you. Despite my reputation, I am not in the habit of making love to innocent young girls.

"I therefore feel it my duty to offer you my name. Will you marry me, Henrietta?"

Henrietta's face was as featureless as a mask. The small French clock on the mantle chimed the quarter hour with faint, silvery, apologetic tones, a birch log in the fireplace shifted and fell sending a sudden blaze up the chimney. The reflection of the flames danced round the room in the gathering dusk, flickering on the gold titles of the calf bound volumes, over the oriental rugs and spindly furniture, on the pale green silk of Henrietta's dress. She raised her head at last and looked at him.

"No," she said baldly, making a move as if to rise.

He held out a restraining hand. "You have not forgiven me then?" The husky voice was very quiet.

Henrietta looked at him thoughtfully. "I have forgiven you and I have forgiven myself, my lord," she said quietly. "Fortunately, I am an heiress and do not have to marry out of necessity. I think I once told you that I would marry only for love. And you do not love me."

For once, Lord Reckford's famous poise deserted him. "I have a great regard for you, my dear," he faltered. "I think that we should deal together extremely well. I must after all get married some time or another . . ."

"That is not enough for me," said Henrietta in a low voice. "As you have said, no one witnessed our . . . our . . . behavior. I intend to forget about the whole thing."

"Very well, Miss Sandford." The Beau rose to his feet. He felt obscurely piqued. Perhaps she preferred his friend, Mr. Holmes. "There is half an hour yet until dinner. Walk with me on the terrace for a little and let us discuss this latest mysterious happening."

Henrietta wished to refuse—to escape to the privacy of her room and relieve her wrought up feelings in a hearty bout of tears. But his lordship had regained his poise. He looked aristocratic, handsome, and very much master of the house. Without waiting for her reply, he draped her fine Norfolk shawl about her shoulders and held out his arm. Silently they moved through the long French windows on to the terrace. A startled peacock screamed in surprise and then paraded up and down in front of them, his tail feathers spread as if to vie with the evening dress of the couple who stood watching him.

The sky was slowly turning purple with a faint green

line on the horizon. A thin crescent moon faintly lit the formal gardens which were spread out in front of them. The woods were already full of mysterious shadows and on the still waters of the lake, a swan seemed made of porcelain set on black glass. The heavy scent of pine, wild honeysuckle, roses, stock and herbs rose about them.

"How can I forget what happened?" thought Henrietta miserably. "How can I ever be the same again?"

She stole a look at the profile of the man next to her, the high aquiline nose, the hooded eyes, the thin mobile mouth that only just recently. . . .

"I have been considering the mystery that surrounds you, Miss Sandford," said the husky voice. "Someone, it appears, is trying to send you mad or prove you mad. Forgive me for asking this, but should you die unwed, who would inherit your fortune? It would go to your brother, I assume."

Henrietta shook her head. "If I die, every penny goes to Miss Scattersworth. But Mattie would not . . . could not . . ."

"No," he agreed hurriedly. "Your friend seems a trifle eccentric at times but I swear there is no harm in her. I must confess," he added with a laugh, "that my poor secretary has appealed to me for protection."

Henrietta blushed for her friend. "Poor Mattie has led such a *narrow* life for so many years that all this sudden society of gentlemen has gone to her head."

Lord Reckford smiled. "I have invited the local squire, Sir Peter Benjamin to dinner. He is a widower of Miss Scattersworth's age. Perhaps he may capture her attention. But to return to your problem.

"Would you consider disappearing for some time? I have tried bringing all the likely suspects together but we seem to be getting no further forward. Perhaps if you and Miss Scattersworth were to go away somewhere quietly for a little while, then perhaps your tormentor would grow tired."

Leave before the end of the Season! Not to see Lord Reckford or hear his voice! Never!

"You must realize, my lord," said Henrietta, "that I have not led a very pleasant life until recently. I always dreamt of having a Season in London and going to balls and parties and routs and I do not wish to have it all taken away from me by some . . . some madman."

"In that case," replied the dearly loved voice, "please allow me to go on protecting you. We are friends after all, are we not?"

"Friends," whispered Henrietta weakly.

He smiled and held out his hand, grasping Henrietta's small one in his long fingers. The night stood still as they stood staring at each other, Henrietta with a kind of mute appeal in her large eyes and Lord Reckford with a curious dawning look of surprise. He felt a tingling in his hand as if it had been very cold and was just coming to life. A little breeze lifted the shawl round Henrietta's shoulders like wings and the faint moonlight silvered the edge of her hair.

"Dinner is served," came a correct voice behind them. Silently Henrietta took his lordship's arm and floated in to the diningroom. Lord Reckford gazed down at her with a troubled expression in his eyes. He had the uncomfortable feeling that just recently, he had made some irrevocable mistake.

Henrietta blinked in the blaze of light in the formal diningroom. Wax candles shone in the crystals of the heavy Waterford chandelier over the long table and flickered round the walls. The squire was already there, a handsome well-built man in his sixties, accompanied by his middle-aged sister. The vicar was also present, a thin aesthetic cleric, a whole world different from Henrietta's overdressed and pompous brother Henry. The final newcomer was the local magistrate, Sir Edwin Lewis, a huge jovial man with small piggy eyes and an unfortunate habit of referring to himself in the third person.

"So Sir Edwin says to himself, he says, 'That fellow's a felon if there ever was one.' " Hanging on his every word was Miss Mattie and from her glowing eyes, Henrietta deduced with a sinking heart that the susceptible spinster had fallen in love again. She had already picked up the magistrate's unfortunate manner of speech.

"When she was in Nethercote, Miss Scattersworth often used to. . . ." Henrietta heard her saying.

Lord Reckford again found himself seated beside Alice Belding and frowned a query over to his secretary who answered with a Gallic shrug and an expressive look at the wooden-faced butler. The secretary then quickly mimed gold changing hands and looked pointedly at Lady Belding.

Henrietta's appetite had failed her and she surveyed the magnificent repast with distaste. There was a boned duck swimming in a tureen of *potage royale*. A huge roast pike scowled at the guests, flanked on either side by a leg of mutton and bombarded veal. These were followed by a grand battalia pie with chickens, pigeons and rabbits, cock's combs and savoury balls smothered in a rich sauce of claret, anchovy and sweet herbs. The cover of the pie was ornamented with the arms of Reckford in raised pastry.

Then came the jellies, custards, syllabubs and flummery and then a dish of oyster loaves and a pompetone of larks.

It was the fashion for ladies to pick delicately at their food so no one noticed Henrietta's lack of appetite. She had just had the proposal of marriage she had long dreamt of. Had Lord Reckford taken her in his arms again or shown the slightest hint of warmth, then she would have gladly accepted him. But to live in terms of friendship with a man she loved to distraction would be torture indeed. With relief she noticed Lady Belding, who had taken over the role of hostess, rising to lead the ladies to the drawingroom and leave the gentlemen to their wine.

Lady Belding had new blood to patronise in the

presence of the squire's sister, Miss Benjamin. Unfortunately for Lady Belding, Miss Benjamin was a tall raw-boned woman whose mind was never far from the hunting field. Lady Belding tried to talk of blood lines. Miss Benjamin thought she meant blood mares and launched into an enthusiastic monologue. Lady Belding brought forward the nose. Miss Benjamin rhapsodised on the nose of her pet Arabian mount. With two spots of angry color in her cheeks, Lady Belding was just about to round on the familiar target of Henrietta, when they were joined by the gentlemen.

"Miss Scattersworth says let us explore the gardens by moonlight," trilled Miss Mattie with an eye on Sir Edwin.

"And Sir Edwin says he would be delighted to escort same," replied that gentleman with a coyness too awful to behold.

As the ill-assorted couple were tittuping happily in the direction of the French windows Henrietta threw Lord Reckford an anguished look of appeal.

"An excellent idea," said Lord Reckford smoothly. "Let us all view the gardens."

Henrietta flashed him a look of pure gratitude but the eyes that met hers were enigmatic as Lord Reckford offered Alice Belding his arm.

The small procession walked sedately down the broad shallow steps leading to the gardens. Henrietta wished the evening would end so that she could take her troubled thoughts to her room. Lord Reckford seemed wholly absorbed in pointing out various landmarks to Alice and her mother. Jeremy Holmes was standing slightly behind them. Miss Scattersworth and her latest beau were cheerfully conversing in the third person, Mrs. Ralston, Henry and Monsieur Dubois had elected to stay behind in the drawingroom and that left Edmund Ralston moving towards Henrietta with an unusually purposeful look in his eye. Henrietta mumbled some vague, incoherent apology and fled down a paved path between the rose bushes until she had left the rest of the company behind.

The calm summer night seemed heavy with the scent of roses. The path narrowed so that the bushes on either side brushed her dress. Suddenly the moon was blotted out as she entered an archway composed of rambling roses draped over arched trellising. She spied an ornate ironwork bench tucked away at the side of the path. It was painted white and glimmered faintly in the gloom. Henrietta sank down gratefully and tried to compose her jumbled thoughts.

Perhaps she should have accepted Lord Reckford's offer. Perhaps to have a little of him was better than nothing at all. She gave a tiny sigh and stared at her shoes. Suddenly, the whole tunnel was plunged in Stygian darkness as far away above the heavy arch of roses, the moon raced behind a cloud. The night seemed to become awake with strange rustlings. Assailed with a sudden uneasiness, Henrietta got to her feet and stood irresolute. She should go back. But it seemed too soon to face the rest of the house party. She moved forward slowly, thankfully seeing a faint pale glimmer of moonlight at the end of the archway.

As she neared the end of the tunnel of roses, she saw the figure of a woman in evening dress walking towards her. Henrietta hesitated and gave a tentative smile. The strange woman did the same. Henrietta moved forward again . . . and found that Miss Henrietta Sandford was walking towards her, into the darkness.

For one second, she stood paralysed with fear. Memories of dark German legends of the döppelganger fled through her mind. If you ever met yourself, you would shortly die. She let out a strangled whimper of terror and turned and fled. Her heart seemed to have moved up into her throat and was about to burst out through her neck. She hurtled from the rose garden as if all the demons of hell were snapping at her heels.

All the guests and their host had left the gardens.

Sobbing and trying to catch her breath, Henrietta paused outside the windows of the drawingroom. Through a crack in the heavy curtains, she could see the party moving elegantly about the room like figures in a minuet.

She took a deep breath. She *would not* burst into the room, crying out that she had just met herself. They would really think she was mad and, as a glimmer of commonsense crept through Henrietta's panic, she realized that that was exactly how someone had expected her to behave.

Draping her shawl to cover her trembling hands, she opened the doors of the French windows and went in. She felt sure that everyone would notice that she had endured some harrowing experience, but they all continued chatting easily. Edmund Ralston waltzed forward and took her arm in a surprisingly strong grip. The room was warm and his pretty face gleamed slightly under its layer of paint.

"Ah, *dear* Henrietta," he breathed. "I must share my marvellous news with you. Mother. had just told me that she will put up the money so that I may publish my first book of poems. I shall dedicate it to you."

"I am honored," said Henrietta faintly. "But there must be many young ladies who would be more deserving."

"But I am not going to marry any other young lady," said Edmund Ralston with an almost insane simplicity.

Henrietta looked wildly round for help. Jeremy Holmes was talking about a fair that was to be held in a nearby village and she thankfully broke into his conversation.

"I have never been to a fair," she said. "I've always longed to go."

"Oh, really," tittered Alice. "How rustic."

"Really, Henrietta," protested Henry. "I do not know what my lord will think. . . ."

"I think it is a splendid idea," said Lord Reckford.

"We can all go on Monday and it will only delay our return to Town by one day."

What it was to be a lord and live in an abbey, thought Henrietta cynically. Immediately the sneers and contempt left everyone's faces as if by magic to be replaced by enthusiasm.

Mrs. Ralston flashed her beautiful smile round the room and remarked that it would be wonderful for Henrietta to meet some *other* freaks. Lady Belding smiled indulgently after suffering a vicious pinch on the arm from her daughter. Only Edmund Ralston protested and said that he would not attend. "The crowds! The common herd! Faugh!" he shuddered and waved a delicate, spider's web of a handkerchief under his nose.

"That's all settled then," said Lord Reckford. "Henrietta shall have her fair."

"And Alice," put in Lady Belding gently.

The squire, the vicar, the magistrate and Miss Benjamin rose to take their leave. Miss Scattersworth fluttered all the way to the door, clinging to Sir Edwin's arm.

Henrietta flushed as she heard Miss Scattersworth positively pleading with the magistrate to escort her to the fair on Monday. "Miss Scattersworth would feel *so* reassured to have a strong protector like Sir Edwin."

"Then Sir Edwin shall go," announced the magistrate with a vulgar wink to the rest of the gentlemen as if to indicate that his path was constantly being strewn with ladies pleading for his escort.

Miss Scattersworth returned to Henrietta's side, her face flushed with excitement. "I must tell you all about it," she whispered to Henrietta. "We shall have a comfortable coze before you retire."

Henrietta groaned inwardly at the thought of having to listen to Miss Mattie enthusing over the pompous windbag that was the magistrate. Then she reflected that the presence of her old friend would be comforting and Miss Mattie's prattling would be enough to drive away the toughest ghost.

Lady Belding stood up and prepared to retire. She obviously expected the ladies all to leave with her. No one had the courage to defy her. It had been too long and exhausting a day.

In the privacy of her sitting room, Henrietta listened with half an ear to Miss Mattie's outpourings. It soon got through to the spinster that her young friend's mind was elsewhere and that she looked pale and tired.

"What is it my dear?" she asked, laying a comforting hand on Henrietta's knee. Henrietta blurted out her story of the ghost. To her surprise, her friend let out a faint giggle.

"My dear child," she said. "You must forgive me for laughing but, believe it or not, I played that trick on an elderly gentleman when I was a young girl . . . and got soundly whipped for my pains."

"Trick," echoed Henrietta faintly.

"Yes, trick," said Miss Mattie, her old eyes looking shrewd and kind. "I was staying with friends of my parents and they had four very mischievous little girls of my own age. There was this very portly old gentleman who was part of the house party and he did not like girls, 'detested 'em' he kept saying. So we all decided to have our revenge.

"Now, he kept clockwork hours and every morning at precisely ten of the clock he would walk in the orangery. We took a huge pier glass from one of the rooms and placed it across the end of the orangery and waited. He was rather short sighted so when he first saw himself in the looking glass, he kept bowing and scraping and saying goodmorning and of course his reflection kept doing the same thing. At one point, it looked as if he were going to bow to the mirror all morning. Then he moved closer and saw what he thought was himself walking towards him. Well, he nearly fainted, then he shouted for help and all the servants came running. We were caught trying to remove the mirror and soundly punished. So there!"

Henrietta looked at her in dismay. "But don't you

see what this means, Mattie? It means that someone is constantly on the watch. We did not know that we were going to walk in the gardens. Whoever it was did not know that I would wander off by myself. So it means that someone is constantly on the watch. Dear God! Someone must really hate me."

"You must make sure that you are never alone," said Miss Mattie firmly. "I will sleep in your room tonight."

Henrietta heaved a sigh of relief. "Oh, thank you Mattie. I should be so frightened on my own."

A wind had sprung up outside. The shutters gave a sudden rattle, making both women jump, and the lamplight flickered and danced round the room.

Miss Mattie coughed nervously. "Do you think it might be childish, dear Henrietta, if we were to leave all the lamps burning?"

"Not at all," said Henrietta. "But I promise you one thing. Whoever it is, is not going to drive me away from my social life or my London Season, Mattie." And on that firm note, the ladies crept off to bed.

The Sunday dawned wet and windy. The only amusement was a visit to church. Lord Reckford shut himself up with his estate books and his steward, leaving his guests to potter about dismally and get on each other's nerves. By evening, all wondered what on earth they were doing in the country in the middle of the Season and by suppertime had resolved to leave for Town first thing the next morning.

But Monday brought back the full glory of the summer to the countryside and, after a hearty breakfast, the proposed visit to the fair appeared to one and all to be a delightful project instead of the dreary peasant outing it had seemed the night before.

The carriages were lined up in the driveway. Henrietta could not help hoping that she would be allowed to partner Lord Reckford but Lady Belding had already made sure that Alice was to have that honor. Lord Reckford had been extremely courteous but very distant to Henrietta at breakfast. Henrietta gave one longing look at his lordship's well-tailored back and turned to accept Jeremy Holmes' escort. Jeremy prattled on easily, pointing out various landmarks with his whip as he drove his curricle down the drive at a smart pace. Henrietta was wearing a poke bonnet which concealed her face so that she found she could indulge her misery and only supply her partner with an appropriate "yes" or "no."

After several miles, they stopped at a pretty inn for luncheon. Lord Reckford and Alice Belding were on excellent terms, noted Henrietta, with a gloom which was so complete and miserable, it was almost comforting. Lord Reckford had obviously asked for Henrietta's hand in marriage only because he had felt he had compromised her. Henrietta began to flirt inexpertly with Mr. Holmes and wished she were dead.

The fair was crowded with sightseers by the time they arrived and Henrietta began to brighten at the sight of the sideshows. The party agreed to keep together for the first part of the fair and there was much arguing about which spectacle they should see first. Jeremy wanted to see the two-headed baby and Alice, the fat lady, but it was Henrietta who decided for them. "A magician," she breathed, pointing to a nearby tent. "I've never seen a magician before."

"Then the magician it shall be," said Lord Reckford, suddenly smiling down at her which turned her limbs to water.

The elegant party moved into the tent and sat down self-consciously on the front benches. Lady Belding said in a loud carrying voice that she detested yokels and Henry Sandford followed suit by staring round at the peasantry with his protruding eyes. The rest of the crowd stared back at him good humouredly and several suggested that Henry was a sideshow in himself. "Ooh, mum, ain't he fat," screamed a child.

"This is intolerable," puffed Henry. "That I should be subjected to. . . ." But several voices told him to sit down and shut up. The show was about to begin.

Two tattered sheets which served as curtains were drawn back to reveal the magician who began rapidly drawing a seemingly endless string of handkerchiefs out of his sleeve to the delight of the crowd. Lord Reckford suddenly grabbed Jeremy's arm. "It's the man . . . the man who tried to speak to me in the coffee house," he said in a low voice. "Take care of the ladies and when he finishes, I'll catch him after his performance."

The magician was billed on a placard at the side of the stage as "Mr. Marvellous Who Has Performed Before the Crowned Heads of Europe. Agricultural Shows and Market Days a Speciality."

Lord Reckford glanced at Henrietta. The magician had just produced an egg from the ear of a shy farm laborer who had volunteered his services as assistant and Henrietta's hands were clasped and her eyes were like stars.

"And now," announced Mr. Marvellous in an awesome voice. "I come to the highlight of the show. I shall produce Satan himself."

"Heathen nonsense," muttered brother Henry, shifting uneasily on the bench. The tent flaps were drawn tightly closed. Mr. Marvellous was helped into a long black robe covered in signs of the zodiac and a large black cauldron was carried on the stage. He raised his arms for silence and then his voice began to rise in a thin high chant. The words he spoke were unintelligible and probably ridiculous but there was something hypnotic about the man, decided Henrietta. Everyone in the audience was very quiet. The voice of the magician rose to a high thin screech and he threw something on the cauldron. Green smoke began to curl heavily into the air and then in the middle of the smoke, the grinning face of Satan began to appear.

Henrietta sprang to her feet. "The devil!" she cried. "It's the face I saw in the woods." No sooner had she shouted than there was a commotion at the back of the tent. A stout farmer's wife had fainted and everyone suddenly seemed to be running about and calling for light. The tent flaps were jerked open. Lord Reckford saw the magician hurriedly leaving through a curtain at the back of the stage and leapt after him.

The curtain opened out into a narrow space at the end of which could be seen Mr. Marvellous making a rapid exit into the bustle of the fairground. Lord Reckford gave chase, never losing sight of his quarry among the crowds, aided by his superior height. At last he reached the magician's side, grabbed his arm, and spun him round. Mr. Marvellous cast a terrified look of appeal up at him. "Now now, my lord," he stammered. "If I should be seen talking to you, it would mean my death."

"What is it you have to tell me? Out with it, man," snapped the Beau, jerking the magician by his dingy cravat.

"Not here, my lord," he repeated. "Oh, dear God. Let me go! Give me an hour and meet me behind the Cherry Tree Inn down the road. Please my lord . . . meet me there. I'll be in the little yard at the back." With that he wrenched himself free and hastened away among the holiday crowd.

Lord Reckford returned slowly to his guests. Someone had obviously been paying this man to use his tricks on Henrietta. Well, the mystery would soon be over. He decided to take Henrietta with him. She should hear with her own ears the name of her tormenter.

Accordingly, when he returned to the party, he drew Henrietta aside and told her of his plans. "We shall say that you are feeling faint after your experience and I shall urge the rest to stay here while I escort you back to the Abbey. No, on second thought, we will leave Mr. Holmes to do the explaining. Perhaps your devoted Mr. Ralston will insist on accompanying us."

Mr. Ralston had languidly elected to join the outing

despite his former protests and was now enjoying all the fun of the fair with the enthusiasm of a schoolboy.

Their only difficulty was in shaking off Miss Scattersworth who was disconsolate because Sir Edwin had not put in an appearance. Henrietta, feeling very guilty, at last begged Miss Scattersworth to fetch her a glass of water, and as soon as the spinster's thin back had disappeared into the crowd, she and Lord Reckford made their escape.

"It is not far to the inn," said Lord Reckford. "Perhaps—if you are not too fatigued, we could walk. . . ."

Henrietta nodded dumbly and took his proferred arm. The noise of the fairground gradually sank away behind them as they walked along the chalky country road. Apprehensive as she was about the magician's news, Henrietta had imagined a leisurely stroll arm in arm with Lord Reckford among the pastoral flowers and grasses of early summer. But the air was heavy with the scent of pig, flies buzzed around piles of horse droppings on the road and the slightest rapid movement stirred the dust up into a choking, wheezing cloud.

"This was not a good idea," said the Beau penitently. "We are beginning to look like ghosts." Both were slowly being covered from head to foot in white dust. "Don't worry," he added bracingly. "It's not far now."

At first sight, The Cherry Tree was an unprepossessing hostelry. It seemed by its walls of timber and wattle to have survived from Tudor times. With its low walls and heavy thatched roof, it had the appearance of crouching beside the road to waylay the traveller rather than to welcome him. No smoke rose from the chimney and no sound came from the taproom.

Henrietta wondered why, although she felt frightened and apprehensive, she had a nagging feeling of pique. Lord Reckford was friendly and gentlemanly. But not by one flicker of an eyelid did he reveal that anything of an intimate nature had recently passed between them.

"We unfortunately must go through the tap to get to the yard at the back," he said. "I will lead the way. Keep close behind me."

The taproom was empty and silent. Sunlight filtered faintly through the dirty leaded windows. There was a sour smell of stale beer and wine and old unwashed bedding. They crept quietly, their feet making no sound on the sawdust covered floor. The Beau waved his quizzing glass at a row of blue rosettes over the mantelpiece. "It seems the landlord keeps a prize pig. He's probably taken it to the fair. 'The Fair Beauty of Upper Wipplestone.' Dear me. Poor animal. I wonder what they call it for short."

Lord Reckford pushed open the door at the back of the tap. There was a small greasy kitchen. The stink of sour milk was very strong. It came from an open churn in the corner and the air above it was black with heavy swollen flies.

"Ugh!" said Henrietta, throwing caution to the winds and marching to the kitchen door. "Let us get out of here." She threw open the door. "Well, there's The Fair Beauty of Upper Wipplestone . . . Oh my God . . . ."

The Fair Beauty, a hugh pink sow, slowly turned its massive head at the sound of their approach. Blood dripped from its mouth and down its chubby legs. Lying nearly under it lay the body of the magician. His throat had been cut from ear to ear, his eyes turned up to the summer sky. Then the horrible face was blotted out as the pig bent its head down again.

Henrietta was aware of Lord Reckford's strong arms round her as he dragged her bodily back into the inn. She could feel a scream forming at the back of her throat. She wanted to scream and scream and scream until the very sound of her voice wiped that dreadful bloody picture from her mind.

Lord Reckford's icy voice cut like a knife through

her hysterical thoughts. "Don't be so damned missish," he snapped.

Henrietta gulped and stared but before she could say anything, he went on, "I am sure you've seen plenty bodies hanging from gibbets and people dying all over the streets of London, so what's another body?"

His callousness had the desired effect. Henrietta forgot her shock and fright in a healthy outburst of rage. She called him every name she could think of, beating her fists against his jacket and trying to kick him in the shins. Then she collapsed into a chair and burst into tears.

"That's my girl," said his infuriating lordship in a mild voice. "Just what you needed. Now drink this."

"What is . . . is it?" stammered Henrietta.

"Brandy."

"Oh, but I can't . . . I . . ." She stopped talking as the glass was forced against her lips by a firm hand and the fiery liquid poured down her throat.

After a few minutes, the brandy began to take effect, and Henrietta managed to say, "We must find the magistrate . . . ."

"My dear, dear girl," drawled her companion. "There are magistrates and magistrates. Our local one unfortunately is that bumbling idiot, Sir Edwin. Can't you imagine it? He will lumber in and start off 'Sir Edwin wonders why my lord and Miss Sandford should have informed Mr. Holmes and party that they were returning to the Abbey on account of Miss Sandford's indisposition and yet are found in a common inn with a pig and a dead body.' Come now, Henrietta. Let us make our escape."

Henrietta got to her feet. She felt suddenly exhausted. "Why is it, my lord, that you refuse to call in the authorities to solve this mystery?"

His lordship flicked the dust from his hessians with his handkerchief and then stood up and faced her. "Miss Sandford. Apart from bringing a lot of scandal and vulgar gossip down about our ears, I fail to see what else the Runners can do. Never fear, I shall catch the culprit."

"And I shall be dead first."

"No, my dear, whoever it is wants you alive and mad. As long as you accept my help, no harm will come to you. I should really have brought the carriage. It is a long walk to the Abbey. . . .", he added doubtfully, looking down at Henrietta's thin slippers.

"Oh, I shall survive, no doubt," said Henrietta sweetly. "Are you sure, my lord, that you would not like to tether me to a stake as bait for the killer the way they use goats to entrap a tiger in India?"

"I may do that yet," he said with a laugh, drawing her arm through his.

They set off down the road at a leisurely pace. Lord Reckford began to talk about the problems of running his large estate, the modern methods of farming he hoped to introduce, and how he intended to leave the London scene after this Season. He then asked her about her past life and whether she ever missed Nethercote. Henrietta began to describe her narrow life of church duties and visits to the poor. A very bleak picture emerged although she tried to make it sound amusing.

He looked down at her. She was staring unseeingly at the dusty road as she talked, swinging her bonnet in her hand. A curl had escaped from its mooring and lay like a question mark on the back of her neck.

He had a sudden impulse to bend down and kiss her on the nape of the neck and then was shocked at the intensity of his feelings. It was not because Henrietta was beautiful—and she had certainly changed into a beauty since she had lost weight—it was, he decided, that she seemed to carry with her an aura of heavy sensuality which revealed itself in small ways, in the way she turned her head and the way she moved when she danced.

She turned and looked up into his eyes, laughing at one of her own anecdotes and he caught his breath. He could not properly analyse his feelings but he felt in some obscure way that he would never think of Henrietta as a comfortable sort of girl again.

He was suddenly conscious of her hand on his arm and immediately released his own to brush away an imaginary fly. The sun was setting behind the woods as they wearily made their way up the long drive that led to the Abbey. Lights were shining from the windows and there was a smell of woodsmoke in the air. Although she had lived most of her life in the modest vicarage of Nethercote, Henrietta suddenly had the strange feeling of coming home. They paused outside the entrance to the hall and Lord Reckford bent his head and kissed her hand. The kiss seemed to burn through her glove and she could not bring herself to look at him. Lord Reckford stood for a long time looking after her until the rumble of carriages in the drive as the other guests arrived diverted his attention.

Chapter Nine

"I SHALL NEVER SURVIVE THIS SEASON."

Henrietta looked mournfully down at her swollen ankles, the result of dancing all night and then accepting an engagement to ride in the Row first thing in the morning.

Her return to Town from the Abbey had been marked with outstanding social success. That arbiter of fashion, Mr. George Brummell, had been warned by Lady Belding to avoid Henrietta. "The girl is quite mad, you know," she had informed him. "And no person of the *ton* should be seen in her company." Mr. Brummell cordially despised Lady Belding and had made a great effort to be seen constantly in Henrietta's company. He even went so far as to label Miss Scattersworth as "a truly charming English eccentric." Poor Miss Mattie found that all her most ordinary remarks were treated as brilliant witticisms and all the attention went immediately to the spinster's head. Henrietta rarely saw her and often had to rely on Lord Reckford's sister, Lady Ann Courtney, to act as chaperone. Most of her social engagements were blessed with the presence of Lord Reckford but there never seemed a moment to talk to him alone.

There had been no more attempts on her sanity and

all the past episodes leading up to the murder of the magician took on a vague dreamlike sense of unreality.

Still wearing her ridingdress of pale blue gaberdine, its severe lines flattering to her new slim figure, Henrietta crossed to the looking glass to adjust her curls.

Lord Reckford was announced and she swung round in surprise, a tell-tale blush creeping up her cheek.

He bent punctilliously over her hand and then straightened up and looked at her with unwonted severity. "You look tired," he remarked dryly.

"Of course I'm tired," retorted Henrietta. "These past weeks have been exhausting. I have been dancing and partying almost every night. I declare I am worn to a frazzle."

"Is that all you have been doing?"

Henrietta stared at him in surprise. "Is that not enough?"

He sat down and stretched out his long legs and tapped his boot with his quizzing glass. At last he said very slowly, "You have not . . . by any chance . . . been gambling?"

"Gambling! Well, I suppose . . . a little faro and silver loo and things like that. Everyone does it."

"Everyone does not however frequent the gambling hells of the demi-monde and behave in a raucous, drunken manner."

Henrietta looked at him coldly. "Out with it, my lord. Speak plain."

"I shall try to put it as simply as possible. Various members of my acquaintance have seen fit to inform me that you have frequently been gambling heavily and drinking heavily. Now, it is all very well for young men to frequent these establishments but any woman who does so is facing social ruin."

"I have not been to any of those places," said Henrietta outraged.

"I had it on good authority that you were at a certain Mrs. Slattery's last night."

Henrietta's eyes were like agate. "I take leave to inform you, my lord, that I attended the Beauchamp's ball last night chaperoned by your sister."

He got to his feet in surprise. "Then what is the meaning of all this. You cannot be in two places at once ... or can you?"

Henrietta stared at him wide-eyed. "What do you mean?"

"I mean, it is starting all over again. Someone is out to discredit you. They hired the magician and then disposed of him. Perhaps they have now hired someone who looks exactly like you. I shall need to try and track this person down if that is the case. Unless you produce your double, all London is shortly going to think you have gone to the dogs!"

He walked forward and took her hands in his. "My dear," he said in a softer voice, "if you would accept the protection of my name ..."

"Never!" choked Henrietta, jerking her hands out of his grasp. "I do not feel for you in ... in ... that way, my lord."

He studied her bent head thoughtfully. Then he put a long finger under her chin and raised it. "I could teach you to feel otherwise." He said it, meaning to sound teasing, but his voice came out assured and arrogant.

"Oh, save your charms for little opera dancers," snapped Henrietta, unforgivably. "You will find me made of sterner stuff. I bid you good day, my lord." He caught her wrist as she stretched out her hand for the bell-rope and slowly drew her towards him.

She came towards him, weakly, as if mesmerised. His arms went round her slowly, taking an infinity of time.

Henrietta's excellent butler was long to regret that that day of all days, he happened to be suffering from a cold. He had quietly opened the door to announce the arrival of Lady Belding and, taking in the situation, had meant to quickly retreat and inform her ladyship that Miss Sandford was not at home. But at that precise moment he sneezed. The couple broke apart and Lady Belding and Alice edged past him and made their way into the room.

"Ah, Lord Reckford," declared Lady Belding, holding out her arm like the wing of a dying swan, "I saw your carriage outside. One of our horses has cast a shoe and I wondered if I could prevail upon you to escort Alice and myself to Bond Street."

The Beau kissed the air above her fingers and murmured that he would only be too delighted. He left, reminding Henrietta that he would see her with his sister's party at Raneleigh after the theater. She stood on the hearthrug, staring at the closed doors, long after he had gone.

That evening, Lord Reckford decided to forego the theater, and search for the fake Miss Sandford. She had been seen at three notorious gambling hells and he proposed to visit each one in turn. He enlisted the aid of Jeremy Holmes. "I do not anticipate any difficulty in gaining admission," he informed his friend dryly. "My fortune is well known if my face is not."

"What shall we do with the woman should we find her?" asked Mr. Holmes.

"Why, pay her," remarked his lordship dryly. "Offer to pay her more than she is getting from her present employer. Then she'll give us his name, I warrant you."

"You think a man and not a woman is behind all this?"

The Beau shrugged his elegant shoulders, "Who knows? Someone, anyway, with enough money to hire people to do the dirty work. Shall we go?"

The couple decided to go on foot as the night was a fine one. Armed only with their swordsticks, they ambled towards an area of London where the distances between the parish lamps grew longer, leaving sinister shadows. "Here we are. This must be the place," said Lord Reckford eventually, stopping in front of a narrow building. He rapped on the door with his stick and then popped a guinea and his card through the judas and waited for results. In a few seconds the door was opened by an enormous footman, his livery bursting at the seams.

"Members only, me lord, this being an exclusive place. But we allus does waive the rules for a gent like yourself," remarked the footman, trying to divest the gentlemen of their hats and gloves.

"We shall, in all probability, not be staying long," remarked Lord Reckford and strode into the club. He paused on the threshold of the first room . . . and caught his breath.

His friend looked over his shoulder. "My God! There's Henrietta!" cried Jeremy. "Why, the little minx."

And there indeed, it appeared, was that lady, much the worse for liquor. She was seated on a dandy's knee and helping herself liberally to snuff. The game was about to recommence and she swung herself off her gallant's knee and settled back into her own chair with the feverish light of the true gambler burning in her eyes. Her eyes!

"It's not Henrietta." Jeremy heaved a sigh of relief. "Henrietta's eyes are hazel, hers are blue."

Lord Reckford felt a momentary twinge of irritation that his friend should have noticed the color of Henrietta's eyes. They both watched the game in silence. The girl was certainly remarkably like Henrietta. Her heavy fair hair had been dressed in the same style, her jewellery had been faithfully copied, and she had Henrietta's manner of turning her head. She was losing heavily. Lord Reckford went to stand behind her. He leaned forward and placed a rouleau of guineas at her elbow. She turned to flash a smile at her latest gallant, looked Lord Reckford full in the face, and turned white. Quickly she popped the rouleau down the front of her gown and rose shakily to her feet.

"Not so fast, my dear," said Lord Reckford, holding her arm in a grip like iron. "If you do not wish me to make a scene, you will smile like the good little actress you are and accompany me."

Her eyes wide and terrified, she nodded dumbly. He pulled her over to a quiet space beside the window and lowered his voice. The people in the room were all intent on their game. Smoke hung in heavy wreaths over the green baize tables and nothing could be heard but the click of the dice and the clink of glasses.

"Who is paying you to do this?"

"La, sir! I don't know what you mean." She made a desperate effort at coquetry and then winced as his grip tightened. "You're hurting me," she whimpered.

"And I shall hurt you a good deal more unless you tell me what I want to know." Really, it was unnerving how like Henrietta this girl looked. "On the other hand," he went on smoothly, "if you do tell me the information I desire, you will be paid handsomely, a small fortune, I assure you."

A gleam of avarice flickered through the wide blue eyes. "How can I believe you?"

"You can't," drawled the husky voice. "But if you do not do what I say, I shall drag you before the Bow Street magistrates for impersonating a lady of quality."

She looked round nervously. "All right, my lord. I'll tell you. But not here. They watches me every move." Fright was disolving her voice into its normal Cockney whine. "I know you is to be at Raneleigh with Miss Sandford. There is a temple there . . . a sort of Greek thing . . . near the river . . ." She suddenly saw the burly footman approaching and wrenched out of his grasp. "Twelve o'clock, my lord. . . ." The slight whisper came back to him faintly. He felt a hand on his arm. "Everything all right, my lord?" said the footman. There was a hint of underlying menace in his voice.

His lordship raised his quizzing glass. "Take your hand from my arm, fellow," he said icily. "You are soiling my coat."

The footman looked narrowly from Lord Reckford

to the fake Miss Sandford who was to all intents and purposes wholly absorbed in a rubber of piquet. He gave a surly grunt and lumbered back to his post by the door.

Lord Reckford collected Jeremy and suggested that they should leave quickly. They walked along, discussing the mystery of Henrietta's impersonator. "Do you think she will come?" asked Jeremy.

"Of course," replied his friend cynically. "Money rules her world as much as our own."

Henrietta was tired of Raneleigh. All the social world flocked to the pleasure gardens after the theater to see and be seen. The ritual was to stroll down one crowded walk bowing or cutting various acquaintance as the case might be and then stroll back going through the whole process again. Miss Scattersworth was surrounded by an audience of bright young men who danced around her in their tall heels, shrieking with laughter and clutching their long walking canes like so many demented Bo-Peeps. The spinster was enjoying her fame as a wit immensely and was almost as noisy as her admirers. She had again begun to dress in clothes too young for her years and had discarded her caps and . . . oh, horrors . . . Henrietta could not believe her eyes. For the one sedate thing in all her vagaries of dress had been Miss Mattie's prim grey hair. Now her head was covered in a mass of improbably golden curls held in place with a baby blue silk ribbon tied in a bow over her left ear.

Henrietta writhed in embarrassment. People were beginning to look at her oddly as well, since the whispers about her supposed debauches in gambling clubs had gone the rounds. She sighed with relief as she recognized the tall figure of Lord Reckford coming towards her. He bent over her hand and then whispered quietly that he had some news for her. "I shall ask Miss Scattersworth for permission to take you for a stroll although Mr. Holmes is coming with us and should be chaperone enough."

His lordship looked round in a puzzled way. "Why, where is Miss Scattersworth?" Henrietta waved her fan faintly in the spinster's direction. Lord Reckford bit his lip to hide a smile. He broke through Miss Mattie's twittering ring of admirers. "I have come to beg your permission to walk a little way with Miss Sandford," he said in chilly formal accents, embarrassed and irritated by the ring of foppish and painted faces.

"Why, of course, you naughty, naughty man," said Miss Mattie with a roguishness awful to behold. She tried to bat her eyelashes at him but she had painted them so thick with blacking that they stuck together. The Beau bowed and left her surrounded by the waving handkerchiefs of her court as they vied for the honor of prying her eyelashes apart.

Henrietta walked a little way, flanked by Lord Reckford and Jeremy Holmes, pleasantly aware of the envious glances cast in her direction. When they had left the crowds behind, Lord Reckford outlined what had happened and their discovery of her impersonator.

Henrietta clasped her hands. "But that is marvellous. Let us go quickly."

They hurried along the more deserted walks. Lord Reckford noticed gratefully that Henrietta was too absorbed in her mission to notice or be embarrassed by the sounds of noisy love-making in the bushes around them.

At the far end of the gardens stood the temple, shining faintly in the moonlight. They mounted the short flight of steps and went inside.

A couple of lovers hurriedly leapt to their feet, adjusting their dress. The woman seemed more enraged with the interruption than the man and she departed shouting raucous advice to Henrietta about how to cope with two men at the same time. Henrietta's escorts were thankful to note that she did not understand one word the woman was saying.

Henrietta sat down on the bench vacated by the lovers, Jeremy sat next to her, and Lord Reckford leaned against a pillar and stared out at the muddy waters of the Thames. After what seemed to Henrietta to be hours, Lord Reckford said in a flat voice, "She isn't coming Jeremy. We should have waited for her at the club and taken the risk. Damme, if I ever find out who's behind this, I'll murder him with my own hands."

Henrietta rose wearily to her feet and stumbled. Jeremy caught her round the waist and led her gently down the steps of the temple. He turned to address a remark to his friend and received such a blazing look of rage that he stepped back a pace. "Oho! So that's the way the land lies," thought Jeremy.

The silent threesome made their way back into the crowds. Miss Mattie had gone on to a party with her admirers. "What! At two in the morning!" raged Lord Reckford stuffily, much to the amusement of his friend. "Come, Miss Sandford, I shall escort you home. Good-night, Jeremy. I shall call on you tomorrow."

"Wait a bit," said Mr. Holmes, an imp of mischief dancing in his eyes. "I ain't your servant, Guy. I shall come with you. Want to make sure Henrietta's right and tight."

Lord Reckford's thin black brows snapped together and he gave in with bad grace. Jeremy chatted pleasantly all the way to Henrietta's home, leaving his furious friend to curse him mentally for a prattling idiot.

They waited patiently while Henrietta searched in her reticule and produced a heavy key. "Why on earth don't you tell at least one servant to wait up for you," snapped his lordship.

Henrietta looked at him in surprise. "I do not think it fair, my lord. I am not a child, you know. I have opened my front door and put myself to bed for some years now. Why, it would be the height of selfishness to expect my butler to lose his night's sleep to perform such a simple chore for me."

"Dash it all," protested Jeremy. "That's what they're paid for."

"They are not paid to perform unreasonable duties or to work unreasonable hours," said Henrietta. "And may I remind you, they are *my* servants."

She opened the door and they followed her into the hall. Henrietta turned and held out her hand, "I must thank you both. . . ." Then she broke off and put a frightened hand to her mouth. "What's that?" From the drawingroom came the sound of an irregular tap, tap, tap.

The very house seemed to hold its breath as if waiting for their next move.

Henrietta gave an impatient shrug as if to dismiss her fears and strode forward and flung open the double doors of the drawingroom. She stood for a second, framed in the doorway, then she fell to the floor in a dead faint.

Her impersonator swung gently in the breeze from the long open windows. She was hanging from a belt round her neck which was strapped to the Waterford chandelier. Her protruding eyes gazed glassily round the room as her body slowly swung round and round, her tiny feet tap, tap tapping rhythmically against the chair she had been standing on. And with every revolution, the crystals above her sent out a chattering unearthly tinkling like the voices of wicked fairies mocking the dead.

A note lay on the escritoire by the window. While Jeremy helped Henrietta to a sofa, the Beau crossed over and picked it up.

The writing straggled wildly across the page. "My dear Miss Sandford," he read. "The man you are seeking is Guy Reckford. He plans to drive you mad because he is mad himself. Ask him what became of Lucinda. I can stand it no more. God forgive me. . . ."

Lord Reckford crumpled the parchment in his hand, and stared unseeingly at a portrait of one of Mrs.

Tankerton's simpering ancestors over the fireplace. Slowly he took down a tall wax candle from the mantleshelf and held it under the paper. His arm was seized by Jeremy Holmes. "For God's Sake, Guy, what's in the note?"

He shrugged his friend off and dropped the letter on the hearth where it crackled and blazed. "Later, Jeremy," he said softly with a glance at the slowly recovering Henrietta. "Later."

There was a commotion in the hallway outside as Miss Scattersworth returned with her admirers. Lord Reckford dashed to bar the door but he was too late.

To his surprise, Miss Mattie neither screamed nor fainted. She glanced quickly from the grotesque swinging figure to Henrietta and then back to her shocked and twittering entourage. "Home gentlemen," she said firmly, hustling and shooing them before her. Then she returned to the drawingroom and looked at Lord Reckford, seeming suddenly old and tired. "I shall take Henrietta to her bedchamber while you summon the magistrate, my lord."

She waited until Lord Reckford and Jeremy had left and then turned to Henrietta. "Come, my dear. Come to bed and I shall find something to make you sleep. Come with Mattie."

Henrietta rose to her feet like a sleepwalker. She was just about to leave the room when the letter which had been burning merrily on the hearth gave a final spurt of flame and went out.

Shaking off Miss Scattersworth's arm, she walked over to the fireplace and picked up the charred paper. It had not burned completely and a few trails of handwriting stood out sharply.

". . . Reckford . . . mad . . . what became of Lucinda. . . ."

Chapter Ten

Two DAYS HAD passed and the mystery seemed darker than ever. The dead girl was identified as a high class prostitute and interest in the case promptly died as far as law and order were concerned. The girl had obviously committed suicide and London was well rid of her.

Henrietta had got rid of the remains of the letter and confided her fears to Miss Mattie. What if the elegant Beau himself were tormenting her as part of some mad game played out by a bored aristocrat? After all, look at the insane and violent crimes that had been committed by the Mohawks. Seeing that her friend, although worried and frightened, at least showed no signs of succumbing to the vapors, Miss Scattersworth had volunteered to solve the mystery of what had happened to Lucinda by discreetly questioning her new acquaintances, many of whom, as she pointed out, were confirmed gossips.

Waiting for her return, Henrietta wished she had never enlisted the help of her friend. She found herself not wanting to know anything at all about Lucinda.

She heard Miss Mattie's brisk step in the hall and sat bolt upright in her chair. Please let him not be guilty of anything, she murmured to herself.

Miss Mattie trotted in and then seemed to spend an unconscionable amount of time divesting herself of many fluttering shawls and several bulky packages.

"Well, well, Henrietta," said the spinster finally, sitting down with a bump. "These Roman sandals of mine are so pretty but I declare, after any amount of walking, they do cut into one's legs so."

"A plague on your Roman sandals," snapped Henrietta. "Honestly, Mattie. I've been sitting here all morning nearly *dying* with apprehension. What about Lucinda?"

Miss Mattie looked rather wildly about the room. "I really would rather not tell you, my dear, and gossip is never reliable and . . ."

"I would rather hear it no matter what," said Henrietta quietly.

Miss Mattie sighed. She began, "Remember I told you that Lucinda Braintree went off with the Marquis of Glenmorrison. Well, it seems that after a year, she had a hankering to see Beau Reckford and managed to get herself invited to a house party at which he was to be present. It was somewhere in Essex, I forget the name of the people. Anyway, it seemed as if the affair was to begin again. Lucinda certainly seemed eager enough but after a few days, Lord Reckford was obviously trying not to be alone in her company.

"Then one night, Lucinda could be heard sobbing and screaming in Lord Reckford's bedroom. The following days, she avoided everyone, but could be seen walking and walking round the grounds with her dress muddy and her hair in a mess. Lord Reckford cut short his visit and returned to Town and afterwards she went completely berserk. She ran down the driveway after his carriage, cursing and screaming and he . . . he never even turned his head.

"Lucinda grew worse and worse and was finally committed to the madhouse."

Henrietta heaved a sigh of relief. "Come now, Mattie, women don't just turn mad over night."

Miss Scattersworth looked at her doubtfully. She said, "But, my dear, I can see it all. Perhaps they were in a great Gothic castle with . . . well, you know . . . bats flying from the battlements and dead gnarled trees all over the park.

" 'I spurn you,' says the handsome lord. 'Have pity on me,' she screams. ''Tis only you I love.' 'Away, woman,' he snarls. And her poor mind becomes unhinged and . . ."

"Really, Mattie, if you go on in this strain I shall think that *your* mind has become unhinged. I shall forget about the whole business. After all, Lord Reckford has been a victim himself. Do you not remember when his staff was drugged and he was imprisoned in his room?"

Miss Mattie shook her brassy curls, "We have only his word for it. He could have made the whole thing up in order to worm his way into our confidence. Perhaps, I could investigate . . ."

"Enough!" cried Henrietta, getting to her feet. "Not another word. I am very grateful to you for your efforts, but please let the subject be forgotten." She paused in the doorway but Miss Mattie was engrossed in removing her tortured foot from its Roman sandal and did not look up.

Perhaps Miss Mattie would have dropped her latest role of Bow Street Runner had it not been for the unexpected visit of Mr. Symes. Mr. Symes explained that the vicar had kindly let him have a free hour in Town while he visited his tailor. He did not, however, explain that Henry Sandford had the irritating habit of using his curate to carry his many parcels back to Nethercote.

"And how do you go on, Miss Scattersworth?" asked the curate politely as he seated himself primly on the edge of the sofa.

"Oh, tol rol," said Miss Mattie, gaily waving her fingers. "I am become all the crack you know. Mr. Brummell himself says I am a notable wit."

"Indeed!" exclaimed Mr. Symes, and repeated "Indeed!" in a more startled voice as he took in the full glory of Miss Scattersworth's hair.

"I am not up to the latest fashions, Miss Scattersworth," he added. "You are wearing a wig, I see."

Miss Mattie blushed. "N-no . . . not exactly," she stammered.

"You have dyed your hair!" shouted the curate, springing to his feet. "This is too much. I cannot stand by and see what used to be a stately lady comporting herself like a . . . like a lightskirt."

Miss Scattersworth leaped to her feet, trembling with a mixture of shame and rage. "Get out!" she shouted. "You have no right to be so insulting. Why, you are nothing but a meek little curate who knows nothing of the ways of the world."

Mr. Symes stood with his hand on the doorknob. He seemed to have grown suddenly taller. "I know enough of the world," he said with icy hauteur, "to mark that it is time you re-hennaed your hair. The roots are black. Good day to you."

After he had gone, Miss Mattie cried very long and loudly. Then she dried her tears. She would never marry. Her role was to be protector to Henrietta.

Lord Reckford sat in his library, staring unseeingly at the book in front of him. He wondered if he should have given the magistrate all the facts. He was sure the unfortunate imposter had not committed suicide. More and more the evidence was pointing to someone close to Henrietta. And if there was another incident and Henrietta herself told the magistrates everything, then he himself would fall under suspicion.

His thoughts were interrupted by a discreet cough from the butler. "Excuse me, my lord, but there is an odd person questioning the staff in the kitchen."

Lord Reckford threw down his book. "What kind of person?"

"A strange-looking woman, my lord, who says she is

a representative of the Foreign Office. She is here, she says, to ascertain whether we harbor Bonapartist spies on the premises."

"She does, by God!"

"Exactly, my lord. But what is very strange is that when I assured this person that we had no suspicious persons on our staff, she began to question me about the night that your lordship was locked in his room."

"Bring her here immediately," rapped out his lordship. "And should she show reluctance . . . drag her!"

"Very good, my lord."

At last, thought the Beau, at last I shall be able to get my hands on someone connected with this plot.

There were screams and scuffles and thumps in the hall outside. Then the library door shot open and an elderly female was dragged in by two burly footmen.

Lord Reckford, who had raised his quizzing glass, let it drop with a sigh. He waved his hand in dismissal and his servants left. When the door had closed behind them, Lord Reckford surveyed the female before him and said in a deceptively mild voice, "And to what do I owe the pleasure of your visit . . . Miss Scattersworth?"

Miss Scattersworth blushed like a seventeen year old and stared at the carpet.

Lord Reckford's voice took on an angry edge. "Out with it," he snapped.

Miss Scattersworth clutched a chair back and faced him. "Never, my lord. Never! Though you throw me in your deepest dungeon, though you brand me with irons. Never!" She threw back her head and closed her eyes.

"We do not have dungeons in Mayfair, Miss Scattersworth nor do we use red hot irons in this enlightened beginning to the nineteenth century. But if you do not hurry and explain your presence in my home then I shall be sorely tempted to put you over my knee and give you a good hiding."

"And drive me mad like poor Lucinda," retorted Miss Mattie.

Lord Reckford surveyed the trembling spinster for a few minutes while his mind worked furiously. Then he said in a kindly voice, "Sit down, Miss Scattersworth. So the note about me driving Lucinda mad was not burnt?"

Miss Scattersworth mutely nodded her head.

"And where is it now?"

"Miss Sandford destroyed it."

"And is Miss Sandford aware of your spying activities?"

"Oh, no," said Miss Scattersworth, recovering her poise. "It was my own idea entirely. Should we not leave the door open, my lord. We are unchaperoned."

"Oh, for Heaven's sake," snapped his lordship. "I may have gained a reputation as a rake but I have not yet got as far as raping elderly spinsters."

To his horror, Miss Scattersworth burst into tears. "Nobody finds me attractive," she sobbed.

Lord Reckford was sorely tempted to order his carriage and take her back to Henrietta then and there.

Miss Scattersworth gave a loud sob, a gulp, and then began to pour out a long explanation about the cruelty of Mr. Symes and her subsequent determination to devote her life to aiding Henrietta.

With her usual mercurial change of mood, she brightened considerably when she reached the end of her tale. "Tell me honestly, my lord, do I look like a lightskirt?"

Lord Reckford bit his lip to hide a smile. "Indeed not, Miss Scattersworth, but your blonde curls *are* somewhat aging."

The spinster clutched her hair and let out a faint moan. "I suggest," his lordship went on in a soothing voice, "that you find an excellent hairdresser to dye your hair back to its natural color and then inform Mr. Symes that you made the sacrifice on his behalf."

"Oh, thank you," she gulped, getting to her feet. "I

should have known that with your experience of the ladies that you would know exactly what to do."

Lord Reckford let that go past. "Now, I will send for my carriage and escort you home. I am anxious to see that Miss Sandford is in good health despite her experience."

Miss Scattersworth paused on the threshold. "You must forgive me, my lord, but I am Miss Sandford's chaperone as well as her friend. Pray, what are your intentions regarding Henrietta?"

"Intentions! I have no intentions regarding Miss Sandford. I fear I am a confirmed bachelor."

Miss Scattersworth peered anxiously into his face. "And you do not feel *anything* for Miss Sandford . . . apart from feelings of friendship that is . . .?"

"Nothing at all," he remarked lightly, collecting his hat and his cane from the butler.

"Now why," he wondered, as the carriage lurched over the cobbles . . . "why did I say that? But surely that is what I feel. After all, the girl will marry some day but that will surely not affect me in the slightest." Having convinced himself of the platonic nature of his feelings, he settled his head back against the squabs and listened with half an ear to Miss Scattersworth's prattling.

He was, therefore, unprepared for the violence of his feelings when he came upon Henrietta and Jeremy Holmes with their blonde heads close together, arguing about the mystery.

"You were, if I recollect rightly, preparing to call on Miss Belding this morning," he said with a lightness he did not feel. "You were taking flowers to her, were you not." He cast an acid look at the bouquet in Henrietta's hands.

Mr. Holmes flushed. "I got half way there, Guy, and I suddenly felt I could not face it. Lady Belding is always so disapproving, you know. And then sometimes Alice is so charming and sometimes it seems she don't want to see me at all. Then, I sort of thought, what fun it would be to call on Henrietta instead."

"Miss Sandford," corrected the Beau in a school-masterish voice.

"Oh, fudge!" declared his friend happily. "You can't go fishing with a girl and then keep calling her by her surname. Henrietta don't care for the formalities."

"Then it is time she did," said Lord Reckford coldly. "You are both in this room unchaperoned . . . and with the door closed."

Jeremy cast his outraged friend a mischievous look. "Turned governess, Guy?"

His lordship did not deign to reply. In awesome accents, he reminded Henrietta that she was engaged to drive with him that afternoon, made a magnificent leg and quickly departed.

"Now, what has put him in such a rage?" said Henrietta wonderingly. "Did you meet him on the door-step, Mattie?"

Miss Scattersworth murmured something which sounded like "so . . . sorry . . . dear . . . hair-dresser. . . ." and fled.

Mr. Ralston was the next caller and it appeared that he too disapproved of Henrietta's friendship with Mr. Holmes. His pale green eyes stared at them and his rosebud mouth pouted like a disappointed child's.

"My dear Miss Sandford," he exclaimed at last. "You must not play fast and loose with my affections. Mama wishes to know when we are to send a notice of our forthcoming nuptials to the Gazette."

"We are not to be married. I've told you and told you," said Henrietta. Mr. Holmes thought her reply was rather sharp but Henrietta knew that nothing really would divert the single-minded track of Mr. Ralston's thoughts. And indeed her protest did not.

"Coy as ever," said Mr. Ralston vaguely. "I see you have bought a new vase." He picked it up and turned it gently round, tapping it with his long polished nails.

"Ming!" he exclaimed, replacing it on its stand with a nerve-wracking thump. "This must stop."

"What must?" said Henrietta.

"All this wasting of money. *I* should decide how to spend it, not you. It is *my* money, after all. Shame on you Henrietta."

"Be damned to you," said Jeremy getting to his feet. "Get out of here you little wart before I land you a facer." He grasped hold of Mr. Ralston's sleeve and tried to drag him towards the door.

Edmund Ralston went quite white under his paint. "Take your filthy clodhopper hands off me," he hissed. And before either Henrietta or Jeremy realized his intent, he had tugged a small dagger from his pocket and slashed Jeremy Holmes over the back of his knuckles. Then he sat down and began to cry.

Jeremy stared at the blood welling from his hand and turned crimson with fury.

"By God, you shall answer for this!" Jeremy picked up his glove and struck Edmund Ralston across the face. "Name your seconds, sir."

Edmund stared up at him. The tears continued to well out of his eyes and pour down his cheeks. He opened his painted mouth and let out a thin, high cry, "Mother!"

As if on cue, the door burst open and Mrs. Ralston ran into the room. She moved like lightning. The bewildered Henrietta estimated it must have taken Mrs. Ralston less than a minute to dry her son's eyes, hug him, swipe Mr. Holmes across the face with her large reticule, and drag her son from the room.

Jeremy and Henrietta regarded each other in shocked silence. Henrietta's excellent butler, Hobbard, had appeared as if by magic with salves and bandages and was already binding up the injured hand. "He's the one," declared Jeremy finally. "Why, he's stark raving mad!"

Henrietta shook her head. "He has neither the ruthlessness nor the intellect to carry out any of the attempts on my sanity. I tell you this, Jeremy. For some reason, I do not feel so frightened. I think the death of that poor girl marked the end of my troubles."

"Talking about troubles," said Jeremy. "Everyone's talking about you and Reckford. Say you're going to make a match of it."

Henrietta blushed and said in a small voice. "Lord Reckford thinks of me as a . . . a sister."

"He does, does he," said Jeremy with a grin. "Then why did he poker up when he found us together, heh? Never known old Guy to be so stuffy."

Henrietta clutched at his injured hand, making him wince. "Oh, do you think . . . do you really think. . . ."

"Now don't go getting all excited," said Jeremy. "I might be wrong. Anyway, it ain't as if you'll die an old maid. I mean to say, take me for instance. We get along pretty well together don't we?"

"You surely aren't proposing to me, Jeremy?"

"Not yet, I ain't," he said cheerfully. "But you never know. . . ."

"What about Alice?"

"Oh, *Alice*. Oh, yes, almost forgot. Love her to distraction," said Jeremy.

Henrietta retired to her room after he had left and rang for her maid and began the long elaborate toilette she considered essential for driving out with the Beau.

Various outfits were inspected and dismissed until Henrietta settled on a demure grey driving dress of a mannish cut, flattering to her trim figure. A dashing little hat with one of the new veils was placed on her elaborate curls and she sat stiffly in front of her looking glass, frightened to move in case she disarranged so much as a hair, waiting for the magic hour to arrive.

At two minutes to three, she made a stately descent to the drawingroom, to be informed that her brother was waiting to see her. She bit her lip with annoyance and then, composing her features into a smile of welcome, followed Hobbard into the room.

Henry wheezed to his feet and tried to clasp her to him in a brotherly embrace, but only succeeded in bumping her backwards with his enormous whale-bone-encased stomach. It would be interesting, mused Henrietta to see what some anthropologist from the future will make of us. Like the strange embrace of the Eskimo who rub noses, he would probably observe that the men and women of the nineteenth century bumped stomachs when they met.

"I have come to offer my services as an escort," said Henry. "There are some prodigious mind-improving books in Hatchard's."

"Then they must wait to improve my mind on another day. I am about to drive out with Lord Reckford."

Henry moved his chair forward and clasped her knee with a pudgy hand. "You must be careful, my sister. Lord Reckford has a bad reputation. Tell him that you do not wish to go. Blood is thicker than water, eh!"

Henrietta was about to reply when Lord Reckford was announced. Henry got to his feet with a determined glint in his eye. "My sister will not be able to accompany you. She is to come with me to Hatchard's."

To his fury, the Beau simply ignored him and addressed his remarks solely to Henrietta. "No, Miss Sandford. Absolutely no. I have my reputation to consider. I refuse to be seen driving a lady wearing a veil."

"But it is the latest thing," said Henrietta crossly.

"The latest thing is not always the most flattering. I shall wait while you find something else."

Henrietta was as furious as only a very feminine woman can be after spending time, money and effort on an article of fashion only to be told that her taste is in error. "I suggest you go without me." She tried to make her voice as disdainful as his lordship's but it came out sounding petulant and disappointed. But she would not have gone had not Henry suddenly demanded that she accompany him instead. She flounced to her room and crammed an attractive bérgére confection on her head only to find that it did not complement her driving dress. In despair, she put on a simple sprigged muslin and found that it was much too tight across the bosom and certainly too low. But she would not change. She had a sudden panicky feeling that Henry might persuade Lord Reckford to leave. She hurriedly tied a fichu round her shoulders and descended the staircase in a most unladylike manner by sliding down the bannister.

There was a silence when she re-entered the room. Henry was looking flushed and furious and the Beau enigmatic. "How charming you look," said Lord Reckford gallantly, mentally thinking that Henrietta had had her clothes thrown onto her from a long distance. "Bid you good day, Sandford," he said over his shoulder. Henry followed them into the hall, entreating Henrietta to stay and, by the time she was handed up into his lordship's carriage, she felt hot, untidy, flustered and embarrassed. Lord Reckford had ignored her brother throughout the whole and he drove off without turning his head to even glance at the vicar who was babbling on the pavement.

He threaded his way in and out of the Mayfair traffic, paying no attention to his companion. Henrietta was too busy with her jumbled thoughts to notice the direction they were taking and it was with some surprise that she eventually noticed that they were not heading in the direction of the park.

"We are going out into the country," remarked Lord Reckford, answering her unspoken question. "For once, we are going away from the Henrys and the Beldings and the Ralstons and the Scattersworths. I declare I have seen so much of them of late that there seem to be hundreds of them."

Henrietta was suddenly afraid of her own emotions. It had been some time since she had seen him alone. Her knees began to tremble and she felt quite faint. "You must hold on very tightly, Miss Sandford," said

Lord Reckford looking down at her with a glint of mischief in his eyes. "My cattle are fresh and I am going to spring them."

The wind and the unfamiliar countryside whipped past them. Henrietta clutched the side of the curricle and shut her eyes tight. One minute it seemed she was sitting in the carriage with every bone in her body being jolted about and the next she was sailing through the air. She landed with a heavy crash in a dry ditch and lay staring wild-eyed at the summer sky. She could hear the horses rearing and plunging and then they were quiet. There seemed to be a sudden dreadful silence and then, as the dizzy whirling of her brain stopped, the little noises of the countryside crept to her ears. Somewhere nearby, a heavy animal was grazing. A lark seemed to hang suspended far above her, the sound of his song tumbling down to her from very far away. The air was heavy with the scent of mown grass, wild honeysuckle and pine.

She cautiously moved her limbs and found that nothing was broken and then painfully raised herself up on one elbow. With a sudden stab of panic, she realized she had not heard a sound from Lord Reckford. Her head did not reach over the edge of the ditch, so cautiously and painfully she struggled to her feet. Lord Reckford lay at the side of the road where he had been thrown from the carriage. His head lay on a stone and a thin trickle of blood was oozing into the dust of the road.

She ran forward and knelt down beside him. He lay as still as death, his face waxy under the blazing sun. Then he groaned faintly and slowly opened his eyes. "My horses?" he said faintly.

Henrietta looked round. His matched greys were grazing unconcernedly at the side of the road. "Your horses are perfectly well," said Henrietta, "and just in case you might perhaps feel some concern, so am I."

He smiled faintly and then sat up with a groan. "Oh, my head. God I feel sick."

"There is a field across the road with a little stream," said Henrietta. "If you can lean on me, I can help you cross it and then bathe your head."

"My sensible angel" he murmured. He threw an arm round her shoulders and they got to their feet and inched their way across into the field. He moaned and sank down on a pile of freshly cut grass beside the stream, dragging Henrietta down with him. She gently extricated herself and tried to rip a flounce from her petticoat to use as a bandage. But the seams refused to break. "No need for such sacrifice," said her companion with a return of something of his usual mocking manner. He held out a large sensible handkerchief.

Henrietta soaked it in the stream and then timidly parted the heavy black hair. "It does not look too bad, my lord," she said, carefully washing the wound. "How do you feel?"

"Sick as a dog," he replied, "but no bones broken. I shall come about presently but at the moment, all I want to do is put my head down on that beautiful bosom and sleep."

He rolled over and casually suited the action to the words. Henrietta had lost her fichu in the accident and felt almost naked. He could not possibly be asleep! But his rythmical breathing showed that he was. She lay back against the pile of grass and stared at the sky, cradling the heavy wet head on her bosom and wondered if she were going to faint from an excess of emotion. Then after some time, the heat of the day and the reaction to the shock of the accident overcame her, and she too closed her eyes and slept.

As the sun was setting behind the trees, Lord Reckford opened his eyes and for a few horrible seconds did not know where he was. His cheeks was pillowed on a well-rounded bosom and far above him, little feathery clouds were turning red and gold in the evening sky. At last he remembered, and cautiously raised his head and stared down at the sleeping girl. Her dress was crumpled where his heavy body had lain on it. Tendrils of damp hair clung to her brow and she sighed gently in her sleep.

He was overcome with a feeling of tenderness and did not wish to wake her and spoil the moment. The countryside was very still. The water chuckled over the stones and far away across the fields, a dog bayed to the rising moon.

Then there was the sound of rough voices on the road and Henrietta's hazel eyes jerked wide open. "Come quickly," said Lord Reckford. "I am afraid of losing my horses."

They stiffly emerged on to the roadway to find a farmer and his son examining the overturned curricle . . . or rather the farmer was down on his knees inspecting the carriage while his son sat vacantly on the farm wagon, bucolically chewing on a piece of grass.

The farmer raised his head at their approach. "This your'n?" he asked laconically. "Ur lynch-pin 'as bin sawn through."

"What!" shouted the Beau, making his audience jump.

"Zactly. Sawn through 'er be."

Henrietta felt a cold knot of fear in her stomach.

"Where is the nearest blacksmith?" demanded his lordship, his features harsh and drawn in the twilight."

"Reckon smiddy's a mile or so down road. But you and your missus 'op on the wagon and us'll have you there soon."

In all her fright, Henrietta felt a warm glow at being taken for the Beau's "missus." The horses were tethered to the back as Lord Reckford helped Henrietta up onto the farm wagon. The farmer clucked to his horse which moved off down the road at a leisurely pace.

After a mile or so they saw the twinkling lights of a village. "There's an inn there. Coach an' 'Orses," said the farmer. "Leave your missus there and us'll get the blacksmith."

The Coach and Horses proved to be a small but comfortable inn and Henrietta wearily trailed after

Lord Reckford into the brightly lit hallway, unaware of her appearance.

She cringed before the basilisk stare of the landlord's wife who was glaring at Henrietta's expanse of bosom and mud-stained dress. The landlord's wife folded her arms and, ignoring Lord Reckford, addressed Henrietta. "We're respectable folk here. You can take yourselves off this minute."

She caught the look in Lord Reckford's eye and fell silent. "My good woman," he said, each word dripping like acid. "You will arrange a bedchamber for this lady so that she may repair her dress, you will arrange a private parlor for the both of us and you will set about cooking dinner. And spare me any further of your damned insolence." He turned to the farmer without looking at her further. His lordship expected his commands to be obeyed and Henrietta found herself envying him. Was he not aware of their appearance? But the woman dropped something like a curtsy and led Henrietta to a bedchamber on the upper floor.

After the woman had gone, Henrietta pushed open the window latch and leaned out. There was a small garden at the back of the inn with a few tables. The heavy scent of lavender and stock drifted up in the evening air. She stayed there, drinking in the peace of the evening, unwilling to move and go back to the real world. Relationships between men and women did not remain static. That much she had gleaned from her observations of the parishoners of Nethercote. Lord Reckford did not love her. Therefore the only logical progression was that they should part at the end of the Season. Henrietta wished that it were mid-winter so that a snowstorm might entrap them in the inn. Then she laughed and closed the window. Miss Mattie would certainly have something dramatic to make of that situation.

The floorboards creaked in the corridor outside and there was a firm knock at the door. She opened it and gazed up at Lord Reckford.

"My carriage can not be repaired tonight, Miss Sandford, and if we stay here, you will be sadly compromised. I have sent one of the ostlers to the nearest town to hire us a conveyance."

Henrietta suddenly became aware of her still dishevelled appearance. Lord Reckford had miraculously managed to transform himself back into his old elegant self.

"I bought this from the landlord's wife," he said handing her a heavy, crimson wool shawl. "Would you like me to send her up to you to help arrange your hair."

She put her hand up to her tangled locks. "No, it will not be necessary," she said, thinking of the landlord's sour-faced wife. "I shall join you presently."

He bowed very formally and left. She washed as best she could and arranged her hair in the dim light of one tallow candle.

Her efforts were not entirely successful. "You look like a gypsy," smiled Lord Reckford when she entered the parlor with the crimson shawl draped round her shoulders. He drew out a chair for her and motioned her towards the table.

They ate in a companionable silence until the farmer's son arrived to tell them that a carriage and pair were waiting for them in the courtyard.

When they were seated in the comfortable, if musty, darkness, Lord Reckford said, "What will you do when the Season ends, Henrietta? I do not like to think of you unprotected. Our madman has turned murderer."

"I had not thought," said Henrietta. "What are your own plans?"

"Oh, I shall follow Prinny and the fashionables to Brighton. This is to be my last year of the social round." She felt his face turn towards her in the darkness. "Next year I shall retire to my estates, marry, and set up my nursery."

"I thought you were a confirmed bachelor," said Henrietta in a small voice.

156

"Ah, but we old roués must settle down sometime. Shall you visit me and play with my children?"

"No," choked Henrietta.

"Don't like children, eh?" he drawled maddeningly. "But you must like mine. We are such good friends, you see."

Was he being deliberately cruel? How could this wretched man sleep all afternoon on her bosom and calmly talk about the children he was to have by another woman?

Just as she felt that she was about to break down into tears, he changed the subject. "I feel you should visit Brighton as well, Henrietta. Who else is going to take care of you?"

How Henrietta longed to scream childishly that she did not wish to go to Brighton but instead she remarked in a matter of fact voice, "It will surely be very hard to find accommodation at this late date."

"Stay with me," said the Beau with maddening unconcern. "My sister has taken a large mansion on the Marine Parade and she and her husband will act as chaperone."

"If I am to take up residence in your household, my lord, the gossips will certainly have something to talk about."

"But nothing disrespectful," he rejoined laconically. "You will keep the scalp-hunters at bay until I decide on a wife."

"Have you considered, my lord, that *I* do not wish the scalp-hunters to be kept away from *me*? I am desirous of marriage, you know," said Henrietta in a quiet voice. "And I despise your arrogance. You will 'decide on a wife.' What if the young lady will not have you?"

"My dear, Miss Sandford, there is no one who would refuse my fortune . . . except perhaps yourself."

"And since you do not want me for a wife, you see no hindrance?"

He leaned forward in the darkness. "But I did ask

you to marry me," he said slowly. "Or had you forgotten."

"That, my lord," she said primly, "was only because you felt you had compromised me after you had been making love to the ghost of Lucinda."

"Damn Lucinda. Ah, I had forgot. I am supposed to have driven the fair Lucinda mad. Well, for your information, that charming young lady was introduced to cocaine by her elderly lover and when I last saw her she was completely out of her wits."

"Poor Lucinda," whispered Henrietta.

"And poor Henrietta," he said, dismissing the subject of his ex-love with seeming callousness. "No one to love you and no one to protect you. You could do far worse than to be married to me."

Henrietta fell silent. If only he would take her in his arms. The silence lengthened and then, to her fury, she heard the sounds of heavy breathing from the other corner of the carriage. His lordship had fallen fast asleep. The infuriating man could go to Brighton for all she cared. She would learn to live without him. Since the Season began, she had been unable to notice any other man. Well, she would begin to change.

With this firm resolve, she made his sleepy lordship a chilly adieu at Brook Street and escaped to the privacy of her bedroom for a hearty cry.

Chapter Eleven

THE SEASON WAS AT last finished. Marriages, as the top ten thousand very well knew, were not made in heaven. They were made in the overheated saloons and ballrooms of London. The exhausted debutantes who had failed to snare a mate returned to their country homes with their vast wardrobes to recharge their energies for the next battle. The successful ones also rested like exhausted warriors after a long campaign and left the worrying of wedding expenses to their parents.

The hardier spirits followed the Prince Regent to Brighton to resume their military tactics by laying seige to every available bachelor heart in the Assembly Rooms of the now famous seaside resort.

Henrietta had joined the lists.

Beau Reckford should discover that he was not the only pebble on the beach and that elegant gentleman was considerably irritated to find that Henrietta never seemed to be at home. And unless he presented himself very early at the assemblies at the Ship Inn, he found that her dance card was always full.

Henrietta and Miss Scattersworth had rented a house on the Marine Parade which had been vacated at the last minute by an impecunious lord who had lost his rent and lease at the faro table.

Henrietta had never seen the sea before. As the heavy travelling coach had rumbled down the Lewes Road and she had caught her first glimpse of the endless stretch of blue water sparkling under the summer sun, a little of the ache in her heart lessened.

She had decided that she would never love anyone else as deeply and completely as she loved the Beau. But if she should have to settle for half measures, then let it be with some other gentleman. There were many who would be willing to marry her for her money. Henrietta had become worldly enough to not object to that idea. Were the impoverished gentleman complacent and kind and comfortable enough, then she would be happy to repair his fortune in exchange for his name. Children would be adequate compensation for any lack of love, decided Henrietta.

Having firmly made up her mind to put Beau Reckford out of her mind and having firmly convinced herself that she was only in Brighton to look for a suitable husband, she settled back to enjoy her holiday. The longing and pain she felt when she saw Lord Reckford's handsome face in the ballroom had become such a habit that by the close of the Season, Henrietta had come to accept it the way one accepts the pain of perpetual illness.

For his part, Lord Reckford decided to ignore her in turn. He had received many rebuffs from the vicar's sister during the first week in Brighton. Enough was enough. If that was all the thanks he was to receive for all his condecension and flattering attention to a little provincial, then to hell with her!

He drank, gambled and flirted as he had never done before and felt immeasurably bored.

His sister, Lady Ann Courtney, anxiously watched him. She had come to like Henrietta and had hoped that her wild brother would settle down and set up his nursery. She watched his haggard face across the breakfast table one morning with disapproval.

"Really, Guy," she sighed. "You are getting slightly

too old to go on in this ramshackle manner. We have only been in Brighton for a week and already tales of your dissipation are coming to my ears."

"Don't refine too much on it," he said lazily. "The old tabbies who come around here would ferret out scandal about a bishop."

The curtains of the breakfast room window were drawn back affording an excellent view of the Parade. Henrietta Sandford floated past on the arm of a military gentleman. She seemed unusually animated and gay. Behind her trailed Miss Scattersworth, for once unaccompanied. The spinster's hair under her cap showed faint glints of green. The re-dying of her hair had not been entirely successful. A mischievous breeze carried the infectious trill of Henrietta's laughter through the open windows to Lord Reckford's jaundiced ears. He cursed under his breath and threw down his napkin.

His sister regarded him anxiously. "Guy . . . I had hoped that you were fixed with Miss Sandford. You are not, by any chance, still hankering after poor Lucinda?"

Her brother regarded her with surprise. "I declare I had not thought of Lucinda in some time. Is she still alive?"

"Only just," said Ann dryly. "But her brother seems to be in a fair way to wasting her fortune."

He gave her a startled look. "Are you sure Lucinda had a fortune? She was always asking me for money and expensive trinkets. And I thought her sudden interest in the Marquis was because his estate was more considerable than mine."

"Oh, yes. Lucinda was greedy. Like a greedy little child. But she had quite a considerable fortune."

"But what has that got to do with her brother . . . ?" Lord Reckford looked at her with a sudden dawning glimmer of understanding.

"Well, of course, Guy. Your wits must be wandering. When Lucinda was put in the madhouse and all the papers signed, her parents being dead, her brother naturally took control of her estate. Why, Guy! What on earth is the matter? You have gone quite white!"

"Her brother," whispered Lord Reckford. "Her brother."

"Now what is there about Lucinda Braintree's brother to put you in such a pucker? A wastral and a rake, I grant you. And talking of rakes," she began severely. But she spoke to the empty air. The crashing of the outside door marked where his lordship had taken hurried leave.

Ann put down her cup of chocolate and ran to the window. Her brother's broad back could be seen disappearing at a rapid rate down the Parade.

She sat down again with a sigh. Ever since her little brother had met Miss Sandford . . . well, she hardly knew him.

Jeremy Holmes was nursing a sore head and a large glass of hock and seltzer when his butler announced Lord Reckford. The Beau hurtled into the room and grabbed Jeremy by the lapels of his magnificent dressinggown.

"The brother, Jeremy. Henry Sandford!"

Jeremy slowly and gently disengaged Lord Reckford's powerful fingers. "Look," he said patiently, "I don't like Henry Sandford myself. But is that any reason to come burstin' in . . ."

"No, listen and I'll tell you." Recovering his usual composure, Lord Reckford bent his head close to his friend's and begean to talk rapidly and urgently.

At that moment, Miss Sandford had given up all pretense of enjoying her companion's company. She had laughed and chatted gaily until they were well past Lord Reckford's residence. Then all the sparkle seemed to go out of her day and she paused for a moment by the rail of the Parade and decided suddenly to leave Brighton. Henry had written to say that he would be joining her for a few days and, although he had been all that was amiable to her for some time, she felt she could not endure him under the same roof again.

Her plan of ignoring the infuriating Lord Reckford was not working out. The only way to get over her unfortunate passion was to keep the cause of it firmly out of sight. She turned her head and addressed Miss Scattersworth. "Mattie, we shall leave in the morning."

Her escort, a Captain Frederick Waverley, tugged his magnificent moustaches in surprise, "Oh, I say, Miss Sandford. Brighton won't be the same. 'Pon rep. Prettiest gel 'bout to leave town. Gawd, what, eh!"

Miss Mattie let out a wail. "But, Henrietta, perhaps Mr. Sandford will bring Mr. Symes with him."

"I doubt it, Mattie. He will want his curate to run the parish in his absence."

Miss Scattersworth sighed dismally and touched her hair under her cap. "Perhaps it is just as well."

"But, the ball tonight. Promised the waltz, Miss Sandford," said the Captain. "Must have the pleasure. Last dance and all, gawd, what, eh!"

Henrietta smiled and nodded and privately thought of another gentleman who she hoped to dance with for the last time. Just once more, she would twirl under the lights of the ballroom in Lord Reckford's arms. And then, she would never see him again. She choked back a sob and, taking her escort's arm, moved off along the Parade.

As soon as she politely and possibly could, she took her leave of the Captain, assuring him fervently that yes, she would waltz with him—so fervently that he walked away jauntily and happily, convinced he had made another conquest.

At the end of the Parade, two elegant gentleman were propped against the rail, watching his progress. Captain Waverley recognized Lord Reckford and Mr. Jeremy Holmes and puffed out his chest. It was common knowledge that the famous Beau had been dangling after Miss Sandford and now he, Captain

Waverley, had succeeded in attaching the affections of the beautiful heiress.

To his surprise, Lord Reckford stepped forward and made him an elegant bow. "Your servant, Captain," said the Beau. "We have not been introduced but I have heard it said that you are a good opponent in a game of chance and I wondered whether you would like to try your skill against mine."

The Captain hesitated. It was indeed flattering to be singled out by the famous Lord Reckford but there was a tightness about his lordship's mouth and a glint in his eye which gave the Captain an uneasy feeling of danger. He opened his mouth to refuse but the Beau went on smoothly, "I had it from your Colonel-in-Chief, Lord Hadrington, that your skill at piquet is beyond compare."

The Captain beamed. Now here was a different matter. He was anxious for promotion and he did not want his Colonel-in-Chief to hear that he had disobliged a friend.

"Well, well, lead on my lord. Delighted to play you. Anywhere you wish."

"My house is hard by," said Lord Reckford, moving to one side of the Captain while Jeremy Holmes flanked the other. Again the Captain had an uneasy feeling of danger and hesitated but Lord Reckford's hand on his arm was most insistent. The Captain shook his head as though to dispel his fears. After all, what could happen to him? Lord Reckford was a friend of Miss Sandford and then there was the matter of the Colonel-in-Chief.

Once inside, all his fears were dispelled. He was introduced to Lady Ann Courtney and her husband, Sir Geoffrey. Admittedly the couple looked startled to hear that Lord Reckford meant to play cards at such an early hour but Sir Geoffrey merely suggested that they use the study on the first floor where they would be sure of being undisturbed.

The Captain surveyed the luxurious appointments of

the house with an appreciative eye. Wait till he told the fellows in the mess!

As he was studying his cards, Mr. Holmes placed a glass of madeira at his elbow and urged him to try it. The Captain waved his hand. "Never drink this early in the day. Wait until the sun's over the yard arm as the navy chaps say, eh, what!"

There was a slight pause and then Lord Reckford's husky voice said, "Ah, but I wish you would give me your opinion. I sent a case of it to Lord Hadrington."

The Captain eyed his glass. A stray sunbeam winked hypnotically on the crystal. He could hear himself saying to Lord Hadrington, "Played a rubber with that fellow Reckford t'other day. Damned fine madeira, what," and how the fellows would stare to hear him discussing the famous Beau in such easy terms.

The Captain squared his shoulders and brought the glass stiffly up to his mouth as if about to salute and took a large swallow. The madeira certainly had a warm and mellowing effect.

"I would like to stake a wager," said Lord Reckford.

"Of course, of course," said the Captain cautiously. "Not too high, mind!"

"Oh, I wasn't thinking of money," said the Beau smoothly. "Not from you, that is. I will wager five hundred guineas. What I want from you is a dance—your dance—with Miss Sandford."

The Captain looked at him in surprise and then a slow, satisfied smile spread over his features. "Surely you can ask her yourself."

The Beau shook his head. "I am unlucky, you see. Miss Sandford's dance card is always full even before the ball begins. Come, come Captain. Five hundred guineas is a fair wager."

The Captain opened his mouth to refuse and then closed it tight. The picture of himself casually discussing Lord Reckford's madeira danced tantalisingly through his mind. And, By George, he could use five hundred guineas in any case.

"Your hand on it, sir," he cried. "Let the game commence."

Half an hour later, the defeated Captain moodily left the house. Why, the man was a master at cards. With his skill, Beau Reckford could earn a fortune playing for gold instead of a dance.

Upstairs Jeremy Holmes laughed at his friend. "Miss Sandford should be flattered. You'll feel silly if her dance card is half empty!"

"Oh, but I am sure it will not be," said the Beau. "Miss Sandford has made a point of having her card completely full almost before the ball begins."

Jeremy looked suddenly worried. "You know, what you are about to do to Miss Sandford is downright criminal."

"I know," drawled his companion. "But it certainly takes the boredom out of life."

Henrietta paused at the doorway of the ballroom and surveyed the scene. She was wearing a white satin slip of a dress with a black lace overdress with long tight sleeves. Diamonds blazed at her throat and wrists and her heavy blonde hair was piled high on her head in a confusion of artfully arranged curls. Behind her stood Miss Scattersworth in a severe burgundy gown and with a matching turban covering her offending greenish hair. It was one of the few times of late that Miss Mattie had dressed in keeping with her years and, as a result, looked considerably younger.

The couples swirled and dipped before Henrietta's sad eyes. Their gaiety seemed to remove them a world away. She breathed in the now familiar Brighton ballroom air of wax candles, scent, pomade, sweat, fish and poor drainage and moved forward across the floor.

She gave a nervous start and dropped her fan as Lord Reckford seemed to materialize in front of her. In the hope of a last dance with him, she had made sure that her dance card was half empty. He took it from her and gave a cynical laugh. "What has happened this evening? I was sure that the gallant Captain would have claimed you for every dance."

"Only the waltz," said Henrietta, as he bent to retrieve her fan.

"Then I must disappoint you. The Captain begged me to inform you that he is . . . ah . . . somewhat under the weather. I shall stand in for him, of course." He began to write busily in her card.

Henrietta gasped. "My lord, you have engaged me for so many dances. More than two would cause a scandal."

"We shall sit most of them out," he remarked with arrogant indifference. "But first of all, I have something of a serious nature to say to you, Henrietta. After the next waltz, please step outside with me. We must have privacy. Do not look so frightened. We shall take Miss Scattersworth with us."

The strains of the waltz started up and he drew her into his arms, holding her much closer than the proprieties allowed. Henrietta shut out the past and the future and concentrated only on the feel of his arms around her. They danced in silence while the gossips turned to stare. Out of the corner of her vision, Henrietta could see the pouting and painted face of Edmund Ralston and then, after another turn of the waltz, the high-nosed stare of Lady Belding and the set white face of her daughter, Alice. Another turn, and Jeremy Holmes was at their side. Lord Reckford stopped and dropped his arms to his side and the sounds and sights of the everyday world flooded into Henrietta's ears. "It's time," said Mr. Holmes simply.

"Come, Henrietta!" Lord Reckford's hand was on her arm, but this time his grip was like a vice.

"Miss Mattie," she cried, looking round the crowded room. A few curious stares were already being directed at their party.

"Miss Scattersworth is already waiting for you," said Jeremy Holmes. She allowed herself to be drawn unresistingly from the ballroom.

She stopped in the courtyard outside and looked round. "But where is Miss Scattersworth?"

"She is waiting in that coach over there," said Mr. Holmes in a soothing voice. "Lord Reckford wishes to talk to you in private but as you can see you will not be unchaperoned."

Henrietta was too bewildered to question why the coachman was seated on the box and why the coach was flanked by two outriders if his lordship wished to be private with her. But she climbed into the coach ... and then tried to draw back.

The light from a passing link boy's lantern shone briefly into the darkness of the coach.

Miss Mattie Scattersworth was propped up in the corner bound and gagged, her eyes dilated with fright. Henrietta received an unceremonious shove in the back and fell forward into the straw at the bottom of the carriage. Lord Reckford jumped in after her and then thrust his head out of the window. "Spring 'em!" he shouted. The coach bounded forward and Henrietta slowly dragged herself up onto the seat. "You may ungag your friend," said his lordship in a quiet voice.

He was seated opposite Henrietta. The passing lamps showed his aquiline face set in hard lines. He held a long duelling pistol in his hand and it was pointed straight at Henrietta.

She put a trembling hand up to her mouth. "It was you. It was you all along . . ."

He did not reply. He turned his head and gazed indifferently out at the lights of the fast disappearing town.

But the long fingers which held the pistol did not waver by so much as an inch.

Chapter Twelve

FEELING SICK AND SHAKY, Henrietta turned to loosen Miss Scattersworth's gag. The spinster immediately opened her mouth to scream but shut it again as his lordship said in a voice like ice, "One word from you Miss Scattersworth and I shall blow Miss Sandford's pretty little head from her shoulders."

Miss Mattie shrieked in alarm and turned wide-eyed to Henrietta. Henrietta motioned her to be silent and turned, grim-faced, to her captor. "What are you going to do with us, my lord?"

"You are to be my guests for some time and provided you do not try to escape, we shall contrive to be comfortable."

Miss Mattie gasped, "He is trying to force you to marry him."

"Believe me, madame, marriage is the subject farthest from my mind at this moment," said Lord Reckford.

The spinster clutched Henrietta's arm. "Then he means to ravish you. He will keep you locked in a tower with only rats and bats for company and when he is tired of you, he will ship you to the West Indies as a slave."

Henrietta fought down an insane desire to laugh. But

Miss Mattie's nonsense had a bracing effect. Her heart may be in pieces, but at least she knew her enemy.

"And where are you taking us, my lord?" said Henrietta in a deceptively calm voice.

"To my home," he rejoined laconically. "To the Abbey. I am sorry it is not a hideous tower, Miss Scattersworth, but we do have dungeons."

Henrietta folded her lips, determined to watch for a chance of escape. The hours passed as the strange trio, resplendent in evening dress, rocked and lurched with the motion of the coach, each with their troubled thoughts.

Miss Scattersworth had settled into a kind of heavy despair. She would never see Mr. Symes again and it must be some divine punishment for all her racketing around. Henrietta felt numb with misery. This was where all her wild romantic dreams had brought her. She now heartily wished that Mrs. Tankerton *had* bequeathed her fortune to Edmund Ralston. She would still be at the vicarage, humiliated and bullied, but safe and with her heart in one piece.

They made several stops at posting houses along the road. The two women were allowed to alight and snatch hurried meals, conscious all the time of Lord Reckford's pistol which he had concealed beneath his cloak, Mr. Holmes who was riding beside the coach was similarly armed and his cherubic countenance looked grim and stern.

Henrietta tried to feign sleep as the night wore on but the hand holding the pistol never wavered. A pale grey dawn finally lit their weary faces and still the coach sped on, lurching and bumping along strange country roads, never slackening speed.

Just as she was thinking she would never sleep again, Henrietta's eyelids drooped. When she opened them again, the sun was high in the sky, the heat inside the coach was nigh unbearable. The horses were slowing and she looked hopefully out of the window. But it was only another posting house.

"We will stop here for refreshments," said the now hateful voice of Lord Reckford. "Remember, not by one sign or one glance will you indicate to anyone at this inn that aught is amiss. I will shoot you down on the spot. Out!"

Neither Miss Scattersworth nor Henrietta had any appetite for the excellent meal that was put in front of them. Then they had to endure the humiliation of being escorted to the privy at the foot of the garden under the armed escort of Mr. Holmes who assured the landlord with a sweet smile that since both ladies were liable to fainting fits, he had better be on hand.

Henrietta was about to tell Mr. Holmes that she would never forgive him for as long as she lived and then realized gloomily that that showed every sign of being a very short span of time indeed.

Henrietta had been long enough in fashionable society to learn that, despite all the appearances of public law and order, the powerful aristocratic families were still able to do pretty much as they pleased on the privacy of their estates.

The long journey began again and night was beginning to fall as the coach lumbered up to the drive of the Abbey.

Both women were hustled into the great hallway, up the stairs and along a bewildering series of passages. Trying to keep her wits about her, Henrietta judged that they must be heading somewhere towards the east wing. At last Lord Reckford stopped outside a door and pushed it open. Both were thrust inside and then they heard the key turn in the lock.

Henrietta clutched Miss Scattersworth and then looked about her. They were obviously in what had once been a nursery. There were two bedrooms adjoining it and a small dressingroom. The key turned in the lock and two footmen came in. One stood guard at the door while the other laid a tempting tray of food on a small table and then lit the fire in the hearth. Both bowed solemnly and withdrew.

"I am going to eat," said Miss Scattersworth. "I absolutely refuse to be frightened," But her voice quavered piteously and she suddenly looked very old and frail. Henrietta began to feel very, very angry indeed. What kind of monster was this man who could make an elderly lady suffer so?

"We shall escape, Mattie," she said firmly. "We shall eat well, sleep well . . . and we *shall* get away. Of that, I am determined."

"But the windows are barred," said Miss Scattersworth, "and the door is locked."

"We will find a way," said Henrietta, sitting down. To her surprise, she found she was very hungry indeed.

The door opened again and this time it was Lord Reckford, looking huge and menacing in the low-ceilinged room. Following him came the two footmen bearing an enormous trunk.

"These are your clothes," he said abruptly. "I am sorry that you have to be confined like this but it is for your own good. Do not be frightened," he added in a gentle voice. "It was necessary to terrify you on the road here in case you thought to escape."

"You are mad," said Henrietta, clearly and distinctly. "Stark raving mad."

"As you wish," he said coldly and withdrew.

Miss Scattersworth clasped her trembling hands together. "Oh, I am sure he means us no harm. There must be some explanation. . . ."

"There can be no reasonable explanation," said Henrietta in a flat voice. "It is all part and parcel of all these strange happenings. Now he has me in his home, caged like some animal. I repeat, I shall escape."

Both women finished their meal in silence and then turned to inspect the trunk. It contained two complete wardrobes.

"He has excellent taste," said Miss Mattie cheerfully, her mercurial nature unable to sustain the one set of emotions for long.

Henrietta surveyed the tumbling silks and satins

sourly. "He probably got one of his doxies to do the shopping for him."

Miss Scattersworth gave a delighted giggle. "Why, Mattie," said Henrietta sternly. "I do believe you are beginning to enjoy all this."

"I am," said the spinster a little defiantly. "I have thought things over and I cannot believe ill of Lord Reckford. I shall simply enjoy the adventure and if he kills me, well then, I have not so many years left after all."

"Well, I have, you selfish baggage," said Henrietta with a grin. "Nonetheless, I shall wear something from his lordship's wardrobe tomorrow and I suggest you do the same. We cannot make our escape in these evening gowns."

Henrietta did not feel so optimistic in the morning. She prowled from end to end of their tiny apartment looking for a loophole and then sat down in despair.

"We may as well be in prison," she sighed.

The two footmen duly appeared with breakfast and Henrietta noticed that the one on guard at the door never took his eyes off them.

After the footmen had left, Henrietta smiled at Miss Scattersworth. "Come, Mattie! There is surely an idea in one of our romances to help us out of this predicament."

Miss Scattersworth nibbled at her toast meditatively. "We could seduce the footmen," she said, after a pause.

"Oh, really, Mattie," Henrietta giggled. "Pray do think of something else."

Again Miss Scattersworth thought furiously. "Eureka!" She screamed knocking over the coffee pot and bringing vividly back to mind Lord Reckford's first call at their home in London. "In 'The Courage of Lady Wimmerey,' if you recall, the wicked Turk had her locked in the seraglio and she escaped by throwing pepper in his face."

Both women looked at the large pepper pot on the

table. Henrietta's heart began to pound. "But there are two of them, Mattie."

"Well, there are two of us. You take the one at the door and I'll take t'other. What shall we hit 'em with?" Miss Scattersworth's face was delicately flushed and her eyes were sparkling. Henrietta gave her a wondering look. "There's the poker," she said faintly.

"Good," said Miss Scattersworth. "Now cup your hand and I'll give you half the pepper."

They heard footsteps in the corridor. They had not time enough, thought Henrietta, appealing silently to her friend not to make the attempt. Miss Scattersworth merely squared her cap and gave Henrietta a vulgar wink.

The door was opening. They were here!

Henrietta rose to her feet and started to sway. She moved towards the door. "I feel faint," she said on a half sob. The footman noticed that she was indeed very white and held out his arms. Henrietta threw the handful of pepper full in his eyes. With superb timing, Miss Mattie dealt with her victim at the same moment and then moving like lightning, she rapped the footmen on their heads with the poker, wielding it competently with one scrawny arm.

"We need to tie them up with something," wailed Miss Scattersworth.

"The sheets," whispered Henrietta. "Quietly now, Mattie, someone might have heard the commotion."

Both women tugged frantically at the sheets with no result. "*Honestly*," said Miss Scattersworth petulently throwing down the crumpled linen sheet. "Ladies in books are always ripping sheets and petticoats and heroes are always ripping dresses or something. They can't have heard of Irish linen."

All seemed hopeless until Henrietta spied a little work table in the corner and triumphantly produced two pairs of scissors. Both women fell to work, Miss Scattersworth pointing out sensibly that if they imagined they were engaged in a household task, then it

174

would be easy. "Like trussing birds," she said, standing back at last to survey the two expertly bound and gagged footmen.

Wearing identical walking dresses and half boots ("The doxie did not really throw her heart into the job," Henrietta had commented acidly.) both women edged into the corridor. The great house seemed very quiet.

"We are in the east wing," whispered Henrietta. "If we can descend to the bedrooms on the lower floor, I can perhaps find a back staircase which will lead to the gardens."

They inched their way to the top of the main staircase. The stairs were narrower, descending two flights before they broadened out into a grand majestic sweep. Far away, a rattling of dishes from the kitchens made them jump. They crept to the next floor and waited holding their breath. Then they crept along the lower corridor and Henrietta stopped before a worn leather door and pushed it open. A steep flight of uncarpeted steps lead down.

There seemed to be an infinity of stairs before they reached the ground level. The noises from the kitchens were louder now but they decided to open the door in front of them. It gave a protesting creak which immediately sent their hearts into their mouths and then swung wide open. They found themselves staring across the lawns at the back of the house.

Perhaps, thought Henrietta later, if they had moved from bush to bush as carefully as they had negotiated the corridors, they would have succeeded in escaping. But the sights and woody smells of freedom were too much for both. They plunged headlong across the lawns as if the devil himself were at their heels . . . and straight into the waiting arms of the head gamekeeper.

"Back!" he ordered, waving a very lethal-looking rifle. Heads bowed and shaking with nerves, they were shepherded round to the front of the house and into the library, where the hated lord was calmly going through his estate papers as if he were in the habit of imprisoning respectable ladies every day of his life.

"That will be all, thank you," he said, dismissing the keeper.

Monsieur Dubois came in and, averting his eyes from them, whispered something in Lord Reckford's ear.

"So!" The Beau threw down his quill and leaned back in his chair. "Take Miss Scattersworth back to her rooms. I wish to have a word with Miss Sandford alone. And make sure you are armed."

After the door had closed, he surveyed Henrietta enigmatically. An apple wood fire crackled in the fireplace and a gust of wind swept round the old house like a sigh, sending the candlelight flickering and moving the tapestries on the walls. It had grown as dark as night outside and far away growled the faint menacing rumble of thunder.

Lord Reckford negligently crossed one booted leg over the other and surveyed his prisoner from head to foot.

"You do not appear to trust me, Miss Sandford?"

"Trust you," gasped Henrietta, outraged. "You frighten us half out of our wits, wave pistols at us and lock us in a barred room. Why on earth should we trust you?"

"I mean you no ill. I am simply keeping you here for your own good."

"Why? In God's name why?" stormed Henrietta.

His calm face betrayed none of the thoughts that were racing through his brain. If he told her of his suspicions of her brother, she would never believe him. Better to let her suffer a little. At least she was alive and unharmed.

"I cannot tell you," said the once-loved husky voice flatly. "Come here to me, Henrietta. We should deal better together than this."

He drew her into his arms but she stood, unrespon-

176

sive, like wood and looked at him, her eyes wide with contempt. "If you mean to ravish me my lord and insult me with your unwanted attentions, there is little I can do about it. I am a helpless female and your prisoner."

Lord Reckford dropped his arms and glared at her in fury. "Helpless, be damned. You have just knocked out two of my strongest footmen and you stand there twittering about being helpless. I tell you now, Henrietta Sandford, when this business is over, I shall spend many nights enjoying those delectable curves of yours. And you will come to me of your own free will."

He jerked the bellrope so savagely, it nearly came away in his hand. "Send an escort with Miss Sandford," he snapped at his butler and throwing himself down at his desk, he bent over his papers and did not turn his head until she was led from the room.

Henrietta could not remember having been so angry before in her life. She stormed up and down the room until poor Miss Scattersworth protested that it was too exhausting just watching her.

Sinking into a chair, Henrietta looked gloomily through the barred windows at the sheets of rain blanketing the park. "It's probably just as well we did not escape. We may have died from exposure."

"But what if we escape and do not leave the house?" cried Miss Mattie suddenly.

"And what good is that? Really, Mattie, of all the crack-brained . . ."

"Wait and listen. If we could manage to escape from this room and hide somewhere in the Abbey. They would think we had escaped and everyone including Lord Reckford and Mr. Holmes would be out looking for us. *Then* all we would have to do is . . . walk out of the front door."

"Why Mattie! You're a veritable genius!" Henrietta hugged her friend warmly. "I shall never laugh at your fantasies again."

"Now," said Miss Scattersworth, very flushed and

excited. "We must plan." The wind howled and the rain beat against the windows as both racked their brains, mulling over and discarding various schemes.

Miss Scattersworth ran her bony fingers through her impossible-colored hair. Henrietta looked at her and laughed. "You look like something the Brothers Grimm thought up. Why. . . ."

But her friend was leaping about with excitement.

She pointed a long finger at a small stove in the corner of the room. "We shall simply soak the door in spirits and burn it down."

"Oh, Mattie!" Henrietta's face fell with disappointment, "It's too crazy an idea. We would probably burn ourselves to death first."

"No, no! Listen! Listen!" shouted Miss Scattersworth, positively hopping with excitement. "I have it all planned. We will wait until everyone is abed and then soak the carpet and everything near the door in water. When the door is burning properly, we will ram it with . . . with . . ." she looked wildly round the room . . . "with that dresser."

"But the noise, the flames . . . everyone in the house will come running," protested Henrietta.

"Ah, but we shall simply retire to our rooms and hide under the beds. No one will think we have gone to all the danger and trouble simply to stay in our rooms!"

"We'll try it," said Henrietta after a few minutes. "I'll try anything."

Accordingly, Miss Scattersworth imperiously rang the bell then waited. After some time, they heard the heavy tread of feet in the corridor and a suspicious voice asked them what they wanted.

Miss Scattersworth raised her voice. "I am feeling faint and wish you to bring me a bottle of brandy with my dinner. I also wish to take a bath after my dinner."

There was a short silence and then the voice said, "Very good, ma'am."

Another voice protested something in a low voice.

The first voice answered, "His lordship says they were to have anything they wanted as long as they didn't get out the room. Rum do if you ask me. But that's the Quality for you. If you or me took to locking up respectable females, we'd be dancing at the end of a rope. Oh, well. Can't be much harm in a bath and a bottle o'brandy. Game old bird, ain't she."

The voice faded off down the corridor and Miss Scattersworth turned to Henrietta, her face glowing with excitement. "The brandy added to the spirits will make a fine blaze and the bath water will do to soak the carpet. I shall tell them I am retiring immediately after my bath and do not wish the water removed till the morning."

The long afternoon dragged on. "I think perhaps we will not have long to wait," said Henrietta. "I think dinner will be served about five o'clock. Lord Reckford probably keeps country hours when he does not have guests. And you can hardly call us guests," she added bitterly.

She was shortly proved right as they heard the chink of china and glass in the passage outside. A nervous footman served the dinner while two other armed footmen stood in the doorway.

"My brandy?" asked Miss Scattersworth with awesome dignity.

"With your meal ma'am?" queried the startled footman.

"Yes. I always drink brandy with my meals. And then please wait outside the door until we are finished. The sight of you puts me off my food."

The footman poured two glasses of brandy and then bowed out leaving the bottle on the table.

When the door closed, Miss Scattersworth leaped to her feet and poured the bottle of brandy into an empty ewer on the washstand, first pouring another generous measure into each of their glasses "just to fortify us, you know."

After they had finished their meal, they sat with

their toes on the fender, sipping their brandy and staring into the flames.

"Do you remember the last time we drank brandy together like this?" asked Miss Scattersworth in a sad voice. "It was in my little lodging in Nethercote. Dear me! What dreams we had then."

"Dreams are for children," said Henrietta bitterly.

The remains of the meal were removed, the footman casting an astonished look at the empty bottle. As the footman confided downstairs later, "The old 'un sat there as cool as cucumbers and the 'ole room jes reeked of the stuff."

At ten o'clock, they reappeared with the tea tray and, shortly afterwards, with a large bath and several copper cans steaming with hot water. And then the two prisoners were left alone.

They sat for several hours chatting and exchanging gossip to while away the hours. Lord Reckford's name was never mentioned. Far away down the long corridors, came the silvery chime of a clock. One in the morning.

Swiftly they got to their feet and began to throw the bath water over the carpet and everything near the door, being very careful not to splash the door itself.

Downstairs, Lord Reckford felt himself sliding into sleep at last. His lips curled in a smile. "Brandy. A whole bottle!" he murmured. "Can't say I blame them. Would be as drunk as an owl, myself, given the same circumstances. Well, at least she'll sleep well."

Miss Scattersworth had succeeded in drenching the door thoroughly with a mixture of brandy and spirit. Henrietta clutched her arm. "What if we set the whole Abbey on fire? We will be roasted alive."

"Fiddlesticks!" said her friend. "I rely on the almost frightening efficiency of Lord Reckford's staff." But her lip trembled slightly as she bent over the fire with a taper. "Here goes!"

At first it looked as if the spirits were going to burn off the varnish and little else. Miss Scattersworth pulled open the windows and the night wind swept round the room. With a satisfying crackle the door went up in flames.

They had had the foresight to soak their dresses liberally with water and to bind up their hair in wet kerchiefs. They stood behind the heavy dresser and waited. The heat was becoming intense and suddenly from the grounds outside came a shout of "Fire!"

"The keeper, damn him," hissed Miss Scattersworth in a very unladylike manner. "Now! Push!"

Fear lending them an unnatural strength, both pushed on the heavy dresser with all their might. It shot through the door with an almighty crash leaving a great cavernous blazing hole.

They ran into the far away bedroom and dived under the bed and lay there wet and trembling. The Abbey bell was clanging out into the night and the floor beneath them reverberated with the sound. Henrietta silently blessed her friend for having had the foresight to open the windows. The night gale was blowing the smoke out and along the corridor, otherwise they would have suffocated. For the next fifteen minutes, all was shouting and confusion. Then they heard Lord Reckford's voice as he crashed into the room.

"They've gone, Jeremy!" He shouted. "Call the horses. Get every servant available out in the grounds."

Then he added in an undertone. "The silly bitch! She's just signed her death warrant."

Henrietta, who had secretly been hoping that somehow he was to be trusted, felt her heart die within her.

In a matter of minutes the shouting died away from outside the door but still they lay listening as the commotion was renewed outside.

Then they wearily stumbled to their feet. Henrietta tied up a change of clothes for both of them in a large shawl. They gained the bedrooms on the lower floor without hearing or meeting a soul. Choosing one which had the least occupied look about it, they climbed into bed together and fell fast asleep.

They waited another day and night in the bedroom until hunger drove them to try to escape. The faint light of dawn was pearling the horizon as they crept from the back door. This time they moved slowly and cautiously from bush to bush until they reached the security of the woods. Faster they walked and faster, cursing the vast extent of Lord Reckford's estate. It was too dangerous to take the first road they came to so they wearily cut across the fields in silence until they reached a smaller winding country road, screened from the surrounding fields by tall hedgerows. They sat down to rest and plan.

"Have we any money, Mattie?"

"Oh, yes," said her friend blithely. "I always carry two rouleaux of guineas in my reticule. I am not used to having any money *at all* and it is still a thrilling novelty to me to actually be able to carry gold around with me."

"Good," said Henrietta in a flat voice. "We shall walk to the nearest village and hire some sort of conveyance. We shall go back to Nethercote, Mattie. Everyone in the town knows us and it will be very hard for my lord to abduct us again."

The road in front of them stretched forward to freedom. Henrietta began to cry as if her heart would break.

"Oh, Mattie," she sobbed. "And I did love him so."

Chapter Thirteen

HENRY SANDFORD RETURNED FROM Brighton in a sour humor. No, he snapped at his curate, he had not seen Henrietta. She had not been in Brighton, nor her town house nor her house in Sussex.

Henry was weary and puzzled. Henrietta had last been seen leaving the ballroom of the Ship with Lord Reckford. But now Mr. Symes had just informed him that Lord Reckford had called but a half hour ago demanding to see Miss Sandford and appeared very worried and upset.

Mr. Symes was just beginning to wonder uncharitably if his vicar were concerned over his sister's welfare or the fact that she had not been on hand to pay his tailor's bills or the extravagant wages he seemed to pay his new servants.

Three men servants for a vicarage, mused the curate. And such men! They would look more at home in a thieves' kitchen than a country vicarage.

"Why," he suddenly exclaimed. "There is Miss Sandford. And Miss Scattersworth too!"

Henry rushed to the window. Both were descending from a hired carriage. He heard his sister's voice faintly through the glass, "Now, Mattie, you must promise not to say a word. . . ."

Henrietta blinked at the massive ugly features of the footman who opened the door to them. But she was too glad to be on safe familiar ground to worry too much about it.

Henry rounded on the curate. "Take yourself off, Symes. You have parish duties to attend to, you know. Can't stand all day flirting with the ladies," he added hurriedly as he caught the look of surprise on his sister's face. Mr. Symes relinquished Miss Scattersworth's hand and went off slowly.

"Now," said Henry, beaming all over his face. "You must have some refreshment." He tugged the bell. "Some ratafia for the ladies," he ordered.

"Where on earth did you find that peculiar servant?" demanded Henrietta. "And where is our housekeeper?"

"In the kitchen where she belongs," answered her brother, ignoring the first question. "Ah, here we are. Now, drink up ladies! I have a homecoming surprise for you!"

Neither lady likes the taste of ratafia but Henry was beaming all over his face and it was so nice to feel safe, secure and welcome.

Henrietta set down her glass. "What is the surprise?" she asked with a smile. "Isn't it exciting, Mattie?" She turned to her friend and her voice faltered. Miss Scattersworth was slowly slipping down in her chair. She was pointing weakly to the empty glasses.

Henrietta tried to get to her feet but the room began to spin. From very, very far away, she heard the mocking voice of her brother, "Surprise, dear sister! Surprise!" And then the world went black.

When she awoke, she recognized her old room. She felt sick and, in a second, realized that she was lying in her bed, gagged and bound. Now she was afraid as she had never been in her life before. All her brother's former petty cruelties returned to her mind. When people say, 'I nearly died of fright,' she thought, they don't know what they are talking about. However, I do.

The one thing that saved her sanity and gave her

courage was the sudden overwhelming realization that Lord Reckford was guiltless. As it dawned on her frightened mind that the Beau had somehow guessed about her brother and had been trying to save her, her strength of mind returned. She would wait and plot and watch for any chance of escape.

A whole night passed and it was well into the next day when she began to wonder if Henry meant to starve her to death. But finally the door opened and he came in wearing a benign smile and carrying a tray. "Hungry?" he asked setting the tray down on a table beside the bed. He reached forward and untied her gag with his plump hands. "Now you may scream all you like. The neighbors have been convinced that you are mad. My Lady Belding has helped vastly in this. She only does it out of spite, of course. She has no place in this plot."

"Just what is this plot?" asked Henrietta, resolutely starting to eat.

"Why to prove you mad, of course," he said calmly, pouring himself a glass of wine. "This evening after dark you will be conveyed to the nearest madhouse and you will stay there for the rest of your life.

"I have all the necessary papers, the necessary corrupt physician and—in case you have any hopes—the necessarily corrupt director of the madhouse."

"Then it was you who murdered the poor magician and that poor girl."

"I! Of course not. I am a man of God and do not soil my hands with murder. I have men who are paid to do that. As a matter of fact, you paid for their deaths yourself, my dear. You remember the gold snuff box I begged for so earnestly. That disposed of the tattle-tale magician. The girl was more expensive. The diamond studs you gave me for my birthday filled the bill admirably."

"Miss Scattersworth . . ." began Henrietta faintly.

"Interfering old ratbag. She shall meddle no more. She has been heavily drugged and is reported to have gone into a decline because of your condition. When you are safely in the madhouse, we shall terminate her decline with a sympathetic overdose. A nice painless death. Like putting down an old tabby." He gave a fat chuckle and helped himself to more wine.

"*You* are the one who should be in the madhouse, my dear brother," said Henrietta.

He merely gave her a complacent smile.

She racked her brains from some way to annoy him. Some way to make him betray a weakness in his plan.

"Lord Reckford," she exclaimed suddenly. "He will be looking for me."

"He already has," said Henry coldly. "He can do nothing. And after several months have passed, he will be married to Alice Belding. I have a plan . . . Lady Belding would reward me amply an' I were to pull it off."

"What need will you have of more money when you have mine?" she asked curiously.

"I need all the money I can get. I shall buy a peerage some way or another. I shall buy an abbey. I shall be my Lord Henry. I shall have power." His bulbous eyes were glittering and flecks of spit were showing at the corners of his plump mouth.

Henrietta felt her new found courage ebbing. "At least have somebody to change my bed linen."

"Smell, do you? All to the good. Mad people are supposed to be smelly."

Tears of humiliation began to form in Henrietta's eyes. "Oh, if you are going to blubber, I'm going. Be back for you after dark." With that he ambled off taking the tray with him.

Henrietta bit her lip to try to stop the tears. Until the gates of the madhouse closed behind her, she would not give up hope. She lay wide eyed all the long afternoon, watching the lengthening shadows on the floor and reliving her happy times with Lord Reckford. By the time night had fallen, she had hit upon a dismal plan of action. When they took her from the house, she would fight for her freedom. If she did not escape, they would have to kill her and she would be better dead than condemned to a life of imprisonment.

But when her brother and his three servants came for her, even that hope died. She was to be taken out to the carriage bound and gagged.

"I have told all our neighbors that you are becoming violent," said Henry cheerfully. "They have promised to draw their blinds and stay indoors as a last mark of respect."

And so Henrietta was carried as easily as a parcel down the stairs and out into the night. She was thrown into the corner of a closed carriage, her large terrified eyes roaming round like a trapped animal.

Henry leaned his great bulk back in the opposite seat and lit a cheroot. "A few miles and it shall be all over. What a Gothic night! Appropriate, don't you think?"

A strong wind shrieked around the carriage and a tiny moon raced through the black ragged clouds. The lights of Nethercote were left behind and Henrietta sent up a fervent prayer for Miss Scattersworth's life.

If only Miss Scattersworth were here, thought Henrietta, she would have some mad scheme. Or even one of her fantasies to enliven this terror-stricken gloom, such as—Lord Reckford would seize her from the gates of the madhouse at the last minute. They would be married by special license that very night. Tears of weakness gathered in Henrietta's eyes and she began to feel ill and faint.

All too soon, Henry announced blithely, "Here we are," for all the world, thought Henrietta, as if they were coming to the end of some pleasurable outing.

She had a glimpse of massive spiked iron gates being swung back. The carriage lumbered forward and the gates swung to behind them with a clang like a death knell. "So this is reality," said Henrietta to herself. "Oh, Mattie. No gallant gentlemen to ride to our rescue and no . . ."

"Hold hard!" shouted a stentorian voice and a shot whistled over the roof of the coach.

The coach jerked to a halt as the horses reared and plunged. "Highwaymen!" gasped Henry, his round face pasty in the light of the carriage lamps.

"What! In the grounds of the madhouse?" thought Henrietta incredulously.

Henry jerked down the window and leaned out, "What is the meaning of . . ." That was as far as he got. The carriage door was jerked roughly open and he tumbled out on to the ground. The air seemed to be full of shouts and shots and the clash of steel. Then the face she never thought to see again appeared at the door of the carriage. Lord Reckford lifted her carefully out, untying the tight ropes that bound her and releasing her gag. A strange sight met her eyes. Henry and his three servants were being trussed up as ruthlessly as Henrietta herself had been. Standing over them, on guard, with a naked sword in his hand and his grey hair standing up round his head like an auriol stood the timid curate, Mr. John Symes.

"Miss Scattersworth," cried Henrietta. "They are going to kill her!"

"I rescued her," said Mr. Symes simply and with great pride. Then he grinned, "Just like a book, she told me."

Relief and reaction were making Henrietta feel faint. She clung to Lord Reckford's arm as if she would never let go.

He lifted Henrietta gently in his arms. "Come, my dear," he said. "Let us go home."

He helped her up onto his horse and sprang up lightly beside her. "We will leave Jeremy and Mr. Symes to take care of the prisoners."

They cantered off in silence while Henrietta leaned back against him. "I will take you to the vicarage at Nethercote. Miss Scattersworth has quite a tale to tell. And so do you, my love, after you have had a bath."

Henrietta wrinkled her nose in disgust and then

blushed. How could she ever hope to marry this handsome lord who had so many fair beauties to choose from? Beauties who did not get tied up in their bedchambers by their brothers and then dragged to the madhouse.

"What will you do with my brother?" she asked eventually. "Will you take him to the magistrate?"

"What a passion you have for law and order." he teased. "No, Miss Sandford, I am anxious to avoid scandal at all costs. Your brother will be forced to sign a confession and then we will send him out of the country. As for his servants, I will leave their fate to Jeremy. He's very good at disposing of little matters like that."

Henrietta shuddered and did not reply.

The house round the vicarage was still ablaze with light and what a tale the neighbors had to tell for many years to come. Of the famous night Miss Henrietta Sandford came home from the madhouse, dressed only in a filthy nightdress, and with no less than the famous Beau Reckford to carry her indoors.

Looking not a whit the worse for her harrowing experience, Miss Scattersworth rushed to meet them, chattering non-stop about her adventures. She knew that she was being drugged so she had only pretended to eat and drink what they had put in front of her. But her door was securely locked and when she saw Henrietta being dragged from the house, she nearly gave up hope. But then Mr. Symes had broken down the door of her room. "He was magnificent," sighed Miss Scattersworth. "Like Sir Lancelot and King Richard and Joan of Arc all rolled into one."

Henrietta giggled faintly, feeling the world beginning to right itself again. "Joan of Arc. Really, Mattie!"

After she was bathed and dressed in clean clothes, Henrietta insisted on going downstairs again. "I must thank Lord Reckford for rescuing me, Mattie," she said firmly.

Miss Scattersworth felt her brow. "You are a trifle

hot, my dear. Do you not think you should go to bed and have some camomile tea or something of that nature?"

Henrietta shook her head and led the way downstairs. She blinked in surprise as she entered the drawingroom. Half the town seemed to be there, congratulating Lord Reckford who, lying cheerfully, had told them that the vicar had been suffering from a *crise des nerfs* and had persuaded himself that his sister was mad and that he, Lord Reckford, had managed to rescue Miss Sandford in time.

Henrietta's head began to feel very hot indeed. Voices rose and fell around her as meaningless as the sounds of the sea.

Lord Reckford appeared very far away and inaccessible. She wanted to be near him, to break down her reserve, to tell him that she loved him and would have him on any terms.

Everyone seemed to have grown a foot taller and her faint "excuse me" as she tried to work her way through the press was to no avail.

"My lord!" she shouted with all her strength. The guests stared, Lord Reckford took a step forward, and Henrietta collapsed in a heap on the floor.

Next day, the house was hushed and silent, the drawingroom deserted except for Lord Reckford and Miss Scattersworth. Both sat silent, listening to the faint sounds above stairs as the physician moved around Henrietta's room.

"She has been through so much," whispered Miss Scattersworth.

Lord Reckford made as if to reply and then they heard the heavy tread of the doctor slowly descending the stairs.

Both rose to their feet and faced the door.

The doctor bustled in and came straight to the point, "Miss Sandford is running a high fever and is much disturbed in mind. She keeps calling for you over and over again, my lord."

Lord Reckford started for the door but the physician caught him by the sleeve.

"I very much fear, my lord, that you might be the root of her problem. She appears to fear you. I regret that if you wish to help Miss Sandford in her recovery, it would be better that you do not see her again."

Lord Reckford stood very still and quiet.

"And Miss Scattersworth," the doctor went on, "as soon as Miss Sandford is in the least recovered and able to travel, it would be as well to remove her from any place or persons that may remind her of her sad ordeal.

"And now, if you will forgive me, I have other patients to see." He looked enquiringly at Lord Reckford who still stood motionless by the door. "Ah, well, well! I shall call tomorrow to see how our patient does. I shall of course not be seeing you again, my lord. I earnestly beseech you to follow my wishes. Perhaps . . . in years to come . . . when Miss Sandford . . . well, well, good day to you."

Miss Scattersworth fluttered around Lord Reckford exclaiming and crying, "Poor, poor Henrietta! I shall do my best to nurse her, my lord. I shall not even mention your name."

Lord Reckford made her his best bow and stood for a few seconds looking round the room. Then he left.

He felt immeasurably desolate.

Chapter Fourteen

THE LITTLE SPA OF Luben in south Germany had suddenly woken up and found itself fashionable overnight. And in the mysterious way of fashion, no one could quite say exactly what had brought about the change. One day, it was a small provincial town and the next, bustling with lords and ladies and their innumerable servants. The walks and gardens rang with high clipped British voices and the hoteliérs had called in all the available labor to build extensions grand enough to please their new clientéle.

"I declare, all peace and quiet has fled," said Henrietta, throwing down her book. "Even the night is made hideous with the rattle of arriving carriages and the eternal bang-bang-banging of the builders.

Miss Scattersworth set another crooked stitch in her tapestry, looked down at her sensible walking shoes and sighed.

"I must say, I welcome all the bustle, Henrietta. Life can be *too* quiet, you know."

"But we are better as we are, Mattie," said Henrietta, looking at her friend anxiously. "We are having a pleasant stay here and I have been able to read . . . oh so many books. You must confess the London Season became boring after we had got used to all the balls and parties."

Miss Scattersworth sighed again and then bit her lip. Her friend's recovery was all that was important and if a certain silly old spinster pined for the noise and excitement of the city, then she must keep her thoughts to herself.

A year had passed since Henry Sandford had tried to lock up his sister. As soon as Henrietta had recovered, Miss Scattersworth had travelled with her to Luben, determined to sacrifice her life in caring for her friend.

Although Miss Scattersworth's moods changed like quicksilver, she was good-hearted and very grateful to Henrietta for rescuing her from a life of genteel poverty. Had her friend shown any signs of remaining sickly, then Miss Scattersworth would happily have given up any thoughts of her own entertainment.

But Henrietta seemed to be completely recovered. Admittedly, she had not mentioned Lord Reckford's name once, which was still a bad sign, but she did seem to be enjoying the fuddy-duddy life of the small spa and had taken to wearing caps again, saying that, since she was doomed to spinsterhood, she may as well look the part.

Miss Scattersworth reflected that her brief Season had spoiled her own tranquility. For years, she had endured a dull tedious life in the rooms above the bakery. So why should she find her present existence nigh unbearable?

The day began with early breakfast at nine o'clock. Then she and Henrietta would stroll along one of the many paved walks and then visit the pump room to watch the octogenarians imbibing the sulphur-laden water. Luncheon at twelve was followed by a long afternoon of reading and sewing, lasting until tea at four. Dinner was served at six sharp and then, to all appearances, the whole town went to bed.

Henrietta had engaged suites of rooms for herself

and Miss Scattersworth at the principal hotel, which, from the sound of frenzied banging, was now rapidly in the process of turning itself into a palace.

Miss Scattersworth watched the tranquil face of her friend, wondering if she ever thought of Lord Reckford or of her brother. The sound of another carriage arriving broke into her thoughts and she idly crossed to the window which overlooked the courtyard. Henrietta heard Miss Scattersworth's indrawn hiss of breath and looked up startled. "What is it, Mattie?"

Miss Scattersworth hurriedly let the curtain fall. "Oh, nothing!" she remarked gaily with an attempt at lightness which even to her own ears rang terribly false. Two rapid steps took Henrietta to the window. She jerked back the curtain and stared down.

Lady Belding, complete with nose and a plethora of bandboxes and trunks was descending from her travelling coach. Her daughter, Alice, was just discernible behind a heavy veil.

"I am not a child," said Henrietta slowly. "There is nothing the Beldings could say or do which would matter to me now. After all it was Lady Belding herself who recommended Luben. She was most insistent and kept informing me in sinister accents that all the most *interesting* people come here. But now it seems that she actually does favor the place herself. I must confess I thought at one time that she might have had a nasty motive and I would not have come here had I been able to think of anywhere else outside of the country to go."

"Then I shall go and investigate," said Miss Scattersworth brightening. The prospect of seeing a familiar face, however detested, was a welcome diversion.

After she had gone, Henrietta picked up her book. After some minutes, she realized she had been reading the same sentence over and over again and put down her book, staring into space, experiencing a dawning feeling of panic.

What if Alice Belding were engaged to Lord Reckford? Or, for that matter, married to him.

Henrietta leaned her head against the cool glass as memories came flooding back. It had been easy to shut Lord Reckford out of her mind after she had endured the first hurt of his seeming neglect. When she was recovered, she had even timidly written a note to say that she was travelling to Luben and would not be back in England for some time. He did not reply. Perhaps, Henrietta had thought bitterly, his lordship is high in the instep after all and does not wish to associate with a family containing a murderer. She had steadfastly schooled herself to forget him since then. Why, she had even toyed with the idea of accepting Mr. Montmorency Evans proposal of marriage.

Mr. Evans had been a visitor in the little spa for almost as long as Henrietta. He was suffering, unromatically, from a complaint of the bowels and longed to be cured and return to England to take up his studies. For Mr. Evans, although hailing from a wealthy Welsh landowning family, was an amateur engineer and pined for the delights of London—different from the delights Miss Scattersworth sighed for. He longed to see Trevethick's locomotive, the Catch-Me-Who-Can, with all the passion that Miss Scattersworth longed for another evening at Ranaleigh with her court of adoring young men.

Henrietta was not allowed to brood much longer for Miss Scattersworth errupted into the room, the ribbons of her cap flying and her eyes shining with excitement. The spinster forgot all about her determination not to mention Beau Reckford's name again, plumped herself down in an armchair, and began.

"Well, I had such an exciting gossip with Lady Belding's maid. . . ."

"Gossiping with the servants. Really, Mattie!"

". . . . and she told me all about the scandal, my dear . . ." said Miss Scattersworth, ignoring her friend's interruption . . . "the scandal involving Lord Reckford and Alice.

"It happened like this. Lady Belding was becoming desperate. The Beau showed no signs of fixing his attention with Alice. So she engineered another invitation to Lord Reckford's home in the country. There were a lot of guests invited. One evening, Lord Reckford sat up later than usual with the men, the ladies having retired to bed. It was about two of the morning, he was headed for his bedchamber, when he saw Alice standing outside his door. He drew into an alcove and watched. She hesitated, looking up and down the corner, then she opened the bedroom door and slipped in, after signalling to someone out of sight.

"Lord Reckford immediately grasped that there was a plot afoot to compromise him so he dashed off and rounded up several of his friends to bear witness that he had not yet gone to bed. I think there were about four of them.

"They hid at a turn in the corridor and waited for results. Lady Belding came along, shouting at the top of her voice, 'I know you have my daughter in there, you lecher,' and other things of that nature. Alice came to the door and said, 'Go away, you silly fool. He is not yet come to bed and I shall never get him to wed me if you do not play your cards aright,' and then both of them turned round and found Lord Reckford and his friends listening to every word.

"Well, there was nothing else to do but for Alice to rusticate. Although Lord Reckford swore them all to secrecy, Mary Britton—and you *know* what a gossip she is—was one of the guests and heard every word. It went round every saloon in London so it was not enough for Alice simply to retire to the country. She had to retire *out* of the country. So here they are!"

Miss Scattersworth finished breathless and excited and then looked at her friend in dismay. "Oh, I am *so* sorry, Henrietta. Lord Reckford's name was not to be mentioned to you again and I forgot."

"What is all this rubbish?" said Henrietta faintly.

"Well, it was the doctor. He told Lord Reckford, the first day you were ill, that it would be best if he never saw you again . . . because of the damaging effect on your poor brain."

Henrietta sat down, suddenly feeling very weak at the knees. "Mattie, I was in danger of going out of my mind because I thought he had forgot me!"

"Oh! Oh! Oh!" screamed Miss Scattersworth. "And we have endured this stuffy town for so long, listening to complaints of agues, humors and disorders. Oh, Henrietta! How *could* you."

As ever, Miss Scattersworth was able to bring Henrietta's strong sense of the ridiculous to the fore and she began to laugh. "Mattie, you will be the death of me. I was bored to tears myself but I did not mind because I had decided that *you* were enjoying this tranquil existence very well."

"Then let us go!" said Miss Scattersworth, getting to her feet and pulling clothes out of the closets and drawers, flying round the room like a whirlwind.

"Wait, Mattie. Wait! You have forgot Mr. Evans."

"A pox on Mr. Evans!" cried Miss Scattersworth, cheerfully throwing a lifetime of ladylike speech to the winds. "That man and his steam engines and hobbyhorses and sewers. Pah!"

"Just another day," pleaded Henrietta. "Poor Mr. Evans. I feel I must explain things to him gently. He will miss me, you know."

"Set him to re-designing the drainage system of this hotel, and he'll soon forget all about you. Ah, well, one more day, it shall be. Now let us go down for tea, my dear. I am sure Lady Belding will not upset you any more."

"No, indeed!" said Henrietta. "I'm quite looking forward to the meeting."

The public rooms and terraces of the hotel were crowded with the new fashionable arrivals. The older residents glared at the silks and satins and elaborate dress of the aristocratic newcomers with disdain.

Mr. Evans was already seated at their customary table on the terrace and for all her new found hope and bravery, Henrietta noticed, with a slight sinking sensation in her stomach, that Lady Belding was at the next table, her high-bridged nose pink with disapproval as she recognized Henrietta.

Alice stared at her plate but Lady Belding said, "Good day to you Miss Sandford," and then stared straight ahead.

Miss Scattersworth greeted Mr. Evans with a cheerful cry of, "Good afternoon, Mr. Evans. Miss Sandford and I consider that the drainage system of this hotel is abominable and we feel you are the man to reorganize it."

Mr. Evans eyes began to burn with an almost religious fervour. He was a small, dark thick-set man in his thirties, plain and correct in his dress, and with the wide-eyed stare of a curious and intelligent child. Henrietta suddenly found that two separate sets of remarks were being addressed to her as Lady Belding turned her head and Mr. Evans rhapsodised on drainage.

"Have you heard from your dear brother! A much maligned man, I fear." (Lady Belding)

". . . put the water closets under the stairs or somewhere like that—*without* a window *or* a ventilated pipe. Why, we could *die* in our beds from the foul gases. . . ." (Mr. Evans)

And so the conversations went on, neither Lady Belding nor Mr. Evans paying any attention to each other.

"Lord Reckford was too high-handed in the matter of Mr. Sandford. No one could deny you were acting strange . . ."

". . . a stink trap is what is needed. Gaillet's trap is not self-cleansing but Cumming's trap is infinitely superior. The valve in the closet takes the form of a *slide* although Bramah gets the credit . . ."

". . . and of course, Reckford is not to be relied on. Nothing but a Dandy. Why, the other day. . . ."

". . . envisage a Golden Age when the *drains themselves* are ventilated. . . ."

". . . looking considerably older, Henrietta, although I am glad to see you are wearing caps . . ."

". . . unless you live in the Strand, *no* sewers in London *at all*," finished Mr. Evans triumphantly.

Lady Belding suddenly took note of Mr. Evans. "The water closet is *not* a subject to be discussed in the presence of ladies."

"And never will be," said Mr. Evans, "so long as pride goes hand in hand with stupidity."

Lady Belding rose to her feet and uttered the classic reply of those who have been left almost speechless. "I have never been so insulted in all my life."

"Then it's time you were," said the unrepentant Mr. Evans seriously.

Lady Belding made a peculiar sound like "Euff!" and marshalling her daughter and her belongings swept from the room.

Henrietta laughed till the tears ran down her face. Mr. Evans looked at her in some surprise. "I was not being funny, my dear Miss Sandford. It behoves every Englishman and woman to take his or her drains seriously."

"Indeed," choked Henrietta.

Mr. Evans turned to Miss Scattersworth who was hiding her head behind her fan. "I had not realized before, Miss Scattersworth, what a highly intelligent woman you are. I shall see the hotel manager directly. Pray excuse me, Miss Sandford."

He bustled off and Miss Scattersworth slowly lowered her fan to reveal her face crimson with supressed laughter. "I told you Henrietta," she giggled. "Drains will outweigh your attractions every time."

Henrietta composed herself. "I shall write to Lord Reckford, then we shall have a whole big bottle of the hotel's best champagne for dinner and then, tomorrow morning, we shall go *home*. Oh, Mattie! I had forgotten so many things. Have you been pining for Mr. Symes?"

"Frequently," said Miss Scattersworth cheerfully. "But we are leaving this dreadful, dreadful place so nothing matters. And if anyone so much as *mentions* Friars Balsam or rhubard or Family Plaisters or roasted onions or agues or humors, I shall . . . I shall call them out!"

Henrietta composed several drafts of a letter to Lord Reckford. They varied from the cold to the coy to the downright formal. At last she wrote a simple, straightforward declaration of love, saying how much she missed him and how she longed to see him again.

Down the corridor, Lady Belding was also composing a hurried letter to a small town on the German border. "My dear Mr. Sandford," she wrote. "You will be amazed to learn that Alice and I met no other than your sister, Henrietta, at tea this afternoon. She was looking prodigious old and her latest beau is an exceeding common young man who discourses on drainage. . . ."

In the morning, the heavy travelling coach lumbered off across the square. Henrietta took a last look at the little town where she had spent such a long year with a tiny twinge of sadness. At least she had been secure from upset and violent emotions. What if Lord Reckford had forgotten her? Mr. Evans already had, she thought with a wry smile. When she had descended in the morning to take her leave, he was seated in the manager's office surrounded by sheets of drawings and he accepted her goodbyes vaguely, his eyes shining with excitement as he assaulted the manager's ears with a barrage of descriptions of intricate drainage systems.

"We shall not *race* back to London," she said slowly to Miss Scattersworth. "We shall travel slowly and comfortably, stopping at places here and there." Miss

Scattersworth gave a resigned nod. They were at least on the road home and that was all that mattered.

Henrietta felt the bulk of her as yet unposted letter to Lord Reckford. Everytime she decided to mail it she stopped and wondered if perhaps this sentence or that could not have been changed. What if he had forgotten her?

Lord Reckford dropped his quill with a sigh and stared unseeingly across the sun dappled lawns of the Abbey. He owed it to his name to find a wife and continue the line and goodness knows, he had tried. He had paid court to pretty debutante after pretty debutante, rejecting each one in turn. They were all so *young* and their more mature sisters were either shrews, vulgar or timid. His masculine pursuits had palled and his fun-loving friends had been startled when he had declared that an excellent race between two pigs in Hyde Park was "damned childish."

It had filtered back to him through the society grapevine that Henrietta was still in Luben where she had been for the past year. She must indeed be ill, he mused, to endure the suffocating life of a small resort peopled with chronic invalids and dowagers though it was said to be becoming fashionable.

The morning post was brought in and he seized on a heavy letter from his friend, Mr. Jeremy Holmes, who had been spending the summer, wandering about Europe. His letters were always lively and full of adventures and had passed many a tedious morning for the Beau.

He settled down to enjoy the latest of Jeremy's adventures and then his mobile face went hard and tight as he read the first paragraphs over and over again. "I called in at Luben to visit Henrietta because, if you recall, the good doctor said nothing about *me* keeping out of her way.

"I was told that Henrietta had already left but she is to be wed! And to a very intense young man called

Evans who talks of nothing but plumbing. Women are indeed strange creatures! And talking of strange creatures, I had this piece of information from none other than Lady Belding herself who assured me it was a definite love match and that Mr. Evans would be shortly returning to London where the marriage is to take place.

"She positively threw Alice at my head but after that little minx's efforts to entrap you, I could not admire her beauty as before.

"Now comes the really worrying part. I escaped from the Belding clutches and travelled post-haste through Germany, stopping at a small town on the border with one of those jaw-breaking German names. . . . Kirchenhause Am Schleinsenstein . . . and there, sitting at the café in the square . . . was none other than the vicar! He calls himself *Lord* Henry Sandford and appears to be a leader of the town society. Now, I had gathered that Henrietta was making her leisurely way through Germany and I searched the towns and villages between Kirchenhause and Luben with no success.

"Feeling she was in need of a protector, I posted back to Luben to apprise her fiancé that she might be in need of protection and did he know which route she had taken.

"Well, the idiot removed his head from a hotel drain as though loathe to leave it and seemed to be surprised that she had gone. I told him the story of brother Henry to which he listened with ill-concealed impatience and then said I was suffering from Gothic hallucinations brought on by bad drainage and then put his head back down the drain. There really is no accounting for love. . . ."

Lord Reckford dropped the letter and stared with unseeing eyes across the room. She was to be married. And to some idiot with his head in a sewer when she might have had him. With a wrenching feeling of anguish, he realized that if he could not marry Henrietta himself, then he could marry no one.

He cursed himself for a fool. The least he could do was to travel to Germany and make sure she was safe. The doctor had said he must not see her but better she have a shock at his reappearance in her life than be murdered by that maniac of a brother.

He spent the rest of the day in feverish preparation for his departure and by the following morning was ready to leave. As he stepped into the coach, his secretary, Monsieur Dubois, came running out with the morning's post. Did his lordship wish to peruse it on his journey? No, his lordship did not. It could be thrown on the fire for all he cared. The heavy coach rumbled off down the drive.

Monsieur Dubois went in to the study and placed the correspondence on the desk and went about his duties.

Henrietta's tender avowal of her love for the Beau—finally posted after much hesitation and mental anguish—lay on top of the pile of unwanted letters as the rumbling of his lordship's coach wheels faded in the distance.

Chapter Fifteen

HENRY SANDFORD LEANED BACK in his customary café chair at the side of the town square. Things had worked out well, very well indeed. His comfortable income from home—and Henrietta would have been horrified if she had realized in the penny-pinching days of Nethercote just how comfortable that income was—went a long way in this little town. He was held in esteem, an English lord—though self-designated—and with none of the rigors of church duty to mar his life.

He sent his recently hired German valet on frequent trips to London to buy his clothes and he felt he looked a very Pink of the Ton in his long swallow-tailed coat with its shining silver buttons and his swansdown waistcoat—the latest thing in Autumn wear.

The leaves were turning red and gold just as they ought and the peasants were laboring hard in the fields around the town adding to his feeling of being some exalted being. The ladies of the town's bourgeoisie fluttered around him—especially since he had carefully put about that the reason for his exile was a broken heart.

With one languid beringed plump hand, he waved forward the local artist.

Henry had his likeness taken almost daily. Not that he was vain, he had explained, but one must make sure these artist fellows earned their bread even if they were forced to draw such an unworthy subject as himself and the ladies fluttered their fans and exclaimed that he was too modest.

The artist, a young man called Heinrich Schweitzer, often woke sweating during the night, dreaming that his multitude of pictures of Henry had come to life and that he was condemned to a lifetime of sketching an infinity of plump and arrogant Henrys.

He had vainly tried to persuade the English milord to return to the land of his fathers. He felt that if he had to go on drawing portraits of Lord Henry that he would become ill. He could not refuse the commissions for my lord was now a social power in the town.

Henry started disparaging himself in his usual way in order to hear the pretty disclaimers of the ladies who formed his court. "Well, Schweitzer old man, all set for another sitting? Must give you some training, all the same. After painting me, it will be a delight to sketch any of the fair beauties here."

Herr Schweitzer gave his hearty assent and then realized he had been too hearty. Henry's plump mouth was forming into a pout. The artist racked his brain for a new subject of conversation.

"My lord," he ventured hurriedly. "You will be interested to know that there is another pretty face in town. Arrived late last night."

"I fear since I was spurned by the Royal lady of my heart, I have little interest in ladies, pretty or otherwise." He gave a fat sigh and his little court sighed sympathetically.

"But this lady was not attractive in the common way," said the artist. "Her features were too round for beauty but she has a certain elegance, an elusive attraction."

"Well, well," said Henry indulgently. "The fair charmer seems to have caught your attention."

Mr. Schweitzer searched in his portfolio. "I made a rapid sketch of her as she was descending from the carriage. I did it very rapidly of course, but I feel I have caught a good likeness."

Henry took the sketch from him. It was unmistakably Henrietta Sandford descending from a travelling coach. His face turned mottled and his breathing became rapid. He could see all his comfort of being lord of the town fading before his eyes. He hated his sister as he had never hated her before.

"What is the matter, my lord?" cried the artist. "You look quite ill."

Henry thought quickly. "This strumpet," he said heavily, "goes by the name of Sandford although she has no claim to our illustrious family name. She is, in fact, a by-blow of one of my uncles.

"It was she who brought about the downfall of my hopes, my romance. She told the Royal prin . . . excuse me, the Royal lady I was to wed that I was a common country vicar, masquerading as a lord. And she was believed for my lady never went into society and was kept apart from the world."

The artist's eyes narrowed speculatively. The fake Miss Sandford's tale held an uncomfortable ring of truth. There was still a lot of the cleric about this English milord. But his court was shrieking and exclaiming in sympathetic dismay.

"So, dear ladies," said Henry, putting his handkerchief to his face, "I beg you to tell everyone in the town not to mention my presence to this . . . this person. My nerves are shattered. I am quite overset."

As he did indeed look quite faint, his sympathetic entourage assured him fervently of their support as he left to retreat to his house.

Henrietta and Miss Scattersworth had planned to spend a leisurely day in Kirchenhause and leave early on the following morning. Henrietta was suddenly overcome with anxiety to reach home. Miss Scattersworth had contracted a minor stomach disorder and had decided to spend the day in bed, leaving Henrietta to her own devices. Accordingly, she asked the hotel manager if there were any sights of interest in the town.

He looked at her in a most peculiar way, she thought, suggested she might like to view a Saxon church on the outskirts which was within easy walking distance, and then abruptly told her that he hoped she would be leaving in the morning as he urgently required her rooms.

With some little surprise, Henrietta assured him that she had already made plans to depart in the morning and could not help noticing the man's obvious relief. She and Miss Scattersworth were the only guests in the hotel so why the desperation for rooms? She decided the manager was eccentric and put the matter from her mind.

Henry Sandford was sitting over his morning coffee. He decided he had been overwrought. The lady in the sketch could have been anyone. Why on earth should his sister be visiting this remote town anyway? Despite a certain itching in the big toe of his left foot which betokened the oncoming of another bout of gout, he felt quite cheerful as he sorted through the morning post, slitting open the letters with a thin silver Italian stiletto, a present from one of his admirers.

He gazed at the opening words of Lady Belding's letter and thought he would faint from rage and bitter despair. There was no doubt left in him. The lady at the hotel must be Henrietta. He crossed to the window, peering down into the sunny street through the Brussels lace curtains.

And there she was!

A poke bonnet with a high crown hid her face but there was no disguising her figure, her walk or the turn of her head.

207

Her scarlet walking dress of merino wool was in the latest fashion and velvet half boots of the same color peeped out from beneath her skirts.

The veins stood out on Henry's forehead and he found he was still clutching the stiletto. He could see himself ending up a fugitive, fleeing from town to town across Europe. He had meant Luben to be his final destination since Lady Belding had so warmly recommended it but had settled happily into his present little kingdom instead. For one awful moment, he was quite sure that Lady Belding had stage-managed this whole disaster.

Henrietta would have to be killed and immediately. His man was in London. Well, he would have to do the job himself.

He searched busily in his wardrobe, cursing his girth and his tight clothes, looking for something which would enable him the maximum of movement. He came across a priest's black robe, grim relic of the austere earlier days of his training in the Anglican church. Stripping down to his small clothes and sending his heavy corsets flying across the room, he quickly donned the robe, pulled the hood over his face and slipped down the backstairs into the street.

Henrietta walked along briskly, enjoying the clear morning air. She soon left the town behind, feeling uneasy as she became aware of the stares of the peasants working in the fields. She had left her maid behind to attend to Miss Scattersworth, feeling it was not necessary to be accompanied in such innocent-seeming surroundings. But it was with a feeling of relief that she saw the square tower of the church a short distance ahead.

The sun was becoming unusually hot for autumn, dispersing the early mists from the fields on either side.

The hedgerows were alive with color, the scarlet of hips and haws mixing with the deep purple and black of brambles. A solitary white rose stood out bravely from the tangled bushes, last survivor of the summer.

Henrietta plucked it from its stem and tucked it into her hair under her bonnet. Tall poplars stood sentinel along the road as it neared the church, their long, pencil-thin shadows stretching across the fields.

She pushed open the churchyard gate and wandered around the moss-covered gravestones but it was a depressing place, rank with weeds and uncut grass and tall nettles.

The heavy door of the church was stiff with disuse but eventually gave as she wrenched the handle. Inside all was cool and dim, the light filtering through the trees outside and the stained glass windows giving her a weird feeling of being in some subterraneous dwelling at the bottom of the sea. Henrietta wandered idly up the aisle, reflecting that there was hardly anything of interest to see. Perhaps she would climb the tower, admire the view, then walk slowly back to the hotel. The door to the tower stood at one side of the altar and proved as difficult to open as the church door. A long flight of wood steps led upward and creaked alarmingly under her tread.

After what seemed to be an unconscionable amount of climbing, she emerged into the bell chamber and stared up at the black mouths of the bells. Motes of dust disturbed by her feet danced around the thin rays of light in the bell chamber. A tottering, crumbling ladder in the corner must lead to the roof of the tower.

But Henrietta was overcome by the mountaineer's urge to go onwards and upwards and firmly set her foot on the bottom rung of the ladder. It ended at a trapdoor. She slid the heavy bolts across and put her shoulder to it. It gave and swung back with an almighty crash and she pulled herself up onto the roof, standing for a few moments to brush the dust from her clothes. A brisk wind had sprung up and tugged at the brim of her bonnet as she walked round the top of the tower admiring the view.

The colors of autumn were emblazoned across the

countryside as far as the eye could see, scarlet and yellow edging patchwork fields of green, umber and gold.

Suddenly the ground beneath her gave an ominous cracking sound and she clung to the stone battlements of the tower and looked down at her feet. For the first time, she realized with a pang of fright that the wooden floor of the tower was rotting and split. Well, she would take one more look around and then cautiously make her descent.

In the distance, on a road leading into the town, she could make out what appeared to be a grand travelling carriage moving at great speed. Then in the immediate foreground, she spied a figure in black, hurrying along the road. As Henrietta continued to watch, the black dot became larger until, as it halted for a moment outside the churchyard, she saw that it was a priest. Good! She would ask the good father about the history of the church.

Below her, one of the bells moved gently sending out a high thin silver note like a warning. The priest must have brushed against one of the sallies, hanging in the room at the foot of the tower.

Then she heard a far away creaking. He must be climbing up the tower. She would wait for him. That was the most sensible thing to do. She would ask for his help in the descent. Henrietta turned back idly to look out over the countryside. The travelling carriage was now leaving the town and taking the road to the church. She turned as the cowled head of the priest appeared above the trapdoor.

"I am glad you are come, Father," she said as the priest hauled his heavy bulk onto the roof. "I had become fearful of the prospect of getting down again. This tower is in bad repair and not very safe."

"I wouldn't let that worry you, my child," said the priest. And then throwing back his cowl, "You are not going anywhere."

"Henry!"

"Yes, Henry," he sneered, his plump features distorted with hate. The sun flickered wickedly on the stiletto he held in his hand. "You are about to meet your Maker, dear sister. Any last words? Scream away. No one will hear you here."

"But why?" stammered Henrietta. "Why? You are my brother. You always said that blood is thicker than water."

"True," he remarked with a fat shrug. "And I'm going to spill some of yours. Why? 'Cause I hate you, Henrietta.

"Always have. You killed our mother. She died giving birth to you. She would have loved me . . . cared for me. Father didn't. Called me a pompous little windbag. Said I was greedy, said I wasn't a man. Talked of nothing else.on his deathbed but his darling baby, his Henrietta. You've always spoiled everything for me. You . . . *you* got Mrs. Tankerton's money after I had slaved and run after her and flattered the horrible old frump.

"*You* dance around London society, fêted on all sides and I . . . I am left to remain a country vicar, nothing more."

Henrietta backed away from him round the roof of the tower, her eyes wide with horror. Henry's face was a mask of rage and hate. She had no hope. She stood still.

"Very well, Henry. Do your worst!" said Henrietta, her back to the parapet.

Henry lurched eagerly forward. There was a tremendous cracking sound as the floor of the tower split right open beneath his feet. His pudgy white hands clawed desperately at the edge of the rotten wood. "Help me!" he screamed. Henrietta stood paralysed with fear. For the rest of her life she would remember those two hands, clutching and scrabbling like two white rats until they disappeared from view.

Henry Sandford's heavy body plunged into the bell chamber, crashing against the bells on his way down and sending their frightening clamor sounding over the quiet fields.

Henrietta sank down to her knees and inched her way to the split in the floor and looked down. Henry Sandford lay on the floor of the bell chamber, his head at an awkward angle, his black habit stretched out on either side of him over the sun splashed floor. There was the sound of horses hooves, then of shouting voices, then steps on the stairs.

"Henrietta!" It was Lord Reckford's voice from the bell chamber below. She would have run forward but his voice stopped her. "I daren't risk mounting the tower or my added weight might make the floor give way altogether. Now I want you to edge forward to the trapdoor very, very slowly."

Feeling as if she were in a long black tunnel and crawling towards light and safety again, Henrietta moved slowly forward on her hands and knees, edging carefully round the hole. The roof creaked and groaned. The tower was now being buffeted by a strong wind and seemed to sway with every gust as the bells below sent out their high clear murmur of warning as they moved gently on their frayed and dusty ropes. Resisting the temptation to throw herself headlong through the trapdoor, Henrietta backed cautiously down the stairs.

Lord Reckford wrapped his arms round her and held her as if he would never let her go. He called her his darling, his beloved. He bent his head and kissed her and they clung together as if to barricade themselves from the wicked world.

Then he put her gently away from him and called to his footman.

"Maxwell will take you back to your hotel," he said quietly. "Leave me to arrange things here."

She looked at him with a question in her eyes, but he merely bowed formally and turned away.

After she had gone, Lord Reckford paused at the foot of the stairs. The white rose Henrietta had been

212

wearing in her hair lay in the dust. He bent slowly and picked it up and put it in his waistcoat.

Crowds stood on the pavement outside the hotel to watch Henrietta being escorted in. Lord Reckford's savage berating of the manager in which he had stated that Henry Sandford was a dangerous lunatic had spread like wildfire round the town.

Miss Scattersworth was in their suite, dressed and waiting for Henrietta. "Come in, my dear and go straight to bed. So Henry's dead, is he? How utterly marvellous!"

Henrietta feebly opened her mouth to protest, to say that Henry was her brother, and then it all seemed so idiotic that she allowed Miss Scattersworth and the maid to undress her and give her a glass of mulled wine with a liberal dose of laudanum. As she drifted off to sleep, the last thing she remembered was Lord Reckford's passionate words and the last worry she had was as to why he had seemed so cold and formal.

Henrietta slept heavily until the next morning. When she was dressed and at breakfast, the burgermaster arrived to tell her in hushed tones that Lord Reckford had arranged all the legal formalities and the funeral. He had expressed a wish that Miss Sandford should leave this town so full of unhappy memories and proceed to Luben.

"Luben!" exclaimed Henrietta in surprise. "What on earth does he mean? No doubt his lordship will explain the matter when he calls."

"But his lordship has already left," said the burgermaster, "He said to present his compliments and something about your love waiting for you at Luben."

How odd, mused Henrietta, after he had left. "What do you think he meant, Mattie?"

"Why he meant himself," said Miss Scattersworth cheerfully. "After what happened in the tower between you, he obviously means himself. He does not wish to declare himself in this atmosphere of scandal and murder."

Henrietta hesitated. "He is so considerate, Mattie. It is not like Lord Reckford to expect me to travel after such an experience."

"Oh, pooh!" said Miss Scattersworth with her eyes shining. "Love is inexplicable, my dear. Let us get packed directly."

Lord Reckford lounged in the corner of his carriage and stared out unseeingly at the passing countryside. He only hoped that fellow Evans realized what a treasure he had in Henrietta. God, he felt like turning round and going to Luben and kicking him into his beloved cesspool. Goodbye, Henrietta, he thought. I shall take care I do not see you again.

Chapter Sixteen

HENRIETTA PIROUETTED IN FRONT of the long pier glass in the bedroom of her house in Brook Street. Her dress of heavy shot taffeta rustled round her ankles, her gold hair rioted over her head *à la Medusa* and a heavy necklace of opals shone at her throat.

This, she decided, was to be her last ball. Then she would remove to the country, wear her caps again and take up Good Works.

Miss Scattersworth came bounding into the room and Henrietta swung round, dropping her fan. Miss Scattersworth's hair was frizzed fashionably at the front and had returned to its natural grey. But she had damped her petticoats and her wet skirts mercilessly outlined all the charms of her rather pitifully thin form.

"Back in London again," cried Miss Scattersworth twirling round the room. "Oh, what bliss. Back to the sophisticated surroundings in which we belong. Oh, that dreadful Luben. Nothing ever happened. I used to dream that the little hill behind the hotel was in fact a volcano and that one day it would erupt and pour molten lava down towards the town and some Count would dash to my rescue. He would throw me on his prancing steed and. . . ."

"You should have mental saddle sores," said Henrietta acidly, "when you consider all the imaginary steeds you have been thrown upon. In any case, a real admirer is calling this evening. I secured an invitation to the D'Arcy's ball for Mr. Symes."

"Is he still at Nethercote?"

"No. I gather that Lord Reckford has become his patron and that Mr. Symes is now studying medieval languages at Oxford University. So Mattie . . . in view of Mr. Symes staid turn of mind, I think perhaps your gown is a little . . . fast."

Miss Scattersworth fervently agreed. "I am indeed looking dangerously seductive and I would not wish Mr. Symes to see how much I inflame other men's passions."

Henrietta turned away to hide a smile as Miss Scattersworth fled from the room. Had it not been for Mattie's nonsense, she reflected, she could never had survived the long disappointing journey from Luben. Lord Reckford had never been near the place. Mr. Evans was still down the drains and Alice was being pursued by an elderly gentleman with gout.

She had asked Lady Belding if she could convey any messages to Lord Belding in London to which Lady Belding gave a definite "No." Lord Belding had cared naught for poor Alice, she had declared wrathfully. Lord Belding had called his daughter a highly insulting name which she would not soil her lips repeating. There had been nothing to do but for Henrietta to leave for England with her cheeks burning with shame. Lord Reckford must have sent her off on a wild goose chase to Luben to be rid of her company.

Pulling on her long white gloves and picking up her shawl she went downstairs to meet Mr. Symes and her escort for the evening, a Scottish gentleman, Charles Lamont, who had just arrived in town.

Charles Lamont was remarkably like Mr. Evans in appearance but fortunately his character was different. He was a jolly young man, only a year older than Henrietta, who was hell bent on enjoying all that London had to offer.

Miss Scattersworth shortly followed, dressed in an attractive crimson velvet gown. "I see Mr. Symes has not yet arrived," she said, pausing on the threshold of the drawingroom.

"Look again," teased Henrietta. "He is very much here."

Miss Scattersworth blinked. Lord Reckford's patronage had extended to franking Mr. Symes' tailor's bills. The ex-curate was dressed in a well-cut evening coat and breeches. His snowy cravat was perfection and his hair had been cut in a Brutus crop. He stood proudly while Miss Scattersworth shrieked her delight and ran round him in little circles.

"I declare my gown is too modest to go with such magnificence. If you will excuse me, I will go and change," said Miss Scattersworth.

Henrietta read visions of transparent petticoats and clinging gowns in the spinster's eyes and ushered her firmly to the door. "No, Mattie. Very definitely no. You look very well as you are."

"Indeed, yes," said Mr. Lamont, who had also suffered from Miss Scattersworth's vagaries of dress. "Splendid. Fine as fivepence."

While their carriage waited in line outside the D'Arcy mansion, Mr. Lamont asked Henrietta if she still meant to retire to the country. She answered the affirmative in a small voice and he shook his head at her.

"I have had enough of the country," he said. "How can you leave all this?" He waved his hand at the mansion. They were nearly at the door and the flambeaux blazing from their brackets on the walls lit up the silks and satins, jewels and feathers. They could hear the faint strains of music. A few thin wreaths of fog were beginning to blur the lights, giving the whole scene the unreal glamor of a fairytale.

"Quite easily," replied Henrietta coldly.

But Mr. Lamont was still shaking his head and declaring he could not understand it, especially after Henrietta introduced him to the famous Mr. Brummell. "You know everyone!" cried the young Scotsman. "There is one gentleman I would really like to meet . . . Lord Reckford."

Henrietta gave him such a blazing look that he took a step backwards in surprise. "Don't glare at me, Miss Sandford. It was a natural enough request," said poor Mr. Lamont. "He is one of the most famous figures on the London social scene."

"He is a lout," said Henrietta, snapping her fan shut decisively. "*Are* you going to escort me into supper, Mr. Lamont, or are we to stand here forever prosing on about some elderly fop?"

Mr. Lamont puctilliously offered his arm but he gave her a nervous look. Miss Sandford was showing all the signs of being a managing shrew.

Why, everyone knew Lord Reckford was a Top of the Trees, a regular out-and-outer. He was all too soon to change his mind.

Lord Reckford had not read Henrietta's declaration of love. He had, however, read one from Alice Belding which was waiting for him on his return. He had torn it up and acidly told his secretary to consign *any* letters at all from Germany—especially wedding invitations and love letters—to the flames.

As the days went by, Lord Reckford was consumed with an awful desire to see Henrietta and her fiancé, Mr. Evans together. He had vowed never to set eyes on the girl again but his pride was badly damaged. He had heard that Henrietta was back in London so that must mean Mr. Evans was there also. What did they talk about? Drains? He must find out. London was thin of company during the Little Season but the D'Arcy ball was always the main social event. He would post to town. Just one more time. . . .

"Good evening, Miss Sandford. How is the sewage

218

system?" demanded a husky voice behind Mr. Lamont's back.

"I haven't the faintest idea what you're talking about," said Henrietta, putting her trembling hands under the table. The fog outside had thickened and had started to penetrate the rooms. Lord Reckford had appeared to pop up like a pantomime demon.

Mr. Lamont turned round eagerly. Lord Reckford was indeed living up to his title of Beau. He was wearing a blue satin evening coat and knee breeches. Sapphires sparkled on his cravat and on his long fingers. Mr. Lamont looked pleadingly at Henrietta. Surely she was going to introduce him.

Henrietta indicated Mr. Lamont with a nervous jerk of her head. "May I introduce. . . ."

"We've already met," sneered Lord Reckford. "How's your water closet."

"Very well, thank you," said Mr. Lamont faintly.

"Cesspool doing well?"

"Excellently, my lord, I'll give it your regards," said Mr. Lamont cheerfully. The wine had been flowing freely and Lord Reckford was obviously all about in his upper chambers and must be humored.

There was an awful silence. Henrietta was white and the Beau's eyes never left her face. Mr. Lamont racked his brains for a topic of conversation. Obviously the drunken Beau was obsessed with drains. "How's *your* commode doin' these days?" he asked cheerfully and then quailed before the Beau's infuriated glare.

"How can you, Henrietta? How can you contemplate spending the rest of your days with this Welsh popinjay?" said Lord Reckford. He was hanging onto the back of Mr. Lamont's chair and his knuckles stood out white.

"Here, I say!" cried Mr. Lamont jumping to his feet. "I ain't Welsh and I ain't a popinjay and if you weren't well to go I'd call you out."

"Good God, man! Your name is Evans. What the hell do you think you are? A Hottentot!"

219

"My name ain't Evans," said Mr. Lamont, slowly and patiently. "It's Charles . . . Charles Lamont."

Lord Reckford looked at him in haughty surprise. "Well, if your name isn't Evans, what on earth are you babbling on about drains for?"

"I wasn't. You were. Asked me how my water closet was. Yes, you did. Plain as day."

Lord Reckford took a deep breath. "And are you betrothed to Miss Sandford?"

"No!" yelped Mr. Lamont. "Not that I wouldn't be delighted but not a marrying man. Please excuse me, Miss Sandford, got to get some air. Feelin' faint."

The Beau looked after his fast retreating back and then held out his hand. "Come Henrietta, we must talk."

She shook her head and stared at the table.

"Come," he said very gently, "or I shall drag you from the room by the hair."

Henrietta looked up at him and what she read in his eyes almost made her heart stop beating. She rose and put her hand in his.

Heads turned and voices whispered as they walked from the room. The fog swirled and the dancers dipped, advanced and retreated as they crossed the ballroom and made their way along to the conservatory. Lord Reckford's mind churned. He would demand to know whether she meant to marry Evans. He would keep her locked in the conservatory until she was compromised. He would. . . .

But he did none of these things. He simply slammed the heavy glass door of the conservatory behind them and pulled Henrietta roughly into his arms and kissed her and kissed her over and over again as if his life depended on it.

When at last she could speak, Henrietta gave a happy little sigh and leaned her head against his coat. "So you did get my letter."

"What letter, my love?"

"The . . . the one . . . in which I said I . . . I . . .
loved you," said Henrietta in a shy whisper.

"Oh, God!" said the Beau, holding her closer. "I
was sure you were to be wed to that fool Evans and I
told my secretary to burn all letters from Germany.
What time we have wasted. Come behind this splendid
species of palm and be seduced."

Henrietta giggled. "You are going to marry me?"

"By special license," he said promptly,

The door of the conservatory rattled furiously.
"Henrietta! Henrietta!" came Miss Scattersworth's ex-
cited voice. "Are you there? I am to be wed to Mr.
Symes."

"Good!" yelled Lord Reckford, wrapping his arms
more tightly around Henrietta. "Miss Sandford and I
are to be wed. Make it a double wedding. Go away!"

"How romantic!" screamed Miss Scattersworth,
oblivious of the crowd of interested guests gathering
around her.

"I can see it all. You are clasped in his strong arms
under the waving palms. Oh, how terribly romantic!"

"The very foggy palms," whispered Lord Reckford
with his mouth against Henrietta's hair. "Now you are
indeed compromised. I, for one, am not going out there
to face that crowd."

"Henrietta!" came another cry—a long petulant
wail. "Is my Henrietta in there?"

"Mr. Ralston," whispered Henrietta in alarm.

"Come away this minute. She is a fallen woman. She
is in there with Reckford and you know what that
means. Why the man is nothing but a loose screw!"

"Mrs. Ralston," laughed Lord Reckford. "Lay you a
monkey she's got a smile like an angel on her face
while she tears our reputations to shreds.

"And now my dear, dear Henrietta, about all that
time we have to make up. Did I ever tell you that I
have an overwhelming passion to kiss your neck . . .
just there . . . and there. . . and there. . . ."

One by one the guests departed into the yellow fog

of London Town. Lady Penelope D'Arcy fixed her lord with a grim stare.

"Are you going to sit there all night leering at them? Go and get that disreputable pair out of the conservatory at once."

"Spoilsport," said her husband cheerfully. But he got to his feet and ambled off to rattle the conservatory door.

"Hey, Reckford!" he yelled. "Got perfectly good beds upstairs you know?"

"Men!" thought Lady D'Arcy bitterly. They were all as bad as Lord Reckford . . . and that was very bad indeed!